Winter Wishes
for the East End Girls

BOOKS BY JEAN FULLERTON

The East End Girls series

The East End Girls

Winter Wishes for the East End Girls

A Wartime Promise for the East End Girls

Stepney Girls series

A Stepney Girl's Secret

A Stepney Girl's Christmas

Felicity's War

East End Ration series

A Ration Book Dream

A Ration Book Christmas

A Ration Book Childhood

A Ration Book Wedding

A Ration Book Christmas Kiss

A Ration Book Daughter

A Ration Book Christmas Broadcast

A Ration Book Victory

Nurse Connie series

Fetch Nurse Connie

Wedding Bells for Nurse Connie

JEAN FULLERTON

Winter Wishes *for the* East End Girls

bookouture

Published by Bookouture in 2025

An imprint of Storyfire Ltd.
Carmelite House
50 Victoria Embankment
London EC4Y 0DZ

www.bookouture.com

The authorised representative in the EEA is Hachette Ireland
8 Castlecourt Centre
Dublin 15 D15 XTP3
Ireland
(email: info@hbgi.ie)

ISBN: 978-1-80550-083-4
eBook ISBN: 978-1-80550-082-7

In memory of the American men and women who, between 1943 and 1945, left their homes and families to stand alongside Britain in the fight against fascism – and who made the ultimate sacrifice.

CHAPTER 1

As the saxophonist blasted out 'Boogie Woogie Bugle Boy' Aircraftwoman Alice Starling of the Woman's Auxiliary Air Force of 906 Balloon Command, stood on tiptoes.

'Can you see George?' her friend and fellow WAAF Nell Reilly shouted over the music.

Skimming her eyes across the couples bobbing about on the dancefloor, Alice shook her head.

'Sure, wasn't she flirting with some officer a while back?' asked Maeve, looking across at the bar at the other end of the dancehall.

George – or rather Aircraftwoman Georgina Hermione Matilda St John-Smythe – was, like Alice, Nell and Maeve, part of the ten-strong barrage balloon team responsible for site 312 situated in the heart of London Docks in Wapping.

They'd all first met on a freezing winter day in January that same year at RAF Cardington in Bedford, where they had signed up to train as barrage balloon operatives.

They had survived the hell of the gruelling thirteen-week barrage balloon operators' training to become one of the first all-female WAAF crews, and despite their different backgrounds,

Alice, Nell, George and Maeve had become life-long friends. And now, after weeks of sleepless nights, heaving a 64-foot canvas balloon filled with helium up and down above London Docks and keeping it there for hours while the Luftwaffe dropped bombs all around, it was one of their rare twelve-hour passes together, and they had decided to let their hair down and enjoy a bit of wartime London's intoxicating nightlife.

Actually, five friends had marched proudly across the parade ground at their graduation almost eight months ago, but Effie, who had been the crew's corporal, was now awaiting the birth of her first child and was therefore not up to a night on the town.

But they weren't the only ones set on enjoying a short respite from duty; the whole of the West End from Oxford Street down to Trafalgar Square was packed with revellers, most of whom were in uniform. As it was the first Saturday night Alice and her friends had had away from their fat, floating silver-grey charge for almost two months, they'd decided to put on their glad rags. In Alice's case, this was a cherry-red crape evening dress with a fluted skirt and capped sleeves. It had been her favourite dress for years, but standing in front of her wardrobe earlier that evening, she'd paused, unsure about wearing it, not only because with just ten weeks until Christmas the weather had turned decidedly wintery, but because she hadn't taken it out of the wardrobe since she'd received the telegram about Arthur.

For a few weeks after she'd read the telegraph that made her a widow at twenty-four, she'd been numb. However, with the Germans sitting a few short miles from them across the English Channel and the war raging overhead during what the newspapers dubbed the Spitfire Summer, Alice pushed through her fog of grief and signed up as a WAAF. She was sure Arthur would have been proud of her taking her place in the defence of the realm he had given his life for. It also gave her a chance to get away from Arthur's overbearing mother and the sadly unneeded nursery, their attempts to start a family before the war having come to nothing. Having reluctantly accepted her lot in life, she now focused on spoiling her many nieces and nephews.

Now, almost two and a half years later and three years into the war, the capital's life had taken on a wartime rhythm all its own. Therefore, at the end of another gruelling week of staying calm and carrying on, it seemed like the whole of London was out and determined to enjoy themselves, and Alice and her friends were no exception. After a slap-up supper in a small, family-owned café behind Shaftesbury Avenue and a few drinks in an overcrowded nearby pub, they had made their way down to where they were now, the Dover Hotel in Leicester Square.

But that was three hours ago and, like it or not, unless they wanted to be up on a charge for being AWOL – absent without leave – they needed to start heading for the tube to whisk them eastwards towards their cosy rooms above the Maid of Norway pub.

'When did you last see her?' asked Alice.

'About an hour ago at the bar with some Yank,' Nell replied. 'He was a right beanpole, too. Six-six if he's an inch, if that 'elps.'

It didn't really. Since the American army had started arriving nine months ago in January every dance hall in London seemed populated with six-foot-plus GIs. The Dover Hotel was no exception – all around Alice were broad-shouldered, chiselled-chinned American soldiers in their pristine olive-green US Army jackets, with starry-eyed young women hanging on their arms.

In the twinkling light of the mirrorball overhead, Alice looked at her watch. 'We've got to be on duty at six, which is why we agreed we'd leave at eleven.'

'You should know what George is like by now,' Nell replied.

She was right. Punctuality wasn't George's strong suit.

'Especially when there's so many handsome blokes around. What are we going to do?' Nell added, as the band blasted out the opening bars of 'Don't Sit Under the Apple Tree'.

'Well, we'll have to find her,' Alice replied. 'You search for her in here and I'll see if she's stepped outside for a breath of fresh air.'

Nell nodded and then, weaving between the couples milling around the dancefloor, headed for the bar. Alice turned in the other direction and made her way towards the hotel's main doors.

Although it must have been close to eleven thirty people were still piling in, mainly Americans with fat cigars clamped between their teeth and their arms draped round smiling girls.

'I'm just popping out to look for my friend,' Alice said to the doorman, as she squeezed past the crowd.

As she stepped out of the ballroom and onto the street, the icy air tingled her cheeks and nose. Like the rest of the West End, the broad thoroughfare that ran from Piccadilly Circus westwards to Park Lane was alive with people strolling back and forth. The blackout had just come into force as they'd set off at seven, and, although the streets were swathed in darkness, dozens of shafts of light from hand-held pencil torches danced around on the pavement to light people's way.

Taking her own torch out of her handbag, Alice switched it on, and pointed it at her feet. She set off towards St James's Palace but after a few minutes, figuring that George couldn't have gone very far, turned back towards the dance hall.

Like almost any street in Mayfair, Soho and Piccadilly, the pavement outside the hotel was filled with small groups of GIs, in their smart uniforms and with bulging wallets, many with brightly dressed young women, with red lips and willing smiles, gathered around them and hanging on their every word.

Giving her the once-over as they passed, a couple of GIs strolled by, as Alice stood wondering where on earth her friend could have got to, someone shoved into her. Frowning, Alice turned, and her torch illuminated four women tottering about on the pavement in front of her.

'Sorry luv,' said a blonde in a blue skirt and frilly blouse. 'I didn't see you in the blackout.'

'We're each going to catch ourselves a lovely American, ain't we, Olive,' said her redheaded friend, waving a half-drunk bottle of gin around as she tried to balance on her ridiculously high heels.

'Yeah, Viv,' Olive replied, swaying slightly.

'One with lots of money and nylons,' her friend in a beaded cocktail dress added.

'I think that's pretty much all of them, isn't it?' Alice said, raising an eyebrow.

The fourth one, a brunette with two enormous victory rolls on top of her head, pulled a face. 'Dotty don't mean no wet-behind-the-ears boys.'

Flicking ash on the floor, Dotty grinned. 'No, I don't, Brenda, I mean big handsome ones so we can be GI brides.'

'Come on,' Viv said, hooking her arm in Alice's. 'You can come wiv us.'

'No thank you,' said Alice, trying to take her arm back. 'I'm just looking for my friend George.'

'Come on luv, forget about this bloke who's left you,' said Olive. 'You stick with us – there's plenty to go around.'

'No thank you,' Alice said again.

She tried to untangle herself again, but her new friend held on, dragging her along the street.

'Yoo-hoo, over here!' screamed Dotty, waving at a group of five American airmen on the other side of Piccadilly.

The servicemen stopped, exchanged a few words and then,

looking the wrong way up the street, they veered across Piccadilly, bringing a taxi to a screeching halt.

'Evening, ladies,' drawled a lanky GI, showing an impressive set of pearly white teeth, as he smiled down at them.

'Evening.' Giggling, the four girls simpered and batted their eyelashes at the American servicemen as they crowded around them, blocking Alice in among them.

'Say, girls,' said a fair-haired soldier. 'We're in town for a few days so would you lovely ladies like to show us the sights?'

Dotty's red lips parted in a huge smile. 'We certainly can, can't we, girls?'

Her three friends squealed their agreement.

'Not me,' said Alice.

She pulled her arm free from Viv and was about to continue her search for George, but then Dotty caught her.

'Come on,' she whispered under her breath. 'There's five of them, so don't be a spoilsport—'

'Oi, you lot!' shouted a woman.

Alice looked around as three girls as lavishly overdressed as the first four barrelled along the pavement towards them.

'We saw 'em first,' said the newcomer, squeezing herself between Dotty and the GI she was clinging to like a limpet.

'Too bad,' said Olive, scowling at her. 'Sling your hook.'

She grabbed the other woman's jacket sleeve. She pulled away and the sound of ripping fabric cut between the rival groups of young women.

'You've torn my friend's coat,' shouted one of the girls in the new group. 'Six coupons that cost 'er.'

'Well, she started it,' yelled Viv.

'And I'll bloody finish it too,' the young woman shrieked.

With her damaged sleeve flapping at her side, she leapt forward, swinging a punch as the supporters on both sides piled on. Alice was knocked to one side, then found herself cornered by Dotty, who was grappling one of the other girls. She looked to the GIs for help in ending the brawl, but they had formed a semicircle and were enjoying the spectacle, encouraging the battling rivals for their affections and cheering them on.

'What the hell is going on here?' bellowed a deep American voice that brought everyone up short.

Alice turned and was almost dazzled by the stark light from a torch. As her eyes adjusted, she found herself looking up into a pair of dark brown eyes set above well-defined cheekbones, and a chin that could break stone.

Although the soldiers around her were all close to the six-foot mark, this newcomer topped them by a couple of inches at least and his olive uniform jacket fitted snugly over his broad shoulders and chest. Like all the Americans, his peaked cap was tipped back, revealing dark curls skimming across his forehead.

Seeing the man's insignia, the GI around them snapped to a haphazard attention.

'J... j... just a bit of fun, Lieutenant, sir,' he replied, almost poking his eye out with a sharp salute.

In the light reflected from the shop window, the American lieutenant's dark eyes ranged over the red-faced, dishevelled group of young women and stopped as they reached Alice, lingering on her for a moment or two before shifting back to the soldiers.

'He's right, Lieutenant,' piped up another GI. 'The girls were just having a bit of—'

'Fun. I heard you,' interrupted their senior officer. 'Trouble is what you'll get, soldier. These sorts of cheap dames are—'

'Cheap dames!' Alice snapped. 'It's *your* drunken soldiers who are the problem. Staggering around the pavement accosting any young women who they meet.'

'They're *drunk*,' he snapped back, 'because women like you get them as drunk as a skunk, then hustle them for nylons, money and anything else you can squeeze out of them.'

Alice bristled. 'How dare you? I'll have you know—'

'Go and find yourself some better company, soldiers,' the handsome lieutenant continued, cutting across Alice. 'Company that won't cost you a night in jail and a month's pay.'

'Yes sir,' the five GIs replied.

The privates snapped to attention, then shot off like their tails were on fire. The lieutenant turned to the groups of women who were about to follow the soldiers back towards Leicester Square.

'Not so fast,' he said, stepping in front of them.

'I don't know who you think you are,' snapped Alice. 'You may be able to order your American troops around, but you can't stop us British citizens walking down the King's Highway.'

The arrogant American lieutenant's gaze flickered over Alice again, then it shifted past her and he raised his hand. 'Constable!'

Alice followed his gaze, and her blood drained to her feet as she saw a police officer heading towards them.

The well-fed member of the capital's constabulary, who had a toothbrush moustache under a bulbous nose, shone his torch over the gathering.

'Evening, sir, what seems to be the trouble?' he asked.

In the dim light from his torch, the American officer's dark brown gaze lingered on Alice again for a second before his attention returned to the stout police officer.

'These *young ladies*,' he said, his tone laced with heavy sarcasm, 'were trying to pull a fast one on one of our soldiers.'

'I'm sorry to hear that, sir,' said the rotund constable. 'It was fortunate you happened by to prevent it. I'm afraid the women who hang around here are a bloody menace.'

A menace! Alice was stunned to silence and her jaw dropped.

The American lieutenant's brown eyes locked with Alice's smoky grey ones again for the briefest of moments.

'They certainly are,' he said, his attention returned to the constable. 'Having young women pouncing on our boys for stockings, cigarettes and anything else they can get out of them doesn't do much to promote harmony between two allies, does it? I've already had it pointed out to me that, while I have jurisdiction over US troops, I can't order British citizens around,' he went on. 'So would you mind doing the honours?'

'Leave it with me, sir, I'll deal with them,' said the officer.

'Thank you, Constable,' said the American. 'Good night.'

Giving Alice a last look, the lieutenant turned, and strolled off towards the Wellington Arch. With rage burning in her chest and having a furious argument with him in her head, Alice watched as his tall frame turned into one of the narrow streets leading to Shepherd Market and out of view.

'Right, you lot,' barked the portly police officer. 'I've clocked all your faces, so you can take this as a warning – if I see any of you hanging around here pestering Yanks, I'll run you in.'

'For what?' asked Viv.

'Don't you worry, I'll find something to put on the charge sheet,' he replied, his eyes scanning over them. 'So don't let me catch any of you making a nuisance of yourselves with the Americans again. Now be off with you.'

He shooed them away, then continued to patrol his beat.

Clenching her fists, Alice stood motionless as the girls around her dispersed.

'Alice, thank Gawd.'

Putting aside the imaginary vision of her giving that conceited American officer the sharp edge of her tongue, Alice looked around to see Nell and Maeve standing beside her.

'Sure, we were beginning to worry that you'd been kidnapped or something,' said Maeve.

'Did you find George?' asked Alice.

'Yer, she was with some American major at the bar,' Nell replied. 'She'll be out in a moment. We got here in time to see that copper giving you and a bunch of girls a dressing-down, though – what on earth were you doing?'

Through gritted teeth, Alice recounted her meeting with the young women and the GIs. '... and the police wouldn't have got involved at all if it hadn't been for this bloody arrogant American who called the copper over...' From nowhere, the contempt in the handsome lieutenant's eyes and the shame of being thought a gold digger on the take swept over Alice.

Nell's arms encircled her. 'Don't worry, we'll soon have you back to the Maid of Norway and tucked up in bed with a cup of cocoa.'

'Thanks, girls,' said Alice, thankful not for the first time that they were billeted in the friendly East London public house. 'But I tell you this,' she concluded, her fingernails biting into her palms as her hands balled into tight fists. 'If I ever run into *that man* again, you'll have to visit me in Pentonville as I will not be responsible for my actions.'

CHAPTER 2

Several days later, Lieutenant Brogan Rafferty of the Office of War Information and Public Relations division of the American Army was standing in the ballroom of the Brook Street Hotel, which was one of the many Mayfair hotels that had been taken over by the US Army to billet troops. The hotel's reading rooms and lounges that had once been a tranquil refuge for visitors to town was now filled with high-spirited young Americans and gramophone music played at full volume.

In front of him were fifty-plus GIs who had recently stepped off the troopships that had taken them away from their homes and families and deposited them in an alien land.

Although some of them were in their mid-to-late thirties, and a few in their forties, the vast majority of the fresh-faced young men had probably only left college a few months before, which, as he was only a few months away from his thirtieth birthday, made Brogan suddenly feel rather old.

When Brogan had been drafted two years before, someone in the recruitment office had concluded that, as a journalist on the *New York Herald*, he would be ideally suited for the American Office of War Information.

As a liaison officer in the US Army's public relations unit, Brogan had many duties, such as liaising with the London civilian authorities, the police, Air Raid Precautions Headquarters and the British Broadcasting Company, along with a variety of other organisations, to maintain cordial and harmonious relations between American and its closest ally, Britain.

His first experience of British ARP committees, town councils and officials from the United Kingdon's Home Defence and War Ministries was in Belfast, before he was transferred to the OWI HQ in London.

This afternoon's audience was on the second of their two 'Welcome to Britain' orientation days. It was Brogan's task this afternoon to put newly arrived GIs wise to the ways of the Brits in the hope, often a forlorn one, that they wouldn't alienate every Brit they met, as it was his job to deal with such incidents, and to ensure they didn't end up in a British police cell.

Yesterday, after taking the roll-call and laying out the two-day programme, Brogan had left them to the straight-talking Major Hanson MD, from the US medical corps. After their midday meal they were handed to the tender care of Staff Sergeant Crocker, who had the temperament of a bull buffalo with a thorn in its hoof. It was his task to instruct the farm boys and factory workers conscripted to fight in the US Army on how best to conduct themselves in such a way as to avoid getting collared by the British police. Crocker Mills graphically laid out the reception they could expect if they did happen to find themselves in a police cell, when they were handed over to the US Army military police or 'snowdrops', as they were commonly called because of their brilliant white helmets.

Brogan's briefing today was to explain the quaint customs and eccentric ways of the Brits, things such as referring to an elevator as a 'lift', a faucet as a 'tap', the difference between bitter and mild ale, and why the beer was served at room temperature and never cold.

Having been through the most common misunderstandings between the Americans and their hosts, at the end of the morning he'd handed out the US Army's 'Instructions for American Servicemen in Britain' followed by a rundown of the army's canteen facilities nearby, and the location of the Post Exchange store, or PXs as it was known, where GIs could buy all sorts of home comforts, and sports clubs. He'd also been through the capital's main historical sites and how best to get around on the city's subway or buses. He was now tackling the subject of British currency, and finding that his audience were predictably full of questions.

'Now hey, as it can be a bit confusing, I'll just run through it again,' said Brogan, tapping the chart on the easel next to him with the two-foot-long pointer. 'A British pound comprises twenty shillings and each shilling is made up of twelve pennies.'

'Geez,' laughed a lanky, fresh-face GI sitting in the front row. 'Why can't it just be simple and add up in tens?'

The soldier behind him sideswiped his hand across the top of his crew-cut. 'Cos the Brits love making stuff complicated, dummy.'

'Complicated or not, soldier,' said Brogan, 'most waiters, storekeepers and taxi drivers are straight-up fellas, but some see you as easy meat, so if you don't want to be taken for a ride you'd better wise up to their money. Another thing you should know about money is that, while Uncle Sam pays you fellas three pounds, eight shillings and nine pennies each week, a British private gets one pound eight shillings. One of the complaints I constantly hear from the Brits is GIs flashing their money around. You won't make many friends if you go rubbing their noses in the fact that you get paid twice as much as they do. And no jibes about running away at Dunkirk. You'll see as you travel around that the Brits have had it pretty tough these past couple of years.' Placing the pointer next to his briefcase on the desk, Brogan scanned his eyes across his audience. 'Now, are there any more questions?' He fielded another couple of the usual questions about the army mail, which he could answer, and a couple about when and where they would be deployed, which he couldn't. He reminded them that there were plenty of Red Cross Clubs for them to make use of when they were off duty, and that there were also several army baseball and basketball teams they could sign up to, plus dozens of clubs ranging from chess to stamp collecting.

'All the information you need to enjoy your time in the United Kingdom will either be in each week's edition of the *Stars and Stripes* or, if it's something close by, pinned on the noticeboard in all our canteens. Now, before I finish, is there anything else?'

There was a bit of shuffling about on seats and muttering, then a freckle-faced GI in the third row stood up. 'Private Ingles, sir.'

'What's your question, Ingles?' said Brogan.

'What are the women like, sir?' he asked, as his buddies around him nudged each other and grinned.

A smile spread across Brogan's face.

'Where you from, soldier?' he asked.

'Arkansas,' Ingles replied.

'Well, don't you have women in Arkansas?' asked Brogan.

Ingles gave him a toothy grin. 'We sure do, Lieutenant. Prettiest gals in the whole damn United States.'

'Well, then you should be able to recognise one over here,' said Brogan.

Laughter rumbled around the room.

'No, I mean, are they friendly, real friendly,' Ingles continued.

'Yes, sir,' added a soldier with jet-black hair sitting behind Ingles. 'Cos we've heard tell that, since their menfolk aren't here, some of the English girls are...' He winked. 'You know.'

Brogan certainly did.

When he'd arrived in London he'd found that despite the bombs and destruction the capital was filled with wine, women and song, and he'd made a vow to enjoy every goddam minute of it.

His smile widened. 'Well, all I can say is the ones I've met are pretty keen to do their bit for Anglo–American relations.'

There were a couple of whoops and two-tone whistles as the GIs grinned at each other.

'But watch out,' continued Brogan. And he told them about the drunken privates and the two groups of women fighting over them in Piccadilly the previous Saturday.

'Some of these gals might look friendly but pretty soon they'll be after you to buy them nylons, soap, shampoo and candy from your PX allowance. Believe me, these broads are a whole heap of trouble,' he added. 'And above all, don't do nothing crazy like falling in love.

'Now, are there any other questions?'

No one spoke.

Brogan glanced at the clock again. 'Well then, if there's nothing further, it's almost opening time.' He gave the room a crooked smile. 'Pub opening times, that's another mystery you're going to have to unravel while you're in Britain. So, attention!'

The rows of soldiers rose from their seats as one.

Brogan gave them a smart salute. 'Dismissed.'

His audience copied the gesture en masse, then broke ranks. Brogan picked up his briefcase and cap from the table and marched down the central aisle, out of the room.

Forty minutes later, placing his hand on the worn brass plate, Brogan pushed open the door, and walked through the heavy blackout curtains into the Jules Club.

'Good afternoon, sir,' said the elderly steward, shuffling forward.

'Good afternoon to you, Harris,' Brogan replied, removing his cap and tucking it under his arm.

The Georgian building in whose antiquated lobby he was now standing had once been the place where the great and good of the British ruling class gathered to drink brandy and puff cigars. However, since the first American troops arrived in London, this establishment, like many others in the streets and squares north of Piccadilly, had been taken over by the American army. It was now one of the dozens of houses, clubs and hotels in Mayfair that housed, fed and watered US troops, specifically junior officers like himself.

Where only the rustle of newspapers, logs crackling in the grate and the gentle snores of aged patrons slumbering in winged armchairs had broken the calm silence, now loud voices, jazz records and heavy footsteps thundering across the upper floor bounced off the 200-year-old walls.

Brogan's billet was home to officers below the rank of major – these obviously were billeted in the more salubrious surroundings of Claridge's and the Albemarle. However, Brogan couldn't complain – the place was kept spotlessly clean by the hotel staff.

'And still no rain,' added Harris, the light above his head reflecting off his thinning hair.

'Let's hope it stays fine for a few more days,' agreed Brogan, wondering not for the first time at the British obsession with the weather. 'Do you happen to know if Lieutenant Robertson is about?'

'I believe I saw him going towards the bar a little while ago,' Harris replied.

Leaving the club's old retainer to greet a couple of officers who had walked in behind him, Brogan made his way along the corridor towards the rear of the building.

Although it was only just after five, there were already a

handful of his fellow officers chatting or reading newspapers in the club's well-worn leather armchairs and chesterfields in the hotel's bar. He spotted his good friend Todd Robertson, reading the latest copy of *Stars and Stripes*, the US Army's daily newspaper, in one of the wing-backed chairs beside the fireplace.

Although he and Todd were both native New Yorkers, they had only met three months ago when Todd was billeted alongside Brogan on the club's top floor. To be honest it would have been astounding if they had met before, not just because their home city had three million people living in it, but because the Robertson family lived in a smart house in wealthy upper Manhattan while the Raffertys, all eight of them, lived in a four-room tenement apartment on the Lower East Side. Unlike Brogan, who had disembarked in Northern Ireland with some of the first American troops in February, Todd had only stepped off the gangplank in Belfast Docks in June. Despite their vastly different backgrounds, they had hit it off immediately and, after spending the summer acquiring a taste for Guinness among other things, they'd both been transferred to London.

In contrast to his own dark hair and brown eyes, Todd, with his broad face and blond crew-cut, was the walking, talking image of an all-American hero.

Nodding a greeting to a couple of his fellow officers, Brogan wandered across to where his friend was sitting.

'There you are. I was beginning to think you'd gone AWOL when you didn't pitch up in the mess last night,' his chum said, as Brogan crashed into the chair opposite.

'Sorry, I had to go for an emergency huddle at Scotland Yard and didn't get back till gone midnight,' Brogan replied.

'Such is the cross an OWI officer carries,' Todd said, solemnly.

Brogan huffed his agreement. He had recognised Hitler for what he was, back in 1938 when he invaded Czechoslovakia. Although at the time he was a reporter on the crime desk at the

Brooklyn Eagle, he had gone head-to-head with the senior editor to print a piece saying as much. He'd won his case and received dozens of letters of support from the neighbourhood's Jewish community. He became the political reporter on the *New York Herald* and continued his campaign to open his fellow New Yorkers' eyes to the events unfolding in Europe, and then enlisted in the army the day after Pearl Harbor, keen to take up arms to defeat fascism. He was therefore bitterly disappointed at first to find that, after basic training, instead of being posted into a fighting battalion he was to be a civilian liaison officer attached to the Office of War Information. However, after only a few weeks Brogan had come to appreciate how vital his role actually was, and that for an army to function effectively it needed much more than just soldiers. 'I see you've got another piece in the old *S&S*,' Todd said, indicating the newspaper he'd set aside on the table.

Brogan nodded. 'And with my name in the credits, not just as "a *Stars and Stripes* staff writer"'.

'Well, it's about time. After all, isn't this the fourth piece you've had accepted?' said Todd.

'Seventh, actually.' Brogan grinned. 'I've got to keep myself sharp if I'm going to be editor in chief on the *New York Times* one day.'

He raised his hand and Cynthia, the Jules' voluptuous redheaded barmaid, sidled over.

'Evening, Lieutenant Rafferty,' she said, fluttering her heavily mascaraed eyelashes at him. 'What's your pleasure?'

'Two bourbons on the rocks, if you please, Cynthia. On my tab,' Brogan replied.

The barmaid gave him a lavish smile and sashayed back to the bar, returning a few minutes later with two tumblers of amber liquid, which she placed on the low coffee table in front of him.

'Thanks, Cynthia,' he said, picking up his drink. 'Cheers.'

He and Todd touched their glasses together.

Brogan swallowed a large mouthful and sank back in the upholstery as the spirit burned pleasantly down his throat.

Todd took a large sip. 'I suppose the London cops were griping about us again.'

'They were,' Brogan replied wearily.

'Well, I can't say I blame them,' said Todd. 'I've just walked back from Horse Guards and could hardly take half a dozen steps without colliding with a drunken GI staggering along the sidewalk. And it's only going to get worse – there's shiploads of GIs arriving on every tide.'

'It can't be helped,' said Brogan. 'The top brass won't think about crossing the English Channel to retake Europe until they have the troops.'

'So in the meantime, we're all here twiddling our thumbs,' said Todd.

'I'm afraid so, but spare a thought for those quaint little thatched villages in Norfolk and Suffolk with a couple of hundred locals living in them. They're about to have their fields ploughed over for airstrips and experience the charms of the Mighty Eighth Army Flying Corps descending on them.'

'God help them,' said Todd with feeling.

'Exactly,' said Brogan. But most of the trouble with GIs I have to deal with is just high spirits. Like the new arrivals I've been educating in the ways of olde England for the past two days. It's their first time away from home, money in their pocket. Most of them are just kids barely out of high school.' He took a mouthful of whisky. 'I tell you, Todd, looking out at that sea of fresh faces made me feel very old.'

'Well, let's hope your words of wisdom soak in – it might stop them having their wallets cleaned out,' said Todd. 'Like those privates you met on Saturday. They were lucky you came by and saved their lives.'

'It wasn't their lives they were after but their money,' said Brogan.

Todd let out a low whistle between his front teeth. 'Some of those girls who hang around on Piccadilly are a grasping bunch.'

The image of the young woman with the captivating eyes came into Brogan's mind.

'Oh,' said Todd, cutting across Brogan's thoughts. 'As you were out when the afternoon post arrived, I picked this up for you.' Delving into his jacket pocket, he pulled out a letter and handed it to him. 'Is it from your sister?'

'No,' said Brogan, turning the flimsy airmail envelope over in his fingers. 'My mother. She's probably going to be on at me again to visit her sister Florrie in London.'

'Why haven't you?' asked Todd.

'I don't know, just busy I guess,' Brogan replied.

Todd gave him a dubious look. 'I'm surprised at you. I would have thought you would have jumped at the chance of a bit of home cooking and change of scenery. Where does this aunt of yours live?'

'Shadwell,' said Brogan.

'Where's that?'

'Somewhere in the east of the city. Near the London Docks, I think,' Brogan replied. 'She runs a pub called the Major of Normandy or something.'

'Well, you should go,' said Todd.

'I know, I know.' Brogan sighed. 'I've got a couple of days furlough owed to me, so perhaps I'll grab a jeep and drive out.'

'All right, boys, can I get you another?' asked Cynthia, as she collected a couple of glasses from the table next to them.

'Brogan?' asked Todd, as the barmaid moseyed over to them.

'Not for me,' he replied. 'I'm seeing Major Jessup ten hundred hours the day after tomorrow. He'll want a full report of the last two orientation days so I'd better write it up while it's still fresh in my mind.'

'You sure I can't tempt you with something else, Brogan?' Cynthia said, pressing her breasts into Brogan's shoulder as she leant across to pick up his empty glass.

Brogan smiled. 'I'm afraid not today, Cynthia.'

'Well, you know where I am if you change your mind,' she sighed, giving Brogan a look that needed no interpretation. Then she sashayed back to the bar.

'It must be hell being you, Brogan,' said Todd, amusement written large across his freckled face.

Brogan looked puzzled. 'What, you mean trying to keep the GIs in line and the Brits happy?'

'No, having to fend off women all the time,' Todd replied.

Brogan laughed but didn't deny it.

'Hey, Todd,' he said. 'There's a new club just opened in Waldorf Street. Me and a few of the boys in the office are thinking of giving it a go later, if you feel like joining us.'

'You're not seeing that singer at the Blue Fountain Club, then?' asked Todd.

'You mean Gloria,' Brogan replied.

Todd nodded.

'Not tonight,' said Brogan. 'She is singing a late set with the band. Are you sure you won't come and shake a leg with us? Do you good.'

Todd smiled. 'I've a letter I need to write.'

Brogan glanced at the sheets of pink paper beneath his friend's newspaper. 'How is Caroline?'

'Very well and says she's missing me loads,' Todd replied. 'Which is reassuring as she's agreed that we should tie the knot as soon as I return.'

'I hope I'm going to get an invitation,' said Brogan, raising the glass to his lips.

'You certainly will,' Todd replied. 'Perhaps by then you'll have your own wife to bring?'

Brogan spluttered.

'Wife? Not me,' he said, wiping his mouth with the back of his hand. 'I'm not the marrying kind.'

Todd gave him a rueful smile. 'No man's the marrying kind until he meets that one special woman.'

Puzzlingly, the image of the young woman with the grey eyes floated into Brogan's consciousness. Smiling at his brain's foolishness, Brogan shoved it aside and, swigging the last of the bourbon, stood up.

'If you say so,' he said, and chuckled, setting his cap at his preferred off-kilter angle. 'But if that miracle ever happens you have my permission to say, "I told you so".'

CHAPTER 3

'How's Bessie doing, Nell?' shouted Alice, looking towards the rear of the balloon where her friend was working.

'Almost there,' Nell yelled back without taking her eyes off the six-inch hose she was holding.

Her knuckles were white with the effort; she was gripping the pipe for dear life. Hardly surprising, really, as the end nearest her was plugged into the balloon's bayonet joint valve while the other was attached by the same mechanism to a long cylinder of helium resting in its cage transporter.

As always at this time of the day they were just finishing off their daily maintenance checks on Bessie, the 30-foot-high, 25-foot-wide and 64-foot-long barrage balloon which was currently floundering like a walrus on a beach on the bare earth of the site's operational area. The last job was always topping up the balloon, which, as it could hold up to 20,000 cubic feet of gas, was often a long job.

Balloon site 312 was situated in King Edward VI Recreational Ground, Wapping, in the heart of East London, and had the Thames lapping at its southern edge.

The park was also between two of the Luftwaffe's favourite

targets, the London Docks and Royal Docks, as the gutted ware-houses and destroyed homes around them testified. As it was one of the few open spaces in the most bombed areas of London, it was the most obvious place to site one of the hundreds of barrage balloons protecting the country's capital.

Because of this, what had once been a place for Sunday afternoon strolls had been completely given over to the war effort and the herbaceous borders were now growing cabbages, onions and carrots. The Air Ministry had taken over the rest of the space so what had previously been a lawn was now a gravel circle about 80 feet in circumference with a ten-foot-square block of concrete in the centre. The balloon was tethered to the concrete by metal cables attached to a petrol-driven winch.

Since her friend and the crew's corporal Effie had left the WAAFs three months ago when she became pregnant, Alice had been appointed acting corporal. It had therefore been her responsibility to rouse the crew at six that morning, and she'd had to drag them from their beds while the blackout was in force. After kit inspection and scrambled eggs and toast in the Maid of Norway's snug bar, she had marched them across the road in the pitch dark to take over from no. 9 crew. After receiving a handover from an exhausted Corporal Millie Wheeler, Alice allocated the crew their various daily tasks. This included repairing a handful of tears in the balloon's rubberised canvas belly and re-splicing a couple of fraying guy ropes. In addition, there was the winch to clean and the brakes to oil and test, before they addressed the maintenance of the countless bolts, blocks and tackle and the concrete anchorage points on the balloon's gravel working bed. Now, four hours later, they had almost completed their essential chores, having left the topping up of the balloon's gas as their last task.

'Turn it off,' Nell called.

With a swift turn of the wrist, Maeve, who was responsible

for the cylinder end of the operation, spun the stopcock to close the outlet valve.

Now buoyant again, the balloon drifted off the ground a few feet until it was halted by the ropes anchoring it.

'We're ready when you are, George,' called Alice.

George, who was in charge of the engine, gave Alice the thumbs-up.

'Right, clear!' Alice instructed, as she stepped back a few yards.

The six WAAFs standing around the balloon moved away as, caught by the wind, it tugged against its restraints.

'Let her go! Five hundred!' shouted Alice.

Standing beneath the domed tarpaulin shelter, George released the cable drum, and then, belching black smoke skywards, the engine spluttered into action. The crew grabbed the guy ropes and held the fat silver-grey balloon steady as it slowly ascended into the October sky, the stabilising fins on either side puffing up with air as it rose.

The cable rattled off the drum for a few moments, then George slammed on the brake. 'Five hundred feet!'

'Good job, everyone,' said Alice, stripping off her heavy-duty gloves. She looked at her watch. 'The dinner wagon will be here soon, but I think we've got time for a well-deserved cuppa before it does.'

'I'll put the kettle on,' said Maeve.

'Make mine a coffee,' said Lily, winding her guy rope into a figure of eight.

'If we have any,' Maeve called over her shoulder as she looped her rope round the concrete anchor.

As the team tidied away, Alice did her last checks on the equipment and then headed over to the hut to join the rest of her crew.

When the idea was mooted of training WAAFs to take over the manning of the barrage balloons, there had been a lot of misgivings. The main objection to the proposal from many of the RAF's top brass was that women weren't strong enough to handle the equipment. It was therefore decided that female crews should comprise ten operatives rather than the eight in male teams.

In theory, no. 3 crew did have ten members; however, theory didn't always translate into practice. As her friend Effie Weston – now Fitzgerald – had left in September to have a baby, they were already down to nine and it was Maureen's day off, so there were only eight of them on duty today.

Leaving the damp autumn gloom behind her, Alice walked into the warm fug of the on-duty hut's interior, just as the kettle's whistle started to rattle.

'You timed that just right,' said Maeve, as Alice closed the door.

George, who was sitting cross-legged on the crew's battered sofa, patted the cushion beside her. 'Take the weight off your feet.'

Alice squeezed beside her as Maeve handed her a cup; however, just as she was about to take a sip the door opened and Sergeant Munroe, the well-built, fair-haired WAAF in her early thirties who was in charge of them, marched in.

'Morning, girls,' she said, planting her polished brogues squarely in the middle of the floor.

The WAAFs stood to attention and returned her greeting.

'We've just made a pot if you fancy a cuppa, Skip,' said Nell, holding the teapot aloft.

'Sadly no,' Munroe replied. 'I've got to be in Stanmore in an hour and after last night's raid goodness knows how many roads are impassable. No, I've just popped by to let you know that Corporal Weston's place on this team has been filled, and she will be arriving in a few days. I also wanted to tell you that Flight HQ has promoted Aircraftwoman Craven to crew corporal.'

Alice's heart sank as her friends stared in disbelief at their non-commissioned officer.

'For goodness sake, Skip! Surely, you can't be putting Lily in charge?' said George.

'George has the right of it,' added Maeve.

Munroe shook her head. 'I'm sorry but that's the decision.'

'Why?' said Nell.

Alice studied her toes. She knew why. Two days before Effie was due to be married, having just discovered she was pregnant, her future husband had gone missing over France. RAF regulations prohibited pregnant women in the WAAF, but Effie had nowhere to turn; her parents disapproved of both her relationship with Nathan and the fact that their only daughter was pregnant out of wedlock. So Alice, Nell and George had helped Effie to conceal her condition, until Lily discovered and out of pure malice telephoned HQ to tell them.

Beneath the peak of her cap, Munroe's grey eyes flickered over Alice. 'I'm sorry, Starling, but you ignored regulations, and this is the consequence. Where is Lily anyway?'

'I saw her heading for the WVS van at the corner,' Alice replied.

'Carry on.' Munroe turned on her heels and marched out.

As the door closed, all eyes turned to Alice.

'It's all right,' she said, blinking away the tightness in her eyes.

'No, it's bloody not,' said Nell. 'And I 'ope HQ remembers it's their fault when it all goes arse up.'

'Do you know someone who can knock some sense into the bloody top brass at Stanmore, George?' asked Dolly.

'Well, I think my brother has a chum who's a flight commander up there,' George replied. 'I could give Rupert a tinkle and—'

The hut door banged open as Lily, a grin spread across her overly made-up face, swaggered in.

'Well, well, well,' she said, putting her hands on her hips and surveying them smugly. 'I can see by the delighted look on your faces that you've heard the good news.'

No one replied.

Slipping off her armband with the corporal stripes, Alice held Lily's gaze for a moment, then offered it to her. 'Congratulations.'

Lily snatched it from her, slid it up her arm, then looked slowly around at the balloon team.

A spiteful smile spread across her face. 'Right, you lot, there's going to be some changes around here.'

After what seemed like a twenty-four-hour shift rather than twelve, and having handed over to the night team, Alice finally arrived back at the Maid of Norway, the century-old four-storey gin palace overlooking their war-site on the corner of Glasshouse Fields and the Highway where she and eight of the other girls in the balloon crew were billeted.

However, instead of going up the stairs where their crew's living quarters were, Alice walked to the end of the hallway and knocked lightly on the door to the landlady's private back parlour. She waited for a moment, then turned the brass handle and walked in.

The room was situated behind the bar at the back and overlooked the handkerchief-sized yard at the rear. It served as both kitchen and parlour. With its faded wallpaper and yellowing paintwork, the room was in dire need of sprucing up but, like the rest of the establishment, it was spotlessly clean. It contained not only a two-seater sofa and two chairs but a painted pine kitchen cabinet. There was also a small table, at which sat a dark-haired young woman.

Effie looked up as Alice walked in and glanced at the clock. 'Goodness, is it gone six already?'

'It's almost half past,' said Alice, unbuttoning the front of her navy boiler suit.

'Good shift?' her friend asked, her pen poised above the open ledger in front of her.

'The usual,' Alice replied. 'What about you, Effie?'

Putting her pen down, Effie rested back, and placed her hand on her swollen stomach. 'Well enough, although this baby hasn't stopped wriggling all day.'

Alice had met Effie Weston during one freezing cold January morning nine months ago and they had been firm friends ever since. Effie's husband Nathan was a decorated RAF flight lieutenant, and, as he was currently stationed in the wilds of Scotland, Florrie had offered Effie lodgings in the Maid of Norway in return for managing the pub's accounts.

'I've just made a pot if you fancy a cuppa,' said Effie, indicating the teapot across from her on the table.

Alice took a mug from the shelf on the dresser, returned to the table and poured herself a cup.

'Well, that's September's accounts all done,' Effie said, dotting her last entry. 'The tobacconist on the corner of St David's Lane asked me if I'd do their books, so I'll make a start in the morning.'

Alice raised her eyebrows. 'Another one?'

'I've only got two other shops, and as bookkeeping isn't a reserved occupation there's plenty of small family businesses struggling to make sense of the wartime regulations,' Effie replied. 'Besides, it keeps me busy, plus I'm adding a few pounds each week to my post office savings bank.' She laid her pen in the tray beside the inkwell, leant back again, and looked puzzled. 'Where's your armband?'

'I gave it to Lily,' Alice replied, and she told Effie about Sergeant Munroe's visit.

'I suppose she's been throwing her weight around already,' said Effie when she'd finished.

Alice nodded. 'The first thing she did was kick Peggy out of the single room because she was "in charge" now.'

Effie frowned. 'It so blooming unfair. You've done a brilliant job since you took over.'

'Well, obviously Flight HQ doesn't think so,' said Alice.

'It's because of what you and the girls did for me, isn't it?' said Effie.

'Munroe didn't say why, but even if it was,' Alice replied, looking her friend squarely in the eye, 'I would do exactly the same again.'

Smiling, Effie looked down and ran her hand over her stomach.

Pain jabbed at Alice. The sort of pain that only nine years of marriage with no sight of a baby can cause. She cleared her throat. 'So what did the midwives at Munroe Clinic say?'

'That everything was as it should be, and that Miss or Master Fitzgerald will be making an appearance in about eight or nine weeks,' Effie replied as Alice sat down opposite her.

A broad smile spread across Alice's face. 'Perfect. Just in time for them to be baby Jesus in the nativity.'

'I might have a girl,' said Effie.

'That's fine,' said Alice. 'Wrapped in swaddling no one will know we've changed the sex of our Saviour.'

'And I don't mind one jot whether I have a boy or a girl,' said Effie, 'as I just can't wait to hold my baby in my arms.'

At her friend's words, Alice felt a familiar tightness in the corners of her eyes, so she buried her nose in her cup.

The door leading to the public bar opened and their landlady Florrie Granger walked in.

Rather than one of her usual figure-hugging outfits, this afternoon she was dressed in her forest green WVS uniform because in addition to her duties in the pub she was also a leading light of the Shadwell Women's Voluntary Service. They ran the relief centre in the old Congregationalist Mission Hall a few hundred yards away. When she wasn't pulling pints in the bar downstairs Florrie could be found distributing clothes and toiletries to those who had been bombed out the night before, running after toddlers in the WVS nursery, which had been set up almost as soon as war broke out for mothers who were doing war work, or making tea for ARP personnel, because beneath whatever she was wearing beat a heart of pure cockney gold.

'Goodness, it's turned nippy,' she said, taking her hat off and patting her strawberry-blonde hair back into order.

'Well, it is the end of October,' said Effie. 'There's tea in the pot if you fancy a cup.'

'Thanks, luv, but I'll give it a miss,' she replied, hooking her coat behind the door. 'I've had half a dozen cups during this afternoon's committee meeting, and I think my teeth are floating! I'm glad I've caught you both, though, as I wanted to see if you can help with the relief centre's Christmas celebrations?'

'We will if we can,' said Alice. 'What are you after?'

'Well,' said Florrie, pulling out a chair at the end of the table and sitting down. 'Christmas Day is Friday so we're going to have the party on Christmas Eve. We're going to kick off the day with a kiddie tea party followed by a visit from Father Christmas, after which we thought we'd get the kiddies to do the nativity play. Then perhaps a bit of a sing-song – perhaps get a couple of people up to do a turn or two – with some carols to round off if we can get someone to play the piano. Miss Worth from the Methodist Chapel usually does it for us but she's gone to be with her brother in Shropshire. I've heard George tinkling the ivories on the pub's old piano, so do you think she'd step in?'

'I'm sure she will,' said Alice.

'It all sounds like it's going to be great fun for everyone,' said Effie.

'And after the last couple of grim months, hopefully it will help cheer people up,' added Alice. 'So, what can we do?'

'Anything you can think of to decorate the hall or that might do for presents in Father Christmas's sack,' said Florrie. 'We're going to get knitting to make woolly hats and mittens, so if you're free and want to join us down at the WVS, then we'd be happy to see you.' She winked. 'There's tea and cake.'

'Count me in,' said Effie.

'Me too,' said Alice. 'And I'll tell the others when I get upstairs.'

'Thanks, luv.' Glancing at the clock on the mantelshelf, Florrie sighed. 'Goodness, is that the blooming time already? Bert will be opening the doors in twenty minutes, so I'd better get changed before the rush.'

Placing her hands flat on the table, Florrie heaved herself to her feet, and headed for the hall door. However, as she reached it she paused, and her pencilled eyebrows pulled together in a frown.

'What's the matter?' asked Alice.

'I dunno, girls,' Florrie said. 'With all the empty windows and shelves in the shops and the blooming government shoving leaflets through your letter box every day about don't use this and save that, goodness knows how we're going to lay on a half-decent spread for the kiddies.'

Effie got to her feet too, and, crossing to where their land-lady stood, she laid a gentle hand on her arm. 'Don't worry, Florrie, we'll pitch in, won't we, Alice?'

'We jolly well will,' Alice agreed, smiling across at the land-lady. 'And I predict, Florrie, that the 1942 Shadwell Relief Centre's Christmas bash will be the most memorable Christmas ever.'

CHAPTER 4

As Brogan walked into the reception of Bow Street police station, Sergeant Mills, the front desk officer, sitting on the other side of the mahogany counter, looked up from the heavy leather-bound book he was writing in.

'Lieutenant Rafferty, how nice to see you again,' he said, in a tone that indicated otherwise. 'And I see you've brought a couple of friends with you.'

It was just after eight in the morning on the last Saturday in October and he was there for the same reason he'd been there two days ago, to collect his fellow countrymen who had disturbed the King's Peace the night before.

The friends Mills was referring to were two officers from the US Army Military Police Corps, who were standing at his shoulders. With hands the size of a baseball fielder's glove and height to match, the two army cops made Brogan look like one of Snow White's landlords. In contrast to Brogan's tailored uniform jacket and civilian-cut trousers, the two officers were dressed in combat trousers and battle jackets, with knee-length webbing gaiters atop their polished black boots and unyielding expressions on their faces.

'Good morning, Officer,' said Brogan, answering the other man's resentful look with a friendly smile. 'What have you got for us on this fine morning?'

Thanks to an agreement thrashed out between the US Army's top brass and the British government, unlike the British population American servicemen stationed in Britain who broke English law were handed over and dealt with by the American authorities. The Brits didn't like it, any more than the Americans would have if the boot was on the other foot, but they needed the US equipment and men to win the war, so were in no position to argue.

'Two drunk and disorderly,' the desk sergeant replied. 'They took exception to vehicles driving on the left in Park Lane and were trying to direct them back onto the right side. They're lucky to be in the cells instead of the casualty ward in Charing Cross Hospital.'

'They sure are,' agreed Brogan.

Reaching into a wire basket beside him, Sergeant Mills pulled out a slim manila file. Brogan took it.

He flipped it open and, after scanning the arresting officer's report, closed it again. 'If you would be kind enough to take us to them, we'll get them out of your hair.'

'Constable Hanson,' the desk sergeant barked over his shoulder.

A young officer with pale eyes, looking like he was wearing his big brother's uniform, sprang out from behind the frosted glass flanking the counter.

'Take our friends and allies here down to the cells,' Mills instructed.

'Thank you, Sergeant,' said Brogan, cheerfully.

Bow Street police station and the adjoining magistrate's court had been there since the middle of the 1700s, about the same time as the ink was drying on the American Constitution. The current building, a solid stone affair with its classical façade, had been built about a hundred years before. However, call it his journalistic imagination if you like, but, every time he made his way down the stone steps to the police station's basement, Brogan couldn't help wondering if the ghosts of long-departed Bow Street Runners were hovering somewhere.

The harsh glare from the strip lighting on the ceiling cut across Brogan's eyes as the small party arrived at the space beneath the police station. Running along each side were heavy cast-iron doors leading to the dozen or so dank police cells.

Hanson took a set of keys from the hook by the jailer's desk and led them between the solid metal doors to one halfway down on the right. After unlocking it, the constable stood back, and Brogan stepped in, followed by the two snowdrops.

The smell of alcohol and vomit from the bucket in the corner hit Brogan in a wave. Slumped on the solid bench that ran across the width of the room were two fresh-faced soldiers. Well, perhaps youthful would have been a better description than fresh, because even in the dim light fixed to the ceiling they both looked decidedly green.

On seeing him enter both attempted to stand, but their legs weren't up to the task, and they fell back.

Brogan flipped open the file again. 'Private Ingles?'

'Sir,' said one, a slender guy with clipped black hair.

'And Kline?' added Brogan.

His freckle-faced friend nodded, then, retching, grabbed the bucket.

Holding his breath, Brogan waited until he'd finished, then turned to the two military police officers behind him.

'They're all yours, officers,' said Brogan, addressing the two men standing behind him.

The military police officers stepped forward and, grabbing a drunken private each, hauled them to their feet, then frog-marched them out of the cell.

Tucking the folder under his arm, Brogan followed them and retraced his steps back up to the station.

'Lieutenant Rafferty,' called the desk sergeant as Hanson led them across the foyer. 'The chief says would you mind having a word with him before you leave.'

'Of course.' Brogan turned to the US military police officers behind him. 'Take them to the barracks and I'll meet you there.'

Dragging the two drunken GIs with them, the officers left the station, and Brogan made his way up the stairs, and into the office at the end of the first-floor corridor.

Pausing, he stared at the frosted glass for a moment, then taking a deep breath, he knocked.

'Come!'

Brogan grasped the handle, forced a friendly expression onto his face and went in.

To his right on the wall was an enlarged map of the west side of London adorned with coloured thumb tacks. Against the wall opposite was a row of wooden filing cabinets labelled alphabetically, above which were a handful of framed citations, plus a couple of silver cups for boxing. However, the room was dominated by a dark oak desk in front of the window, behind which sat Chief Inspector Richard Crosby.

In his early fifties, Chief Inspector Crosby was of middling hight and slightly built. He had a pencil moustache and a gaze that would cut through glass. A native Londoner, he had managed to survive both the Somme and Passchendaele and had joined the Metropolitan Police on his return to England. He had a reputation for being hard-bitten and ruthless, which was just as well as his patch covered not only the well-heeled streets of Mayfair but also Soho, London's red-light district and centre of vice.

Dressed in his Metropolitan Police uniform, he was reading an open file in front of him, but looked up as Brogan walked in.

'Good morning, Chief Inspector,' said Brogan, smiling artlessly at the man behind the desk. 'You wanted a word.'

Without offering him a seat, Crosby rested his elbows on the table and steepled his fingers together.

'Can you tell me what this building is called?' he said.

Guessing where this conversation was going, Brogan stood to attention. 'Bow Street police station.'

'Correct,' barked the chief inspector. 'Did you know that this is the place that gave its name to the Bow Street Runners, the first recognised police force in the country?'

'I did,' said Brogan.

An enraged expression replaced Crosby's genial one in an instant.

'So it is *not* a bloody dosshouse for drunken American servicemen, Lieutenant Rafferty,' he bellowed. He jabbed the file in front of him with a fat index finger. 'Fifteen we've had this week. Fifteen bloody inebriated GIs we've had to arrest for drunk and disorderly behaviour, criminal damage and assault.'

'I'm sorry,' said Brogan. 'But I can assure you that the US Army takes these matters very seriously.'

'Your top brass might,' barked Crosby. 'But it doesn't stop your countrymen taking up our officers' time and clogging up our cells. We've got enough to do trying to catch black-marketeers, looters and thieves without having to deal with dozens of drunken Yanks each night.'

'I do understand the problems,' said Brogan. 'And I'm sure that—'

'They get a forty-eight-hour pass and head straight to London,' continued the chief inspector. 'They're already half-cut when they roll off the trains and then make a beeline for Piccadilly. They steam into clubs flashing their money buying drinks, then stagger around the streets looking for women.'

'When the new Red Cross canteen is opened at Rainbow Corner in a few weeks it will help alleviate some of these problems by offering the soldiers in London on furlough somewhere else to go,' Brogan offered, soothingly.

'To get drunk, don't you mean?' snapped Crosby.

Brogan shook his head. 'None of the US Red Cross canteens have a liquor licence and Rainbow Corner will be the same.'

'Well, that's a small mercy I suppose,' Crosby said grudgingly. 'But with so many young Americans with time on their hands and cash in their pockets, I doubt this new canteen of yours will stop young women from all over the country flocking to London to "catch themselves a Yank".'

The memory of the young women mobbing the group of sozzled GIs the previous week returned. Well, truthfully, just the auburn-haired one with the lovely eyes, whose image seemed to have stuck with him.

Brogan raised an eyebrow. 'I doubt even the United States of America Army is mighty enough to fight against the birds and the bees, Chief Inspector.'

The hint of a smile lifted the corner of Crosby's lips.

'But,' continued Brogan, 'it will offer all our men a bit of home from home and many recreational activities and entertainments to keep them occupied.'

'I hope you're right, Lieutenant,' said the chief inspector. 'Now if you don't mind.'

'Of course,' said Brogan. 'Thank you for your time, Chief Inspector, and I will pass on all your concerns.'

He turned but, after taking a couple of steps towards the door, an idea sprang into his head, so he turned back.

'I'm putting on a guided tour of Rainbow Corner for some of the members of the London Civilian and US Army liaison committee,' he said. 'I'll send you an invite too so you can come and see for yourself.' He smiled innocently at the older man behind the desk. 'We'll be serving complimentary hot dogs and doughnuts.'

The chief inspector chewed his lip for a moment. 'I'll see.'

Smiling, Brogan headed for the door. He'd never met a cop yet who'd say no to a doughnut.

~

'Do you know, I've never been as happy to see Millie and her crew as I was when they turned up tonight,' said Alice as she walked through the Maid of Norway's back door.

'You and me both,' said Nell, stripping off her dripping raincoat. 'Although I don't envy them stuck in the hut all night.'

As she had predicted, when Alice relayed Florrie's request for them to help with the WVS Christmas celebrations the rest of the crew had been keen to do their bit to put a smile on the local kiddies' faces. All, that is, except Lily and Maureen, who indicated they had better things to do with their time than spend it knitting.

That was yesterday. Today, they'd spent most of the day wrestling Bessie down in the teeth of a force nine gale, and were now soaked to the skin. Thankfully, no. 9 crew had turned up for night duty half an hour ago, so Alice and the rest of no. 3 crew were now in the upstairs lounge of the Maid of Norway. Along with the incessant rain, the mercury in the thermometer had plummeted in the last hour, so they were all grateful to find that Florrie had already lit the fire and there were glowing coals in the cast-iron grate.

The main living room was a decent size, but like so much of wartime London was in desperate need of renewing and redecoration. However, the heavy furniture had been polished, the chandelier sparkled, and Florrie ensured that the worn Indian carpet covering the floor was swept three times a week.

'Is someone putting on the kettle?' asked Alice.

'I'm on my way,' Dolly replied, hooking her coat on the hall stand.

'Make sure you put some brandy in mine,' George called, taking off her hat and starting to dry her damp blonde hair.

With every bone in her body aching, and utterly exhausted, Alice flopped onto the sofa, but the moment she closed her eyes the lounge door opened and Florrie's head appeared round it.

For her time behind the bar this evening Florrie was wearing a straight black skirt, white V-neck blouse with a fluted collar and a pair of red high heels that made Alice's feet ache just looking at them. Her only concession to domesticity was a handkerchief-sized frilly apron.

'Yoo-hoo, only me, girls,' she trilled. A look of horror spread across her powdered face as she stepped into the room. 'Oh, my Gawd, you lot look like drowned rats.'

'We feel like it too,' said Dolly, spreading her coat across the back of a dining chair.

'Well, never mind,' Florrie replied, her heavily mascaraed blue eyes warm as she looked across. 'I've made you some nice rabbit stew for supper and I even managed to get a couple of onions to give it a bit of extra flavour. I'll get Ernie to fetch it up in twenty minutes after you've got yourselves dry.'

'Thanks, Florrie,' said Alice, giving her a grateful smile.

The landlady turned and was about to leave the room when she turned back.

'Honestly, what am I like?' she said, rolling her eyes. 'I'd forget my blooming head if it wasn't screwed on.' Delving into her apron pocket, she pulled out a handful of letters. 'I came up to bring you the post.'

Maeve got out of the armchair and took them from her. 'Thanks, Florrie.'

'It's no trouble,' their landlady replied, as Maeve started to sort through them. 'I know how I am waiting for a few lines from my boys, and I'm sure you're the same.'

'This one's yours, Florrie,' said Maeve, holding up an open envelope with red and blue markings round the edge.

'Silly me,' said Florrie, taking it and tucking it back in her apron pocket. 'It's from Bridget, my sister in New York. Her eldest boy's just been posted to London, and she says he'll be popping by to say hello.'

'Tell him to bring half a dozen of his friends,' said George, taking an expensive-looking envelope from Maeve.

'And some nylons,' added Nell.

Florrie raised a pencilled eyebrow, a smile hovering on her cherry-red lips. 'Don't forget. Supper should be here?'

The door burst open again and a skinny boy of about ten or eleven, wearing shorts and a Boy Scout shirt, tie and woggle, marched in carrying an enamel bowl and a pint jug on a tray.

'Where do you want this, Mrs G?' he asked.

'On the table, ta,' Florrie replied.

The boy, whose fair hair seemed to grow at a variety of different angles from his head, placed the tray next to the pot.

'This is Stanley,' Florrie said. 'Our barmaid Daisy's kid brother. His Scout troop have just signed up to be ARP messengers.'

As if to prove her point, Stanley proudly indicated the ARP armband round his right upper arm with the word *Messenger* stencilled on it.

'Thanks, luv,' Florrie added. 'You'd better make tracks now or you'll end up being late.'

The young lad dashed off and clattered down the stairs.

'Enjoy your meal,' said Florrie and followed the young lad back downstairs.

'I wonder what he looks like?' asked Nell.

'Who?' asked Dolly as she walked in carrying a try of tea.

'Florrie's nephew,' Nell replied. 'He's an American GI who just arrived in London.'

'Well, let's hope he looks like the ones we met on Saturday night,' said George, taking a mug. 'Very tall and very handsome.'

'You have the right of it, George,' Maeve laughed. 'Because I'd say they left all the ugly Americans at home.'

The memory of her run-in with the American lieutenant the week before, who certainly fitted that description, floated into Alice's mind.

'Well,' she said, shoving the image from her mind. 'Handsome is as handsome does, so let's hope Florrie's American nephew isn't like that blooming arrogant American lieutenant who I ran into in Piccadilly two weeks ago who had the nerve to call me a cheap dame...'

CHAPTER 5

'What'd you reckon then, chief?' asked Len Truman, rubbing his unshaven chin with a grubby finger.

Brogan gazed around at the stepladders, buckets of paint, rolls of flooring and the half a dozen workmen lolling about on the dust-cover-draped furniture drinking tea.

'You do know we're planning to open the place very soon, don't you, Mr Truman?' he said, trying to keep a lid on his rising panic.

Rainbow Corner comprised two places: Del Monico's restaurant on the corner of Shaftesbury Avenue and the Lyons Corner House next door, both of which had been requisitioned by the British authorities for their American allies to use.

Brogan was standing in what would be one of the two restaurants, each of which could feed at a squeeze two thousand men at any one time for the princely sum of twenty-five cents.

Although under US Army control, the setting up and the day-to-day running of the club was the responsibility of the American Red Cross, whose aim was to create a little piece of America for the troops. This wasn't the first American club that the redoubtable ladies of the ARC working parties had set up, but, situated where the upmarket area of Mayfair met the hedonistic streets of Soho in what the newspapers were now calling Little America, when it opened it would be by far the largest. That was if it *did* open, Brogan thought glumly, because with walls still awaiting paint and bare wooden floorboards underfoot the chances of him opening the club when he planned were growing increasingly remote.

'I do,' Truman replied, the roll-up stuck to his lower lip moving up and down as he spoke. 'So as soon as me and my lads have wet their whistles, we'll crack on.'

'Lieutenant Rafferty!'

Brogan turned to see a tall freckle-faced youth dressed in transport corps combats and with a ginger crew-cut standing in the doorway.

'I've got the pinball machines outside, where do you want them unloaded, sir?' he asked, waving the clipboard in his hand.

'I'll show you,' Brogan replied.

Leaving Len and his builders slurping their third cup of tea of the morning, Brogan led the delivery driver back down the sweeping staircase to the room in the basement.

With elegant plaster columns and fancy architraves, the space Brogan had designated as the games room had once been a late-night eating area. However, the small bistro tables with their pristine white tablecloths and candles had been replaced by two full-sized pool tables with low light over them and comfortable benches running alongside. There were also half a dozen slot machines to the right and a jukebox tucked in the corner.

'The pinballs are going there,' said Brogan, pointing at the space along the far wall.

The transport soldier gave a quick salute and headed off upstairs. Giving the underground sports den a cursory glance, Brogan followed him back up.

'There you are, Brogan!'

He looked up to see Todd Robertson striding towards him. 'Todd. Shouldn't you be rubbing shoulders with that Free French General Depole?'

'It's De Gaulle,' corrected his friend. 'And I would be except he's postponed the meeting until tomorrow because Churchill summoned him to Whitehall. How's it going?'

'Slowly,' Brogan replied. 'Honestly, these Brits. I mean how many damn tea breaks can you have in one day?'

Todd gave him a sympathetic look. 'When is it opening?'

'Soon,' Brogan replied. 'Supposedly with the canteen serving hot dogs and doughnuts, but, as neither the ovens nor the refrigerators have arrived it might be cold sandwiches and warm beer. I've got the band booked, and the ladies of the management committee are halfway through drawing up a list of suitable young women to invite.'

'Very sensible,' said Todd. 'As I doubt the GIs' mothers and girlfriends back home would be very happy to hear we'd allowed their sons and sweethearts to fraternise with Piccadilly's army of *un*suitable ones.'

From nowhere the image of the auburn haired young woman he'd encountered the Saturday before last in Piccadilly flashed through Brogan's mind.

'No sir. They sure wouldn't,' he said, pushing the memory aside. 'And two weeks after the grand opening we'll be having a full Thanksgiving dinner, including apple pie just like "Ma used to make".'

'Put my name on that ticket,' Todd laughed. 'Say, man, are you almost done here?'

'Pretty much,' said Brogan.

'Well then, what say you and me head across to that little Italian restaurant in Frith Street,' said Todd.

'I'd love to but I've got a date,' Brogan replied.

His friend looked puzzled. 'Who is it this time?'

'Florrie,' said Brogan. 'Or more correctly my aunt, Mrs Florence Granger, landlady of the Maid of Norway.'

'So, you decided to go,' said Todd.

Brogan nodded. 'I've got to, really, especially as Ma sent me a Christmas parcel to give Florrie and strict instructions to take something nice from the PX,' he said. 'I'm off to spruce myself up before I head east but— Hey fella,' he shouted as a couple of delivery men struggled in through the door carrying an espresso machine. 'That needs to go upstairs to the coffee bar at the back.' He looked back at Todd. 'Perhaps I'll catch you later.'

'You certainly will,' said Todd. 'As I want to hear all about your expedition into the uncharted territory of East London.'

Humming the chorus of 'The Yellow Rose of Texas', which was blasting out from the radio in the corner of the hut, Alice had just scrubbed the last dollops of lunchtime stew off the enamel stove with wire wool when the hut door opened and Nell walked in.

'Do you mind if I put the kettle on?' she asked, hovering on the threshold and letting in a blast of cold air.

'Of course not,' said Alice, wiping a stray lock of hair from her forehead with the back of her hand. 'Have you all finished?'

'Pretty much,' Nell replied, as she held the kettle under the tap. 'Once Dolly and Rosie have secured the gas cylinders and George has topped up the fuel tank, we're done.'

Just as well, because it was almost three o'clock in the afternoon and, after starting duty on the dot of six that morning, they'd all been hard at it ever since.

The door opened and George and Maeve strolled in, bringing a swirl of river fog with them.

Maeve gave Alice a puzzled look. 'Aren't you supposed to be on a half-day?'

'I was but Lily cancelled it,' said Alice, wiping the last residue of soap from the hotplate.

'Why?' asked George, stripping off her coat and hooking it on the wall peg.

Alice rolled her eyes. 'Because, apparently, Maureen had to go somewhere this afternoon.'

'Round to the ARP hut to shag that skinny warden with the buck teeth, no doubt,' said Nell as she set the mugs on the table.

'She's welcome to him and his dandruff,' said Dolly, who had just walked in.

Everyone laughed.

'Even so,' said Nell, as she handed out the tea. 'Since she was made up to corporal last week, she's changed all the off-duty rotas and given her and her mate Maureen all the cushy jobs each day.'

'Never mind about crab-face Lily,' said George, who was sprawled in one of the armchairs. 'What's more important is who's up for a wild night up west with me on Saturday?'

'Count me in,' said Nell, dropping the knitted cosy over the enamel teapot.

'And me,' said Maeve, who was sitting beside George on the sofa.

'Well, it won't be me and Peggy as our dear corporal has us down for on-call,' said Dolly.

'I'm afraid I can't either,' said Alice, squeezing out the wire wool square.

'Why not?' said Nell.

'Because there's a recital on the wireless that me and Effie are keen to hear,' Alice replied, popping the scrubber into the handless cup behind the tap that served as a soap dish.

Four pairs of eyes looked at her in disbelief.

'Let me see if I have this right,' said Maeve incredulously. 'You're telling us that instead of spending the night sinking

G&Ts and jitterbugging around some grand-looking GI you'd rather drink cocoa and listen to some high-falutin' concert?'

'Well, it *is* Dvořák's serenade in E,' said Alice, looking innocently at them. 'Perhaps next time.'

To be honest she wouldn't have minded going with them, but she couldn't bear it if she came face to face again with that tall American lieutenant who'd thought she was one of those girls hustling GIs. Perhaps if she left it for a couple of weeks, if she did run into him again he might have forgotten her.

The door opened and Lily walked in.

'On your feet, you lot,' she barked. 'The phone line's down, so a rider from HQ has just arrived with instruction to bring the balloon down to five hundred feet.'

'And a good afternoon to you too, Lily,' said George.

Lily's eyes narrowed. 'Never mind the old swank. Just get a move on.'

Grumbling, the girls threw back their drinks and got up, then, donning their greatcoats and scarves as they went, they trudged out.

As the door banged shut behind them Lily picked up Alice's unclaimed tea and sank back onto the sofa.

Taking a sip, her eyes slid on to Alice. 'Carry on.'

Answering Lily's smug expression with a cool one, Alice rolled down her sleeves and then snatched her coat from the peg and marched out to join the rest of the team.

'So,' said Brogan, cradling the hot mug between his large hands. 'That's pretty much all the Brogan family news from our side of the pond.'

'I can't believe your sister Maisey is going to be married,' said Florrie, her powdered face lifting in a sentimental smile. 'It only seems like yesterday your mum wrote to say she was expecting her.'

'Yes, time does fly,' Brogan agreed.

It was the middle of the afternoon, and he was sitting in a rather comfortable fireside armchair in the back lounge of the Maid of Norway public house.

Only slightly larger than his family's tenement room, his aunt's private room was at the rear of the public house and with a cast-iron range instead of fireplace it served as her kitchen and parlour. There was an India rug on the floor, well-worn sofa and chairs and black-and-white photos with smiling children and upright seniors staring out of them – homely would be the best way to describe it. And opposite, sitting in the chair on the other side of the cast-iron grate, was his aunt, Florrie Granger.

When his mother had told him that, like her, Florrie was in her late forties, Brogan had imagined his distant relative to look very much like his ma. However, nothing could be further from the truth. Instead of grey hair scooped back into a discreet bun, Florrie's copper tresses were piled high on her head, and, instead of the mute autumn colours his mother favoured during the day, the woman smiling across at him wore a figure-hugging purple dress with a lacy collar. Her glitzy appearance was enhanced by her bright red lipstick and black patent stilettos. However, the genuine delight and warmth of her welcome made him feel very much at home.

'And you're a newspaper reporter,' said Florrie.

'I am, with the *New York Herald*,' said Brogan. 'But the *New York Times* has published a couple of my pieces so, when I get Stateside again, I'll be knocking at their door. I'm keeping my pen sharp by writing a few pieces for the US Army's own newspaper, the *Stars and Stripes*.'

'Good for you,' said Florrie.

'We were all sorry to hear about your husband,' said Brogan.

'Thanks,' said Florrie. 'It was good of your mum to send a lovely card.'

'Was it sudden?' asked Brogan.

Florrie nodded. 'My Sid was pulling pints Sunday lunchtime and lying in the London Hospital's morgue teatime on Monday,' she said. 'It were 'is heart, you know. Same as his father and his father before him. Almost twenty-three years we were married.' She pulled a handkerchief from her sleeve and blew her nose.

'And with never a cross word, I imagine,' said Brogan.

'Oh, I wouldn't go that far, luv,' she said, looking at him with a twinkle in her eye.

'And your two sons,' said Brogan, shifting the conversation onto a safer subject. 'They're in the thick of it, I hear.'

'They are. Alex is somewhere in Atlantic on HMS *Dorsetshire* and Steve chasing the Italians across the Sahara with the Eighth Army,' Florrie replied. 'So, goodness knows when I'll next see them.' A fond look spread across her powdered face. 'So until I do I 'ave Ernie and Daisy helping me in the pub and the WVS to keep me busy.'

Brogan gave her a querying look.

'Women's Voluntary Service. I'm on the committee of the Shadwell branch. We meet in the old Congregation Hall along the Highway.' Florrie's eyes flickered down to his untouched drink. 'Is your coffee all right?'

Smiling, Brogan took a sip and smacked his lips. 'Yes, ma'am,' he replied. 'Just like we have back home.'

Truthfully, what he was drinking was more like a mouthful of the East River, but, as he always told newly arrived GIs in his orientation talks, the Brits had been bombed and half-starved for three years, so he took pains to be respectful and polite.

Making a mental note to bring a tin of Nescafé when he next visited, he swallowed the last mouthful.

'What is it exactly that you do at the WVS?' he asked, swallowing it down.

'What *don't* we do?' Florrie replied. 'Collect stuff for salvage. Run a relief centre with two dozen beds, with a welfare officer and a clothes exchange for people who have been bombed out. We send out our mobile canteen after an air raid to keep the ARP going with tea and buns and man the refreshments in the Johnson Street shelter under the old boys' orphanage. At the moment, though, all our efforts are going towards putting on the kiddies' Christmas party followed by a Christmas concert and singalong for the adults. Of course, with all the shortages and rations we'll have to put our thinking caps on in order to lay on a half-decent spread, but Peggy Smith's 'usband has agreed to be Father Christmas so that's something.'

'It sounds like a lot of work, especially on top of running the bar,' said Brogan.

The sentimental expression returned to Florrie's face. 'It is, but it'll be worth it just to see the nippers' faces light up.' She frowned. 'Of course, we'll have to make sure we've a toy for each child. The blokes in our local ARP are making wooden trains, aeroplanes and boats for the boys and my girls, bless 'em, are knitting all sorts and stitching new clothes for the girls' dollies.'

Brogan looked puzzled. 'I didn't know you had daughters.'

'I don't.' Florrie chuckled. 'I'm talking about my balloon girls, who are in charge of Bessie, the barrage balloon in the park across the road. Surely you spotted her.'

'I certainly did,' Brogan replied.

To be honest he couldn't very well miss the great bloated grey cigar-shaped thing hovering overhead as he parked his jeep outside the Maid of Norway.

'I have a dozen of them all billeted upstairs,' continued Florrie. 'And a real pleasure it is too. Work their socks off they do, at all hours of the day and night and in all weathers, to keep the blooming Luftwaffe up 'igh so our guns can take a pop at them. But do they complain? No, they blooming well don't. Just roll up their sleeves and get on with it, they do.'

'So, you've got British WAAFs billeted here?' said Brogan.

Florrie nodded again. 'I have a crew of them lodged upstairs on the two top floors. And I'm pleased to have them, that's the truth. They've all signed up to help with the children's Christmas party and George has volunteered to play the piano for the concert after. And it's all down to Alice, who has been getting them to knit some scarves and mittens as presents and to save their sweet and sugar rations so we can give the children something a little special in their stockings. Alice has even put in for a day off so she can help out all day at the relief centre.' She cocked her ear as footsteps sounded on the other side of the door. 'In fact, I think that's one of them now.'

Florrie rose to her feet, crossed to the door and opened it.

'Oh, Alice, I was just talking about you,' she said. 'Come into the parlour, there's someone I'd like you to meet.'

'All right,' said a rather pleasant woman's voice from the other side of the doorway. 'Let me take my wellies off so I don't traipse mud across your carpet.'

There was a pause, then Florrie held the door wide and a slender young woman with auburn hair walked in. She was dressed in a navy-blue boiler suit that was at least two sizes too large for her, and thick woolly socks. There were streaks of mud across her cheeks and beneath her peaked cap her hair looked like a sweep's flue brush. However, as her gaze met his, her rather lovely grey eyes grew wide with surprise.

Brogan wondered why for a moment, then his brain caught up with his vision. Standing in her RAF Women's Auxiliary Air Force uniform in the middle of his aunt's oriental carpet was the very same young woman he'd handed over to the police on a Piccadilly sidewalk two weeks before.

As Alice's gaze fell on the American soldier lounging in one of Florrie's comfortable fireside chairs, she seriously wondered if she'd inadvertently inhaled some helium when she'd topped up the balloon that morning. However, as her gaze locked with the same pair of dark brown eyes that had repeatedly flashed through her mind for two weeks, there was no mistaking that he was the same cocky GI lieutenant who'd called her a cheap dame.

He was wearing the same olive uniform jacket as when she'd first met him and, annoyingly, in the full light of day he looked even better in it than she remembered. It also meant that she could see his lightly tanned skin and the deep cleft in his chin. Freed from his cap, which was lying on Florrie's dresser, above his regulation short-back-and-sides crop his jet-black curls ran riot.

Also, by the look of utter shock on his clean-cut face there was no mistaking the fact that he also recognised her.

Time paused for a second or two, then he unfolded all six foot two of himself and rose to his feet.

'Alice,' said Florrie, from what seemed like a long way away. 'I'd like you to meet my sister Bridget's son, Lieutenant Rafferty. Brogan, this is Aircraftwoman Alice Starling.'

There was another couple of seconds' pause, then a friendly smile spread across his chiselled features.

'Aircraftwoman Starling,' he said, offering her his hand.

Alice hesitated for a moment, then took it. 'Lieutenant Rafferty.'

They shook once, then Alice removed her hand.

She forced a smile. 'Well, I'll let you get on.'

'Don't be daft,' said Florrie. 'In fact, I was just going to offer Brogan another coffee, so stay and have one too.'

'I wouldn't want to intrude—'

'Florrie was just telling me about how grateful she is for you helping her with the children's Christmas party, miss,' Brogan cut in. 'I'd love to hear more.'

'Go on. Take the weight off your feet, Alice,' Florrie urged.

Not seeing a way of getting out of making small talk with Florrie's swaggering GI nephew without seeming rude, Alice let out a long breath and sat on the upright dining chair furthest from him.

Brogan resumed his seat and Florrie took his empty mug from the coffee table and went through the open door to the lean-to scullery beyond. With the sound of their hostess refilling the kettle in the background and Brogan's eyes on her, Alice kept her eyes fixed on the portrait of the king hanging above the sideboard.

Brogan cleared his throat, and she looked round.

He swallowed hard. 'You're in the Women's Auxiliary Air Force.'

'Obviously. But don't worry.' Alice gave him a brittle smile. 'I'm not going to "pester" you for "nylons, money and anything else I can squeeze out of you". Although I must say I am very surprised to see an American soldier actually *sober*.'

To Alice's great satisfaction, annoyance flashed across Brogan's face and he frowned. 'Look, about that—'

'Brrr, it's turned right chilly,' said Florrie, coming back into the room. 'Still, I expect you and the girls know that, Alice, seeing how you've been out in it since six?'

Alice gave her a polite smile as Florrie handed her a mug, but didn't reply.

Brogan took his drink from his host and, after thanking her, his attention returned to Alice.

'It must be tough on you gals manning the barrage balloons being out in all weathers, especially this time of year.'

'We manage,' Alice replied.

'I was telling Brogan all about our plans for the kiddies'

party and concert at Christmas,' Florrie chipped in. 'Although I'm still worried about the spread.'

A confused look settled on Brogan's face. 'Spread?'

'The buffet,' explained Florrie. 'I only 'ope the government ups the ration allowance for tea, and if they give us the one-off suet allowance again that would help. And then there's the presents for the kiddies.'

'I've told you not to worry, Florrie,' said Alice. 'The girls upstairs are already thinking through some ideas for decorations and presents, plus we've been putting the odd tin of fruit and packet of biscuits away in one of the cupboards for the party.'

As she looked across at her, Florrie's worried face lifted in a fond smile.

'Have you been on the balloon crew long, Miss Starling?' Brogan asked.

'Since January,' Alice replied, giving him a frosty smile.

'January,' said Brogan, seemingly unperturbed by her less-than-friendly response. 'So, about the time I was embarking on the *Queen Mary* to sail over here.'

Alice gave him a tight smile. 'Of course, I keep forgetting that America has only just joined us in the fight against Hitler and his Nazis.'

Annoyance again flashed across Brogan's too-handsome face. He opened his mouth to speak but then thought better of it and pressed his lips together instead.

Savouring her small victory, Alice drank the last of her coffee. 'Well, I ought to go and get changed.'

'Of course,' said Florrie. 'I'm glad I caught you. Supper's at seven as usual. It's mutton stew and dumplings. Perhaps you'd like to stay and join us, Brogan.'

An easy smile slid across his face. 'That's very good of you, Aunt Florrie.'

'It's no trouble. I can do a few more spuds, so it'll stretch to one more,' Florrie replied.

'Thank you but I really can't,' Brogan replied. 'I have to get back to HQ for a meeting at five. Perhaps another time.'

'Don't worry, Florrie,' said Alice, looking at Brogan as she spoke. 'I'm sure Lieutenant Rafferty won't go hungry – he'll be able to get himself a steak in one of the American-only canteens later.'

Brogan's eyes narrowed and he pressed his lips together. Feeling more than a little smug at scoring so many points, Alice stood up.

Putting down his coffee, Brogan did the same, and then crossed the space between them and offered his hand again.

Alice hesitated for a second or two, then took it. However, as his long fingers closed round hers and his square palm pressed into her smaller one, an odd tingling started up her arm.

A guileless smile spread across his irritatingly handsome face.

'It's been real swell meeting you, Miss Starling,' he said, in a low voice, his warm brown eyes oozing charm all over her.

Feeling her irritation with him dissolving a little, Alice pulled herself up short.

With his angular face and tousled hair, Brogan was no doubt used to flashing that smile and having women fall at his feet, but he was also the same condescending officer who had so outraged her that she had spent two whole nights staring up at the forty-watt light bulb overhead while arguing with him in her head.

Extracting her hand, Alice gave him a syrupy smile and, as she didn't want to upset lovely Florrie, bit back the words 'I can't say the same' and left the room.

With her pulse thundering in her temples, Alice closed the door and then fell back against the wall, locking her knees to stop her legs shaking. Thankful for the cool air in the hallway, she closed her eyes and took a couple of deep breaths.

Of all the thousands and thousands of Americans in London, why on earth did Florrie's nephew have to be *that* one?

She needed a drink!

However, as fetching herself a double gin and tonic would entail her walking back into Florrie's lounge, Alice decided to settle for a cup of tea, and, once satisfied that her legs weren't going to give way, made her way upstairs.

As the rest of the team were either upstairs in their rooms or had gone out for the afternoon, the lounge was empty. Alice turned towards the kitchen. She put her hand close to the kettle and found it warm, then struck a match and relit the gas beneath.

She was mulling over her encounter with Brogan Rafferty as she made the tea when Effie's head appeared round the open door. 'You're back,' she said, walking into the room.

'Yes, finally,' said Alice. 'Tea?'

'Please,' said Effie, pulling out one of the chairs tucked under the kitchen table and sitting down. 'I've just spent the past hour unravelling the Maid of Norway's monthly orders and invoices, so I could do with a cuppa. Plus, Mr Goldman left his account ledger and monthly shoebox full of bills about an hour ago, too.'

'Well, at least it keeps you out of trouble.' Alice took out two mugs, set them down on the counter and poured milk into them.

'What's with the padlock?' asked Effie, nodding towards the sideboard with a shiny new bolt fixed to it.

'Lily got Ernie to fit it on last week,' Alice explained.

'What's in it?' asked Effie.

'I've no idea,' said Alice. 'As she and Maureen don't put into our weekly housekeeping fund, I guess they put any little extra bits like biscuits or fruit in there.'

'When the rest of the crew came back without you, I

thought perhaps you'd got lost,' said Effie, as Alice brought their drinks over.

'Not lost but waylaid,' Alice replied, taking the seat opposite her friend. 'By Florrie and' – she drew in a deep breath – 'her nephew.'

Effie's eyes opened wide. 'You met Florrie's GI nephew!'

'In passing,' said Alice.

'What's he like?' asked Effie.

'I saw him for a few moments so I couldn't say,' Alice replied, lowering her gaze and blowing across the top of her drink.

'Well, at least tell me if he's tall and handsome?' said Effie.

'He was tall, probably six one or two,' she replied. 'And I suppose he was handsome enough, but honestly; he's not my type.'

'Oh, that's a shame,' said Effie.

'Effie!'

'Don't Effie me,' her friend replied. 'I'm determined to be your maid of honour when you walk down the aisle again.'

Alice rolled her eyes. 'Honestly, Effie, you're such a hopeless romantic.'

'Romantic yes but hopeless no,' said her friend. 'I didn't know when you and I met in January that by Christmas I would not only have fallen in love but would have got married and be expecting a baby.'

'Have you heard from Nathan?' asked Alice.

'I have and he's very well,' said Effie. 'But don't change the subject.'

Alice opened her mouth to speak but Effie jumped in first.

'And before you tell me you've already been married,' continued her friend, 'I'd like to point out that, at twenty-seven, you're much too young and beautiful not to have some handsome man fall desperately in love with you and beg you to marry him.'

'Perhaps there is some tall, broad-shouldered, handsome man out there who will sweep me off my feet but...' An image of Brogan Rafferty's face in the dim torchlight calling her a cheap dame floated back into Alice's mind. 'But I tell you this, Effie, whoever that man might be it will *not* be Florrie's flashy American nephew.'

CHAPTER 6

'And another thing,' said Cyril Lambert, the City of Westminster's senior ARP controller, sitting to Brogan's right. 'Why does every GI on furlough have to immediately jump on a train and head for London?'

Brogan smiled. 'Because, like me, they are fascinated by the ancient buildings and world-famous landmarks in your lovely capital. And of course the culture.'

It was just after three on an overcast Wednesday afternoon and Brogan was sitting in the oak-panelled meeting room in the Portman Club at the top end of Pall Mall. He wasn't alone; ranged around the polished boardroom table were a dozen or so members of London's civil authorities. Some of them were in civvies while others were dressed in their ARP uniforms, but all of them wore disgruntled expressions on their faces.

The Portman was a short walk away from Brogan's office in Chesterfield Gardens. As a liaison officer in the US Army's public relations unit, one of Brogan's roles was to manage civilian relations, which meant that each week he had the dubious pleasure of meeting with the representatives of the civilian authorities in London. The gathering was supposed to offer an opportunity for mutual cooperation and a friendly exchange of ideas. However, in reality, it was a weekly opportunity for Old London Town's representatives to whine and gripe as they stuffed their faces with the cakes sent over from the US Army canteen three floors below.

'Culture!' sniffed an elderly woman swathed in a mink coat, giving the chairman an exasperated look. 'Don't you mean drink?'

Lambert's close-set eyes flickered briefly onto a woman sitting opposite him, wearing an expertly tailored WVS uniform, her hair in a tight chignon.

'You took the words right out of my mouth, Mrs Farley,' he continued, a flush colouring his jowls.

'Any time of the day or night you can find American soldiers staggering around the street half drunk,' chipped in Mrs Willis, a motherly-looking woman wearing an ARP uniform who was sitting halfway down the table.

'You 'ave the right of it there, Mrs Willis,' agreed Tom Smith, the City of London's fire-watch coordinator.

'So, young man,' said Mrs Farley, regarding Brogan coolly through the veil draped over her hat. 'What are you going to do about it?'

Brogan cleared his throat. 'Well, ma'am, as I've mentioned before, we have an ongoing orientation programme that all our troops attend, plus a number of educational films to help them respect the way you folks do things in this lovely country, and I'll certainly add your concerns to—'

'On top of which,' cut in the young WVS woman, 'with a few drinks inside them these GIs just hang out on street corners in Mayfair skylarking about. It can make one feel quite unsettled when one walks past.'

'It certainly can, Lady Biddeford,' agreed Mrs Willis.

Heads nodded as a murmur of agreement went round the table.

'But I can't help but feel sorry for them, really,' Mrs Willis continued, her expression softening a little. 'Some don't look much older than my youngest, Terry. I shouldn't wonder if they aren't homesick, being stuck miles away from their families with nothing to do except drink and get into trouble.'

Brogan gave her his most appealing smile. 'Well, ma'am, you're absolutely right. I'm pleased to tell you that Rainbow Corner, the new American Red Cross Club on the corner of Shaftesbury Avenue and Piccadilly will not only be alcohol-free but it will also have a number of activities to keep our boys occupied while they're off duty. I'll be sure to get you all an invite to the grand opening.'

'But what are you going to do practically to stop your countrymen turning our streets and parks into saloons?' asked Mrs Farley, fixing Brogan with her grey flint-hard eyes.

'I will most certainly have a word with the military police regarding your concerns, ma'am,' Brogan said, trying not to imagine the duty officer's face when he turned up yet again at their HQ in Piccadilly.

'Of course, the problem isn't so much the young soldiers but the young women,' cut in a plummy voice from the other end of the table.

Brogan's attention shifted onto Reverend Waverly, the stick-thin rector of St Agnes Church.

'That's to say, American servicemen throwing their money around tempts otherwise respectable young women to behave disgracefully,' he said, his close-set pale eyes boring into Brogan's brown ones.

As it had done a few times before, the memory of Alice and her drunken friends flocking around the GIs in Piccadilly returned to Brogan.

'Young women,' continued the stiff-necked clergyman, cutting across Brogan's thoughts, 'who once only dreamed of finding a husband and making a nice home are now throwing caution to the wind and behaving in a most disgraceful manner. Apart from entreating them to indulge in the very unladylike drinking of spirits, your soldiers are also teaching them certain *dances*. Dances that require them to swing around in such a manner as allows their unmentionables to be visible to others. What's wrong with a good old waltz or a polka, I ask you?'

'As I say, Reverend,' said Brogan. 'I understand your concerns, but—'

'So,' boomed Reverend Waverly. 'What are you going to do to prevent your soldiers corrupting our young women, Lieutenant Rafferty?'

Resisting the urge to give the stuffed-shirted churchman the same reply about birds and bees as he had Chief Inspector Crosby, Brogan managed to keep his affable expression and held the other man's challenging gaze.

'Let me assure you all,' he said, in the sombre tone he had used many a time to tease out a news story from witness to or victim of crime, 'that the American army takes the matter of protecting British women as seriously as you do. Many of us have sisters or sweethearts at home. I will discuss the matter with our welfare officers and let you know what we come up with.' Brogan gave them his well-practised professional smile. 'Now I'm afraid the clock on the wall has beaten us again.' He snapped the top back on his fountain pen and stowed it in his breast pocket. 'Unfortunately, I'm going to have to bring this meeting to a close. Same time same place next week?'

Everyone nodded.

Brogan rose from his chair.

'Have a good evening,' he said, maintaining his convivial expression as he tidied his papers back into his briefcase.

As the other members gathered themselves together, Brogan stepped out from behind the desk and, ignoring Reverend Waverly's jaundiced look as he passed, headed for the door with an inward sigh of relief.

CHAPTER 7

'What are you knitting, Alice?' asked Maeve, sitting on the threadbare armchair opposite.

'A teddy bear,' Alice replied, slipping the stitch off the end of her needle and jabbing the point through the next loop. 'What about you?'

'Some mittens to match the hat and scarf I made last week,' said Maeve, holding up the pink handiwork hanging from her knitting needles.

It was late afternoon on a cold and miserable Thursday afternoon in October. She and Maeve were sitting in the balloon 312 on-duty hut, either side of the glowing cylindrical stove.

Perhaps glowing was a bit of an exaggeration because, with just a handful of coal in the grate, the stove barely kept the interior of the wooden hut above the outside temperature so both she and Maeve were wrapped up in their duffle coats.

'How are the plans for the kiddies' Christmas party going?' asked Maeve, as she resumed her task.

'Not too badly,' said Alice. 'The WVS members who work in clothing factories are scrounging every scrap of fabric to make soft toys for the babies or dollies' dresses, plus all our knitted teddies, dogs and sheep for the toddlers.' She frowned. 'Bert Willis – you know, the churchwarden at St George's – is sorting out the show, but what Florrie and the rest of the relief centre's committee are worried about is the food for the kiddies' tea and the adults' spread.'

The door opened and Dolly hurried in, bringing a gust of cold and wet weather in with her.

'Well, I'm pleased to report the balloon is still in the air and the tethers still attached to the winch,' she said, stripping off her gloves.

'Where's Lily?' asked Maeve. 'Have you done us all a favour and shoved her in the river?'

Dolly laughed. 'No, she was chatting to some bloke at the gate. What time is it?'

'Twenty past five,' Alice replied.

Although the barrage balloon operational manual stated that each barrage balloon team should comprise nine aircraft-women plus a corporal, it was a rare day when the whole crew was on duty. As Effie's place on the crew was still vacant, George was on a family visit to her ancestral pile in the country and Maureen was sick, only six of them had reported for duty that morning. After working their way through the daily maintenance duties, four of them had retreated to the hut. The remaining two were charged with ensuring old Bessie continued to behave herself and patrolling the site perimeter to stop anyone stealing any of the equipment. They did this for an hour, after which Rose and Peggy had left the warmth of the hut to relieve them for the last patrol of the day.

Thankfully, there'd been no messages to adjust the balloon's height or haul it down, so for once it had been a quiet day.

'Thank goodness the night crew will be here soon,' said Dolly. 'It must be close to freezing out there already, so I don't envy them.'

'At least it's overcast and there's fog along the river so the Luftwaffe are unlikely to put in an appearance,' said Maeve.

'You'd get more heat by sucking a peppermint and breathing on them,' said Alice as Dolly held her hands out to warm them in front of the stove.

'We're not down to coal dust again, are we?' asked Dolly.

'Sure, don't we know it,' Maeve replied.

Dolly gave them a puzzled look. 'But we only had a delivery last Monday. Has anyone asked Lily for the key so we can get another bucketload?'

'I did when we came on duty,' said Alice.

'And what did she say?'

'That we're to put up with it,' Alice replied.

Coal was strictly allocated by the Balloon Squadron HQ to each balloon site and a truck arrived with it every two weeks. Half went to the Maid of Norway for use in the billet while the rest was stored in a concrete bunker behind the hut. As coal was a lucrative commodity on the black market, it was kept under lock and key. A key that, since her promotion, Lily held.

'Oh, well, there is a war on I suppose,' Dolly sighed. 'Any tea left in the pot?'

Alice nodded. 'We made a full pot ten minutes ago.'

Dolly went over to pour herself a hot drink while Alice and Maeve picked up their needles again. However, as Alice swapped her needles over to start the next row the hut door opened again, but, instead of Lily, Sergeant Munroe marched in. In her wake was a dark-haired young woman wearing a new WAAF uniform and carrying a haversack almost as tall as she was.

Alice and Maeve rose to their feet and stood to attention and Dolly, cup in hand, did the same.

'As you were, girls,' said Munroe.

Alice and Maeve resumed their seats while Dolly poured a drink. 'Do you want tea, Sergeant?'

'Thank you, but no, I've got another two sites to visit yet and one of them is right out on Wanstead Flats,' Munroe replied. 'However, this is Aircraftwoman Evans. She just finished at Cardington, and she's been posted here. I spoke to Corporal Craven as I arrived and she said to leave her in your charge, Alice.'

'My pleasure, Skip,' said Alice.

'Very good, now I must push on.' She spotted the colour of the knitting on Maeve's needle and horror spread across her face. 'Please don't tell me another one of you is in the family way?'

'No, not as far as I know,' Alice replied. 'We're knitting toys for our local WVS children's Christmas party.'

The sergeant let out an audible sigh of relief. 'Thank goodness. I've already had to find two replacement crew members because of expectant WAAFs this week. I wish you girls would learn to keep your knees together. Carry on.'

She left the hut and Alice turned to the new WAAF, who was still standing in front of the door.

The newest member of their crew looked as if she'd reached the WAAF's minimum height restriction of five foot two by a whisker. With the physique of a pixie, fine-boned features and large blue eyes, Alice wondered how she'd ever survived the brutal regimen of Corporal Jones, Cardington's PE instructor, but, by the newly sewn balloon squadron insignia on her shoulder, she clearly had.

'I'm Alice and this is Maeve and Dolly,' said Alice, giving the newcomer a friendly smile.

'Gwendolin,' said the young WAAF in a distinctive Welsh accent. 'Although everyone calls me Gwen.'

'Well, Gwen, do you want a cuppa?'

'Oh, yes please,' the young WAAF replied. 'I could murder one.'

'Well, take a pew,' said Dolly. 'I'll fetch you one.'

Maeve patted the space next to her on the sofa.

Gwen dumped her kitbag with a thump on the floor and came over.

'Sounds like you've brought the kitchen sink with you?' Alice laughed.

'Not quite but I did bring a few extra bits,' said Gwen, as she sat down. 'All day it's taken me to get here.'

'From where?'

'Abergavenny on the Welsh border,' Gwen replied. 'I was supposed to get the eight thirty to Newport but that was cancelled, so I missed my connection to Bristol and well it just put everything else out. I finally got to Paddington at four thirty and then got lost on the Underground and ended up in some place called Earl's Court. Thankfully, some Australian soldiers put me on the right line, but I ended up arriving at Stanmore three hours late.'

'Well, you're here now,' said Alice as Dolly handed Gwen a mug.

'That I am,' said Gwen, blowing across the top of her hot drink.

'Where were you stationed before Cardington?' asked Dolly.

'I wasn't. I joined the WAAFs six months ago to be a balloon girl,' Gwen replied. 'I was at the cinema with my chum Dorcus about six months ago when there was this bit on the news, showing girls just like me joining up as barrage balloon operators to free up men for the front line. One of the girls was a Welsh housemaid and Dorcus said, "That could be you, Gwen." And she was right because I was a housemaid up at Royston Grange, so the day after I turned eighteen I jumped on the bus to town and signed up right there and then.'

'Good for you,' said Maeve.

'And don't worry, we'll look after you, and show you around,' said Alice.

'Thank you,' said Gwen. 'And I'm glad to hear it because, look now, I didn't realise London was so big. I mean I thought it might be a bit like Cardiff but it's blooming huge.'

'You'll soon get used to it,' Alice laughed. 'And thank your lucky stars you've been posted here and not camped out in a tent on some desolate dock or factory site like some poor WAAF squads. Here, not only have we've got a warm billet over a pub, but a landlady who can cook.'

'Plus' – Maeve looked at her watch – 'in ten minutes, the night team will arrive and your first day on duty as a member of the 312 crew will be over.'

'So as you can see, this is our sitting room,' said Alice, as she and Gwen stood in the middle of the Maid of Norway's lounge on the first floor. 'And the kitchen is just through there.'

She pointed through the open door and Gwen dutifully turned in the direction indicated.

Millie and her team, had taken over duties from Alice's crew about half an hour ago and had returned to their billet very soon after. While Alice showed Gwen around her new home, the rest of the team were upstairs sorting themselves out ready for when Florrie brought their supper up at seven.

'Although we have our grub delivered to the hut from central when we're on duty, the rest of the time Florrie, who runs the pub, provides us with food,' continued Alice. 'Porridge or cooked something for breakfast, then whatever she can get from the butcher's hot for dinner and supper, but if you want to chip in a shilling each week to our kitchen club then you'll be able to help yourself to whatever's in there if you're peckish, even if it's just bread and jam.'

'As long as you don't try and take anything out of the locked cupboard next to the pantry,' said Nell, walking in dressed in a dressing gown with a towel wrapped round her wet hair.

'If you want in, give me your shilling later when you've unpacked,' said Alice. 'Talking about unpacking, let me show you to your room.'

Leaving Nell and Dolly in the lounge, Alice led the new recruit upstairs and after showing her the bathroom and toilet took her up the next flight of stairs to the top floor.

'I'm afraid it's a bit of a climb as we're up here in the eaves,' said Alice as they reached the top. 'Maeve and Nell are in the room at the back and we're in here.'

Grasping the handle, Alice opened her bedroom door. 'I think the rooms up here were where the pub's staff lived before the war.'

'This is nice and cosy,' said Gwen, dropping her kitbag on the rag-rug beneath their feet and glancing around at the patchwork covers on the two beds.

'You can thank Florrie and the Shadwell WVS group for that,' said Alice. 'They've taken us under their wing, so to speak, and are constantly sending over cake to the duty hut. Plus, they'll find you an adopted family to give you a break from the site that you can visit off duty. That's your bed and wardrobe. I'll leave you to get unpacked.'

'Thanks, Alice,' said Gwen. 'You've all been very kind.'

'Well, we try and help each other out as much as we can. Oh, just one more thing.' Alice indicated the sloping ceiling. 'Mind your head.'

Gwen laughed. 'Thanks for the warning.'

Alice turned to leave but as she reached the door she paused and chewed her bottom lip.

'Is there something else I should know?' asked Gwen.

Alice hesitated for a couple of seconds. 'Perhaps I shouldn't say this, but just be a little careful with what you say when Lily and Maureen are around.'

. . .

Half an hour later Alice was slouched sideways in one of the fireside armchairs with her legs draped over one arm and her head resting on the other, listening to a brass band on the Bakelite wireless sitting on the sideboard.

Nell was slouched on the sofa reading that morning's edition of the *Sketch* while Dolly was sewing up a ladder in her stockings in the chair opposite Alice's.

'Do you know what's for supper?' asked Maeve, who, having laid the crockery and cutlery out ready for their evening meal, was now painting her nails at the table.

'Mutton stew, I think,' said Nell, without looking up. 'And what are you getting all dolled up for?'

'I've got a date,' said Maeve. 'With that tall sergeant stationed at Wapping police station.'

'Well, don't do anything I wouldn't do,' said Nell.

The musicians on the radio struck up for the next piece of music but before the end of the introduction the door opened, and Effie walked in.

As she looked at her very pregnant friend the all-too-familiar yearning tugged at Alice's heart. If she and Arthur had been blessed with children, she wouldn't have been able to sign up as a WAAF and make such firm friends – but, not for the first time, Alice asked herself why she hadn't ever been blessed like thousands of other women.

'Hello, Effie,' said Nell, looking up from her newspaper. 'How are you feeling?'

'Not so bad,' said Effie, lowering herself onto the sofa alongside her. 'Considering I've got a blooming football up my jumper.'

'Have you heard from Nathan?' asked Alice.

'I got a letter this morning,' Effie replied. 'He can't say too much but I get the impression that he's been constantly flying missions for the past month. But he's hopeful that he'll get posted nearer to London before the baby arrives. I hear my replacement has arrived.'

'No one could ever replace you, Effie,' said Maeve, waving her hands around to dry her nails.

The door opened again and Florrie staggered in, carrying a pot between her tea-towel-wrapped hands.

'There we are, ladies,' she said, placing her burden on the square of cork in the centre of the table. 'Mutton stew with potatoes, carrots and peas. I'll bring your afters up in a while. Right, girls, are Lily and Maureen around?'

'No, they went out ten minutes before you came up,' said Maeve.

'Good,' said Florrie, tucking the tea towel in the top of her apron. 'Because I wonder if a couple of you could do me a bit of a favour.'

''Course, if we can,' Alice replied.

'Effie's already said yes but it's my nephew, Brogan...'

Unexpectedly, an image of her landlady's tall, broad-chested, square-jawed, brown-eyed American nephew materialised in Alice's mind and before she could stop it her stomach fluttered.

'Aren't you, Alice?'

Alice snapped her mind back from its wandering. 'Sorry?'

'I said you're free on Sunday, aren't you,' said Effie, looking across at her.

'Er, yes I am—'

'So that's me, Alice,' said Effie. 'Anyone else?'

'Hello.'

Pulling herself together, Alice looked around to see Gwen, dressed in a pair of slacks and jumper, standing in the doorway.

'Florrie, this is our new crew member, Gwen,' said Alice.

'Well, it's nice to meet you, luv,' said Florrie. 'And now you're part of the family you can come too.'

'Can I?' said Gwen.

''Course you can,' said Florrie. 'The more the merrier.'

'Oh, all right, if you say so,' said Gwen, giving her a nervous smile.

'Right now, I've got a pub to run, so tuck in before it gets cold,' said Florrie.

Alice and her friends headed over to the table and Florrie disappeared back downstairs.

Effie went to follow.

'Why don't you join us, Effie,' said Nell. 'There's enough for you too.'

'I'm not supposed to, am I?' said Effie.

'Well, I won't tell HQ if you don't,' said Dolly, as she started handing out the supper.

Gwen took the seat next to Alice.

'Thanks,' she said, giving Alice a little smile as she handed her a bowl. 'And can you tell me where I'm going with Florrie?'

'Downstairs to her parlour on Sunday for dinner, with her American nephew who's over here with the US Army,' said Nell.

Gwen gripped her spoon and her hazel eyes opened wide with wonder. 'There's an American soldier coming here?'

'Yes, there is, and it seems we're having Sunday dinner with him,' said Alice, trying to stop the image of Brogan returning and failing miserably.

CHAPTER 8

'Gee, Brogan, is that the Tower of London?' said Todd, staring open-mouthed at the grey curtain walls of the medieval castle.

'Yep,' said Brogan, steering the jeep between the piles of rubble left behind after the previous night's air raid. 'And that' – he indicated to the left of the edifice – 'is Tower Bridge.'

'And your aunt lives within walking distance of these places,' continued Todd, still looking at London's ancient fortress.

'She sure does,' Brogan replied. 'And we should be there real soon.'

It was just before midday on the first day in November and he and Todd were on their way to the Maid of Norway to take up his aunt's invitation for Sunday dinner.

Having skirted around the centuries-old stronghold, Brogan steered left past the Royal Mint and into East Smithfield. Here, the six-storey granite Victorian offices, company headquarters and professional associations gave way to brick-built Regency wharves and warehouses and the smooth tarmacked road changed to cobbled ones.

In peacetime, today would have been a day of rest, but

instead the docks were alive with porters shouldering boxes onto lorries while others, pushing barrows laden with sacks, dodged between the dock traffic.

However, alongside all this hustle and bustle of activity were smouldering piles of splintered timbers and broken brick-work with ARP personnel still clambering over them as they searched for survivors. Although it was midday the air was heavy with pulverised brick dust and the acrid smell of spent munitions still lingered from the previous night's bombing raid.

As the shimmering waters of Wapping Basin came into view so did a yellow-and-black barrier. Brogan brought the jeep to a halt and a portly London cop with grey mutton-chops and matching bushy eyebrows ambled across.

'Sorry, chum,' he said, displaying a set of nicotine-stained teeth as he spoke. 'The road's closed because of a UXB – that is to say an unexploded bomb. The whizz-bang crew are down there. Where you going?'

'The Maid of Norway public house.'

'First left then at the end of the street right on the Highway and you'll be there in a jiffy,' the policeman replied.

'Thanks, pal,' said Brogan.

He backed the jeep up a few yards, turned the steering wheel and headed off.

'But mind how you go,' the officer called, as Brogan sped off. 'The end of the street was flattened last night by a direct hit. Give my regards to Florrie.'

Bumping over the cobbles, they drove between a five-storey warehouse with only jagged glass in its window frames. Fire was still raging in the gutted office block further along the street.

They continued on, and reached a block of redbrick flats that looked as if a giant hand had reached down and scooped out the middle, exposing wallpapered walls and leaving carpets dangling from damaged floorboards, while the contents of wardrobes and chests of drawers were scattered on the rubble below.

Brogan made his way past a group of ARP rescue workers having a hot drink at a WVS mobile canteen and motored on, but as he was nearing the end of the thoroughfare a large dog ran out from one of the wrecked buildings and stopped in front of the jeep. Brogan slammed on the pedal and skidded to a halt.

'Geez,' said Todd. 'That was close.'

Brogan pulled on the handbrake and then jumped out, and the dog, a large floppy-eared black-and-tan cross of some kind, sat with its tongue hanging out and waited.

'Hey there,' Brogan said, smiling and walking slowly towards the animal. 'How ya doing today?'

The dog thumped its tail in response and gave a little yelp.

Stopping a few yards from the animal, Brogan held out his hand. 'Here, boy.'

The dog stood up, trotted over and nuzzled Brogan's hand.

Hunkering down, Brogan stroked its head and tickled behind its ear, which set off another bout of tail-wagging.

'Where did you come from?' he asked the dog.

'Is it injured?' called Todd.

'Not as far as I can see,' Brogan replied, casting his eyes over the dog. 'It's a young'un though. Only a year or so I reckon, and judging by its paws it's still got a way to go.'

'Has it got a collar?' asked Todd.

Brogan shook his head. Looking into the dog's intelligent eyes, he stroked it again and was rewarded with a wet nose nuzzling his palm.

'It's all right, Mike, I've found him!'

Brogan looked up and saw a stout middle-aged man dressed in a navy uniform with a flat cap, slipping and sliding over a pile of rubble. Finding his feet on the pavement, he hurried over to Brogan.

'Thanks for catching 'im, mate,' said the man, puffing to a stop in front of Brogan.

'Glad to help you find your dog,' said Brogan.

'Naw, 'e ain't my dog.' The man tapped the badge on his chest. 'Royal Society for the Prevention of Cruelty to Animals. We're rounding up strays. There's always a bunch of 'em after a raid. Can't have 'im just roaming wild.'

'What are you going to do with him?' asked Brogan, his hand still stroking the dog's head.

'Back to our kennels at Beckton,' the RSPCA officer replied. 'There's always a slim chance someone might claim 'im but we've got hundreds so, well if not' – he gave a regretful shrug – 'you know...'

As if understanding the animal officer's words, the dog sat down beside Brogan, who continued to stroke his head.

'I'll have him,' said Brogan.

The RSPCA officer looked puzzled. 'Do what?'

'I'll take him with me,' said Brogan. 'Save you the trouble. What do you say, deal?'

Lifting his hat by the brim, the animal officer scratched his bald head. 'What if his owners turn up?'

'My aunt's the landlady of the Maid of Norway, so leave a message with her and I'll return him. Here.' Brogan rummaged in his pocket and pulled out a half-a-crown. He offered it to the dog warden. 'A donation.'

The RSPCA warden chewed his lip for a moment, then took the coin. 'I suppose that'll be all right.'

'Come on, boy,' Brogan said, and patted his thigh as he headed back to the jeep.

The dog sprang up and bounded after him and into the back seat of the vehicle, looking rather pleased with himself.

Brogan climbed in behind the wheel.

'Got a new friend, have you?' asked Todd as Brogan started the vehicle.

'I sure have,' Brogan replied.

'What's his name?'

'I don't know.' With his hands on the steering wheel, Brogan looked behind him. 'What's your name then? Rex, Rover, Patch, Sam?'

The dog barked.

'Okay, Sam it is, After our good ol' uncle,' said Brogan, slamming the gearstick into first. 'But right now we're late for our Sunday roast.'

~

Feeling ridiculously nervous, Alice glanced at her watch, and noted that it was just a few minutes before two o'clock.

'I'm sure he'll be 'ere any minute now,' said Florrie, turning the gas beneath the cabbage down to a simmer.

'Yes,' said Effie, giving their landlady a reassuring smile. 'He's probably just got held up somewhere.'

They were sitting in Florrie's parlour awaiting their Sunday dinner and had been for the last half an hour.

'You look nice, Alice,' said Gwen, who was alongside Effie at the table. 'That colour really suits you.'

'Thank you,' Alice replied. 'But it's just some old thing I had in the back of the wardrobe.'

Actually, that wasn't strictly the truth. The dress she was wearing was certainly a few years old and had been in the back of the wardrobe, but it was the dress she'd worn in April 1940 as matron of honour at her younger sister's wedding. As Arthur had died a month later and she had signed up for the WAAFs a month after that, she'd had very little chance to wear it since. And the colour, a pale lilac with Honiton lace round the neck and cuffs, did suit her, which, having tried on and discarded half a dozen other dresses, made her wonder why she'd chosen it, given she was only going down to have Sunday dinner with Florrie. Or rather, Florrie and that flashy American nephew of hers.

Damping down the irritation Brogan Rafferty always caused, Alice smiled. 'You look very nice, too, Gwen.'

'Thank you,' the young WAAF replied. 'And I'm so excited because I've never met an American before.'

Effie gave her a querying look. 'Haven't you?'

Gwen shook her head. 'We don't get many strangers in our valley.'

'Well, don't worry,' said Effie. 'Now you're in London you'll meet plenty of them.'

'And are they all tall and handsome like film stars?' asked Gwen.

'Well, I can't answer for all of 'em,' said Florrie, crouching down to check the meat roasting in the oven. 'But I think my nephew will send a few hearts into a flutter, don't you, Alice?'

The image of square-jawed, broad-shouldered Brogan Rafferty rising up from Florrie's easy chair returned to Alice's mind.

'W... well, I... I...' she stuttered. 'He is certainly tall—'

The door opened and the image in her head became flesh as Lieutenant Brogan Rafferty strode into the room. Despite schooling herself to remain calm and collected when he arrived, before she could stop it Alice's heart flipped over. However, to her surprise Brogan wasn't alone as half a pace behind him was another American officer, similarly dressed but a few inches shorter, with straw-coloured hair.

'Sorry I'm late, Aunt Florrie,' he said, grinning across at her. 'And I hope you don't mind me bringing my pal?'

''Course not,' said Florrie.

'Lieutenant Todd Robertson, at your service,' said the newcomer.

'Nice to meet you, too,' said Florrie, giving him a warm

smile. 'And this is' – she introduced Effie and Gwen – 'and you've already met Alice.'

Brogan's eyes shifted onto Alice. They flickered over her and something in their dark brown depths altered.

'Nice to meet you again, miss,' he said.

'And you,' she forced out, a sudden tightness in her throat. 'And it's Mrs.'

An odd emotion flickered across Brogan's handsome face. 'My apologies.'

They stared at each other for a long moment, then Brogan's attention shifted back to his aunt. 'Well actually, Aunt Florrie, if you don't mind, I've brought the reason I was late with me too.'

Looking slightly mischievous, he gave a shrill two-tone whistle.

A huge black-and-tan dog loped in and, after circling him once, it sat, looking adoringly up at him.

'Oh, my, 'e looks just like my old dog Rex,' said Florrie, stroking the dog's head. 'Where did you find him?'

'Well, rightly speaking, he found me.' Brogan hunkered down and fussed the dog. 'We ran into a roadblock on our way...'

Although she tried not to, as Brogan told them the tale of how he'd rescued the dog from a one-way trip with the RSPCA wardens Alice felt her heart soften a little.

'What's his name?' asked Effie when he'd finished.

'Sam,' Brogan replied.

As if knowing it was his turn to say hello, the dog, with his tail wagging, plodded around the room sniffing his greetings to everyone, but when he got to Alice he sat down and placed his head on her lap. Smiling, Alice stroked the dog's soft brown fur, then tickled behind his ear. Sam turned his head into her fingers and Alice's heart squeezed a little.

'He's a handsome fella,' said Gwen, gazing at Brogan in much the same way as the dog was.

To be fair, Alice couldn't altogether blame her because annoyingly, dressed in his fawn trousers and olive-coloured jacket, Brogan looked as if he'd stepped out of the silver screen.

'Well, I'm sure we can find him a bit of something, too,' said Florrie, stroking the dog's head. 'And he seems to know his Ps and Qs.'

'Plus we also come bearing gifts, Aunt Florrie.' Brogan held his index finger up for a second, then disappeared back through the door, only to reappear a few moments later carrying a large cardboard box with *USA PX* stamped across the side.

He placed it on the sideboard and beckoned Florrie over.

'My goodness,' she said, her eyes lighting up as she delved into the box. 'I haven't seen the like for three years.' She took out a tin of pineapple. 'This neither.' She held up a tin of ham. 'And where on earth did you find these?' she asked, pulling out a string bag with half a dozen oranges. 'And these?' She produced two chocolate bars.

'At the PX,' said Todd.

'What's that when it's at home?' asked Florrie.

'It's the Post Exchange, which is like a department store full of things the GIs would find in their own general stores back home,' Brogan replied. 'Ships all the comforts of home across the ocean for the American troops over here.'

'That's nice for you,' said Alice, giving him a sweet smile.

Something flickered in Brogan's eyes. 'Yes, it is.'

Again, they stared at each other for a long moment, until the hiss of the water boiling over onto the stove brought Alice back to the here and now.

'That's my signal that says dinner's ready, so if you all find yourselves a seat,' said Florrie returning to the stove, 'I'll dish up.'

'Do you mind if I sit next to you?' Brogan asked Alice, smiling down at her.

'Why don't you sit here, Lieutenant,' said Gwen before

Alice could reply, and indicated the chair beside her at the top of the table. 'There's more room.'

Despite telling herself that Brogan Rafferty was the last man she'd want to sit next to at any table, Gwen's suggestion that he should sit by her caused a niggle of annoyance in Alice's chest.

'That's right, more room to stretch your legs,' said Florrie, holding the lip on the lid tight as she drained the saucepan. 'And, Todd, you take the chair this end.'

'Down, boy,' Brogan said to Sam as he took his seat.

Without needing a second telling, the hound sloped off and curled up by the fire.

'I hope you don't mind me asking, Mrs Fitzgerald,' said Brogan. 'But when are you expecting your happy event?'

'It's Effie, and the baby's due sometime around Christmas,' said Effie. 'My husband's a pilot in the RAF up north some-where, but I'm hoping he'll be able to get some leave when they arrive.'

'Are you hoping for a boy or a girl?' asked Todd.

'I don't mind as long as they have ten fingers and ten toes,' Effie replied. 'Are you married, Lieutenant?'

'No, ma'am,' said Todd. 'But I've got a gal back home and I'm hoping to tie the knot someday soon.'

'So am I,' said Gwen breathlessly and gazed wide-eyed at Brogan.

Taking her napkin from across her lap, Alice placed it on the plate, and stood up.

'Let me give you a hand with the dinner, Florrie.'

'So, Lieutenant Rafferty, what exactly does a liaison officer in the Office of War Information do?' asked the young WAAF who was sitting beside him.

Brogan was sitting in pride of place, at one end of his aunt's dining room table. The three women who'd joined them for lunch were ranged around the table. To his right and opposite his aunt was Gwen, who looked only a year or two older than his fourteen-year-old kid sister, Margy. On the other side of her and on Todd's right hand was the expectant Effie and opposite her was Alice.

They'd sat down an hour ago and since then had talked a little about the Russian advances and the Royal Navy's recent success, then more home-grown topics such as families and hometowns.

'Well, it's a great number of things really, like orientating newly arrived GIs into the way you Brits do things, and meeting with the civilian staff,' Brogan replied. 'At the moment, I'm also spending a great deal of time helping to set up Rainbow Corner, the Red Cross's newest canteen, which hopefully will provide GIs with somewhere to spend their furloughs while they are in London rather than getting drunk in bars and clubs.'

'Your job sounds so interesting,' said Effie.

Brogan gave a short laugh. 'I suppose it does but, honestly, half my job is dealing with GIs and trouble, and the other half is taken up with trouble and GIs.'

Everyone laughed.

'Actually, most of the time, thankfully, it's nothing too serious,' continued Brogan. 'Nine times out of ten it's just fishing out young GIs from police cells after a night on the tiles.'

'Lucky them, to have someone so caring like you, Brogan, to keep them out of trouble and look after them,' said Gwen, her eyes wide with fascination.

'Yes, lucky them,' said Alice, looking coolly down the table at him.

Unfathomably and somewhat annoyingly, throughout dinner Brogan's gaze and attention continually returned to Alice.

Actually, there was nothing mysterious as to why really because, with her auburn hair cascading in soft curls over her shoulders, the colour of her dress highlighting her flawless complexion and grey eyes, it was quite simply because she was utterly lovely and any man with blood in his veins would agree.

Pity really, because judging by the icy looks she sent his way she hadn't forgiven him for their somewhat fractious first meeting, but more to the point because she was married, and therefore completely out of bounds.

Brogan held her gaze for a moment, then Gwen's voice cut between them.

'The new canteen in Piccadilly sounds so exciting,' she said.

'It ought to be,' said Todd. 'Brogan spends enough time there and it's not even open yet.'

'Well, it'll be a complete disaster,' said Brogan, pulling his mind back to the conversation, 'unless I can get everything up and running by the opening on the thirteenth.'

'Friday the thirteenth,' said Effie. 'I hope you're not superstitious.'

'I'm not,' said Brogan. 'But it's also Thanksgiving at the end of the month, so I want to make sure I've ironed out any teething troubles by then.'

'What's Thanksgiving, Brogan?' asked Gwen, gazing dreamily up at him.

'It marks the first harvest after the Pilgrim Fathers landed and founded the United States. Families celebrate with a turkey dinner, beans, cornbread, and roasted sweet potatoes, followed by pumpkin pie, apple pie and sugar plums and sweets for the children.'

'Sounds like Christmas,' said Effie.

'Except I doubt we'll see any turkey again this year,' said Florrie, sadly. 'And with no sugar to be 'ad in the shops for love nor money there won't be any sugar plums or sweets for the kiddies either, poor little mites. I thought Christmas last year was bad, but this year's shaping up to be even worse.'

'Oh, Florrie,' said Alice, placing her hand on her forearm. 'We'll make do.'

'Make do!' Florrie rolled her eyes. 'We've been doing that for three years.'

'And we'll keep on making do for the duration,' said Alice. 'And as long as the children have some games, cake and a present from Father Christmas they'll have a great time.'

An image of the shelves laden with sweets, chocolates, cakes and potato chips in South Audley Street's PX store flashed through Brogan's mind.

'Rainbow Corner,' said Gwen with a sigh. With her chin cupped in her hand, she was staringly wistfully up at him. 'I wish we had somewhere like that to go to.'

'Well, you can come too,' said Todd. 'There's going to be regular dances with some of the big-name bands playing, and GIs are allowed to invite young women.'

Gwen's eyes opened even wider. 'Oh, can we?'

'I don't see why not. After all,' Todd replied, 'you've got the man in charge of the whole kit and caboodle sitting right here.'

He grinned down the table at Brogan.

'Oh, Brogan, please, please, please say you'll get us some tickets to the Thanksgiving dance,' said the young WAAF beside him, looking imploringly up at him.

Brogan smiled. 'I'll see what I can do. You'll all have to be vetted by the committee first, of course. But as you're all members of the British armed forces I can't see that being a problem.'

Gwen looked puzzled. 'Vetted?'

'To make sure they don't let in any young women just after nylons and anything else they can get out of the GIs, Gwen,' Alice explained. Turning to Brogan, she gave him a glacial smile. 'Isn't that right, Lieutenant Rafferty?'

Brogan matched her unwavering stare with one of his own as, out of the corner of his eye, he caught Effie giving her friend a querying look.

There was a long silence, then Brogan turned to his host.

'Well, Aunt Florrie, that was truly delicious,' he said, giving her a dazzling smile.

'Are you sure you've had enough?' asked Florrie, who was sitting between him and Alice.

'More than enough.' He puffed out his cheeks and patted his stomach. 'I couldn't eat another bite.'

That was a complete lie Truthfully, although the roast meat and potatoes were both well cooked and tasty, they barely covered the central pattern on the plate. Although he'd stood in front of newly arrived GIs dozens of times explaining about British wartime rationing, sitting down to dinner at his aunt's table was the first time he'd actually experienced it. It certainly made him glad he'd had the forethought to bring his box of PX provisions.

'What about you, Todd?' asked Florrie, cutting across Brogan's musings. 'There's still some crumble left.'

'Thank you, ma'am,' said Todd. 'But I'm full to the brim.'

'I imagine our traditional Sunday roast is a little different to what you're used to,' said Effie, wiping her mouth with her napkin.

'A little,' said Todd. 'We have potatoes and beans but Brussels sprouts, well, they're something quite different.'

That was a bit of an understatement; American service men had yet to figure out what the hell they were! One commander writing in the *Stars and Stripes* advised that any pilot having to make an emergency landing on his way back to base should aim to do so in a Brussels sprouts field for the sake of his comrades' taste buds.

An amused smile flickered across the young woman's face. 'Sounds as if you don't approve of our sprouts.'

'Let's just say they're an acquired taste,' said Brogan.

Everyone around the table laughed politely again.

'I've heard that the way to a man's heart is through their stomach,' Gwen said, gazing wistful up at him.

Alice gave a short laugh. 'Whoever said that didn't know very much about men.'

As four pairs of eyes fixed on her, she felt her cheeks start to glow. To be honest, she wouldn't have bothered to respond had it not been for the fact that Gwen had spent the whole meal fluttering her eyelashes at Brogan Rafferty.

Amusement flickered across his too-handsome face, and he raised an eyebrow. 'It sounds as if you have a low opinion of us poor men.'

'Not *all* men,' Alice said, giving him the sweetest smile.

There was a pause, then Florrie placed her hands on the table and stood up.

'Well, then, if we're all finished,' she said. 'Why don't you all make yourselves comfortable and I'll put the kettle on.'

Todd, Effie and Gwen pushed back their chairs and started making their way across to the easy chairs. Someone had switched on Florrie's Beko wireless and as the valves warmed up the sound of a dance band drifted across the room.

'You've done enough, Florrie,' said Alice, taking a couple of plates from her. 'I'll wash up.'

'I'll help,' said Brogan, starting to collect the empty bowls.

'There's no need,' said Alice, snatching a pile of dishes and heading for the sink.

She placed them alongside the pile of gravy-smeared dinner plates, then took Florrie's flowery wraparound apron from the hook, slipped it over her head and tied it round her. She turned on the cylindrical hot-water geyser fixed to the wall above the sink, filled it with water, then, throwing a handful of grated soap into the water, stirred it into froth. Then she plunged a small stack of side plates beneath the bubbles.

A faint smell of bay rum wafted over her, announcing Brogan's arrival.

'I'm guessing you're still mad at me for that night in Piccadilly,' he said, placing a stack of used crockery among the rest on the draining board.

Painfully aware of his tall presence beside her, Alice didn't reply.

'Look, I'm very sorry,' he continued as she scrubbed furiously at a submerged plate beneath the soapy water. 'What happened that night when we ran into each other in Piccadilly was a mistake, that's all. I shouldn't have jumped to conclusions.'

The humiliation of the incident two weeks before flashed across Alice's mind.

'A mistake!' she said, stacking a bowl in the draining board. 'Looking left instead of right when crossing the road is a mistake, or thinking ten pennies make a shilling is a mistake. Not accusing a woman who was just looking for her friend of being out to take advantage of drunken GIs.'

Brogan picked up a tea towel, 'I understand you being sore at me but—'

Alice rounded on him. 'I didn't even know those girls! I only got tangled up with them because I happened to be in the wrong place at the wrong time. Thankfully the police officer you called over didn't take it any further, just warned us that we'd be run into the station if he saw us again.'

'I'm sorry,' said Brogan, picking up a dripping dish. 'But—'

'Which is just as well,' she continued, ignoring him. 'Because had I been hauled up in front of the magistrate for breach of the peace or something I'd have been dishonourably discharged from the WAAFs. So no, I'm not *sore*, as you so eloquently put it, I'm damn well bloody furious!'

'Look, Alice—'

'Aircraftwoman First Class Starling to you,' she cut in again, glaring at him.

Brogan's remorseful expression wavered for a second, then weariness replaced it.

The opening bars of 'Pennsylvania 6-5000' sounded and Gwen appeared, and started bobbing around on Florrie's Indian patterned rug.

'Oh, I love this one,' she said, turning the wireless dial. 'Do you do that new jitterbug to this?'

'No, it's a swing number,' said Brogan, throwing the tea towel down. 'Let me show you.'

Giving Alice a scathing look, he turned, and, taking Gwen's hand, twirled her around.

Sam, who had been snoozing by the fire, padded over and sat beside her. Absentmindedly stroking the dog's head, Alice watched Brogan and Gwen for a few beats, then, feeling unexpectedly annoyed at seeing him take the young WAAF in his arms, returned to her task.

As she wiped the dishcloth over the last plate her conscience niggled at her. Yes, she knew he was apologising. And yes, she should of course accept it. After all, everyone jumped to the wrong conclusions some time or another. Even so, there was something about his breezy, self-assured manner and the way he thought he could get away with anything by applying that debonair charm of his that made her feel... That's to say, well, it just made her feel blooming well annoyed!

CHAPTER 9

'Thank goodness,' said Alice later that night, as the strident two-tone pitch of the all-clear cut through the cold night air.

'About time too,' said Maeve, blowing on her hands and rubbing them together. 'Sure, isn't it cold enough to make the devil wear a jumper.'

Although Alice couldn't quite imagine the prince of hell in a double-knit Fair Isle jumper, her friend's observation couldn't be faulted. If the frost creeping across the puddles and whitening the foliage was anything to go by, the temperature was a degree or two below freezing. Hardly surprising, really, as it was the start of November and almost midnight. Of course, standing in the balloon site's five-foot-deep air-raid trench up to your ankles in icy water didn't help matters.

'Right, let's get out,' said Alice. 'Before we both turn into blocks of ice.'

She sloshed through the mud to the end of the trench and then climbed up the short, wooden ladder as a fire engine clattered past, its brass bell ringing furiously as it sped along.

'Looks like they've hit downriver at Silvertown and the

Royal Docks,' she said, gazing eastwards along the river at the red glow lighting the sky.

The warning siren sounded a little after eight, just as Lily and Maureen finished the second two-hour patrol of the shift. Having done their stint, and unlike all the other members of the crew, who crashed out for their allocated two-hour rest period in the on-duty hut's bunks, they had gone back to kip at the Maid of Norway. Nell and Peggy weren't there either, as they were on half duty, meaning if they were lucky they'd have a full night's uninterrupted sleep, but they could be called back on duty if needed.

'Poor souls,' said Maeve, scratching a cross between the buttons of her overcoat. 'Here come Dolly and Rose.'

Like them, the two WAAFs coming to relieve them were dressed for the elements with scarves wrapped round up their necks and up to their ears, heavyweight overcoats and stout hobnail boots.

'How's it going?' asked Rose as she and Dolly reached them.

'Not so bad now the raid's over,' said Alice, stomping her feet in an attempt to warm them. 'Although we had a scary moment a while ago when a high-explosive bomb landed a couple of streets over. The force of the blast nearly ripped Bessie away from her cable. Any orders?'

Dolly shook her head. 'I'm guessing HQ thinks we might be having another visit tonight.'

Tilting her head back, Alice studied the barrage balloon floating 300 feet above them. Her bloated body swayed gently in the night air, her silver skin alive with the flickering red and orange of the flaming dockland around them.

Before she could stop herself, a yawn escaped her. Hardly surprising really as Alice, along with the rest of no. 3 crew, had been on duty for six hours already – and they had the same again in front of them before they finished their shift.

'Come on,' said Maeve, nudging Alice. 'Let's get ourselves some shut-eye. See you later, girls.'

'Not if we see you first,' said Rose and Dolly together.

Leaving them for their two-hour stint on guard duty, Alice and Maeve crunched through the icy puddles on the concrete balloon base back to the hut. Thankful to at last be getting out of the freezing cold, Alice lifted the latch on the door and pushed it open, and entered the hut's warm interior.

'George,' she said, spotting her friend sprawled on one of the old sofas. 'I thought you weren't back until tomorrow.'

'Well, technically speaking,' said George, blowing a stream of cigarette smoke towards the dangling light bulb overhead, 'it is already tomorrow, but as I was able to cadge a lift back from Repton with my cousin I thought I'd head across and see how you've managed to survive without me.'

'Very well, thank you,' said Alice, hanging up her wet-weather gear on the row of pegs beside the door.

'So it would seem,' said George, raising a pencilled eyebrow and looking pointedly across at Gwen perched on the other sofa.

'I was just saying, Brogan' – covering her mouth with her fingers, Gwen gave a girly giggle – 'I mean Lieutenant Rafferty,' she said, her eyes shining as she said his name, 'was so friendly.'

Annoyingly, Alice couldn't deny it.

'... And so tall!' the newest member of no. 3 crew continued. 'About six foot I'd say, wouldn't you, Alice?'

'Was he?' said Alice nonchalantly, crossing to the Primus and relighting the hob under the kettle. 'I can't say I noticed.'

That of course was a complete lie – she would have put him a good eight inches taller than her five foot five.

Gwen gave her a disbelieving look. 'I don't see how you could not have, Alice, seeing as how you and he were standing at the sink together for a good twenty minutes talking.'

Maeve, who was sitting cross-legged next to George on the sofa, gave Alice a knowing look. '*Was* she now?'

Feeling her cheeks start to glow, Alice lowered her eyes and measured a couple of spoonfuls of tea into the pot.

'Oh, yes,' agreed Gwen. 'As soon as Alice started collecting the crockery he got straight up to help with the washing up. ''Cos he's like that, see. Kind and helpful. And so handsome. And don't say you didn't notice, Alice, because you'd have to have had your eyes shut all through dinner not to have.' The adoring expression lit up her pretty face. 'Oh, he is, more handsome even than Dylan Evans from Twigonran Farm and he's reckoned to be the most handsome man in the valley.'

'Most handsome man in the valley, you say?' said Maeve, exchanging an amused glance with George.

'Kind and helpful, tall *and* handsome,' said George, 'He sounds like the perfect man, don't you think so, Alice?'

An image of Brogan Rafferty, who was undeniably tall and irrefutably handsome, loomed up in Alice's mind.

'Well, George,' she said, rattling a spoon around the teapot as she looked across at her friend. 'I go by the old saying, handsome is what handsome does.'

'And even better,' continued Gwen, adoration filling her green eyes, 'you'll never guess what else?' She looked expectantly from George to Maeve and back again. 'He's only going to get us tickets for the Thanksgiving dance at Rainbow Corner!'

George and Maeve sat bolt upright.

'Rainbow Corner!' said George. 'You mean the new American Red Cross Club off Piccadilly Circus?'

Gwen nodded. 'He works there.'

The two WAAFs sitting on the sofa looked at Alice.

'Actually, Gwen,' said Alice, pouring teas into four mugs, 'Lieutenant Rafferty is part of the US's Civilian and Military Liaison Unit.'

'Doing what?' George asked, flicking ash into an ashtray.

'Well now,' said Gwen. 'I think... although I'm not a hundred per cent sure, like, but he meets with different people like the police and wardens, that's to say... at important meetings and...' She shrugged her shoulders. 'Truth is, I'm not too sure what Lieutenant Rafferty really does because—'

'Because you spent the whole meal making eyes at him,' said Alice, handing her a mug.

'I did not!' young Gwen snorted. The same dreamy look she'd worn all afternoon spread again across her face. 'But he *is* very, very handsome.'

'More handsome even than Dylan Evans,' said Maeve, cradling her tea in both hands.

'And *he's* the most handsome man in the valley,' added George, as Alice handed her a hot drink.

'Give over, you two,' said Alice, laughing, lowering herself onto the other sofa.

Gwen put her thumb on her nose and poked out her tongue.

'And anyway,' she said, giving Alice a meaningful look, 'I wasn't the only one who couldn't keep their eyes off Lieutenant Rafferty, was I? Because I saw you giving him a bit of glad-eye when you thought no one was looking.'

Over the tops of their mugs, George and Maeve's eyes fixed on Alice.

Alice forced a laugh. 'Don't be silly.'

Actually, Alice had found that her gaze and attention seemed to return to Brogan Rafferty a little too often for her liking, but it was quite understandable given how furious she still was with him.

'Look,' said George. 'I don't care which one of you wants to get inside Lieutenant Rafferty's trousers—'

Irritatingly, the vision of said trousers hugging Brogan's long muscular legs flashed across Alice's mind.

'—and for all I care, he could look like Quasimodo,'

continued George. 'As long as he's getting us on that guest list to attend Rainbow Corner's Thanksgiving dance.'

Alice let out a silent sigh.

As Rainbow Corner was Brogan's baby he would obviously be at the Thanksgiving dance, so, annoyingly, there would be no way of avoiding him. However, what was even more annoying than having to be in his company was the realisation that she actually wanted to be.

CHAPTER 10

As rivulets of rainwater trickled down the window, Brogan studied the top of Major Jessop's head as he read the list on the table in front of him.

After a few moments Brogan's commanding officer raised his head. 'And this is just this week?'

'I'm afraid so, sir,' Brogan replied.

It was eight thirty on the morning after Sunday dinner with his Aunt Florrie, and he was sitting in Jessop's office, which was situated on the second floor in Wiltshire House on the opposite side of Grosvenor Square from the US Embassy.

Ten years older than Brogan in his late thirties, the man on the other side of the desk had a mass of carrot-red hair cropped to within a half-inch of his head. With a physique like a buffalo and a fat cigar clenched permanently in the left corner of his mouth, Waylon Issac Jessop III was almost a cartoon version of a senior US officer. However, in reality the head of the US Army's Office of War Information and Public Relations in London had before the war been a tenth-grade history teacher in Pennsylvania.

For once it wasn't just him and Jessop in the room, though

Sam, who was lying patiently at Brogan's feet, wasn't contributing much to his weekly reporting session with his commanding officer.

'Thankfully, because of our agreement with the Brits I was able to get them released from the police station without any trouble,' added Brogan. 'But as you can imagine, it's causing a lot of bad feeling with the local cops.'

The list of names Jessop had been scrutinising was of all the GIs Brogan had rescued from police stations in the past week.

'As you'll see, most of them were hauled in by the cops for drunkenness and fighting,' continued Brogan.

'What about the soldier who put one of the Met officers in hospital?' asked Jessop.

'He and the other GI who was arrested for assault were passed over to our officers for full investigation,' Brogan confirmed.

Jessop grunted by way of reply and then returned to his contemplation of the twenty-seven names on the list.

After a moment he looked up. 'What are we going to do about it, Rafferty?'

'Well, sir, I am hopeful that once the new Red Cross Club at Rainbow Corner opens next week our boys who come to town on furlough will spend their evening there eating, playing pool and watching films rather than getting drunk in the West End pubs and clubs,' Brogan replied. 'There'll be dances too, the first being to celebrate Thanksgiving in a few weeks. To be honest, sir, most of the GIs I've had to fish out of police cells have never been out of their home state, let alone halfway across the world. They get themselves into trouble because they're scared, homesick and lonely, so if we can bring a bit of home to them here it might stop some of the problem.'

Jessop gave him a jaundiced look. 'I think you have an overly optimistic view of your fellow man. I can't see your pinball machines and doughnuts being more of a lure than a show at the Windmill or a nightclub full of giggling young women.'

'Perhaps not,' said Brogan. 'But if it stops the station sergeants in Bow Street inwardly groaning when I walk in, I'll count that as a win.'

Jessop grunted again. 'Any other plans to keep the Brits sweet?'

'Now you mention it, sir,' said Brogan. 'I wonder if I could run something by you?'

'Run away, Rafferty,' said the major, the chair creaking as he leant back.

'Well sir, last Sunday...' He gave a brief account of his visits to his Aunt Florrie and the discussion over the previous day's lunch. 'My aunt's WVS are doing the damnedest to put on a Christmas party for the kiddies, so I wondered if we could get involved to help.'

'How?'

'Well, many of our servicemen have children back home who they miss, so perhaps we in the OWI could encourage a platoon or company to adopt a local church or WVS and help them celebrate Christmas. I know that several of the squadrons in the Eighth Army Air Force based in East Anglia and Lincoln are already planning such like in their local towns and villages,' Brogan replied.

Pursing his lips, Jessop nodded. 'Sound idea. I can see how it'd be easy to organise in a small community but I'm not sure it'll work quite as well in London?'

'I thought I'd kick it off by getting a piece in the *Stars and Stripes* asking for volunteers and take it from there,' Brogan said. 'I might ask the newspaper's editor to put in a Willie and Joe cartoon about it. If I can get it off the ground, then it will not only show the local population that we're not just a bunch of loud-mouthed drunks but also let our boys have a family Christmas even if it's not with their own kith and kin.'

'That sounds swell, but haven't you still got problems at Rainbow Corner to figure out without signing GIs up to help with a kiddies' Christmas party?' the major asked.

Brogan shook his head. 'Rainbow Corner's just about ready.'

Actually, that wasn't strictly true, because with just over a week until it was due to open, the carpet in the library and quiet room had yet to be laid and the half of the table tennis tables he'd ordered from the States were still on the dockside in Belfast. However, after gazing across the dinner table at Alice the day before, getting involved with the Shadwell Relief Centre's Christmas events gave him the perfect excuse to visit the Maid of Norway despite his strict rule about getting involved with married women.

A thoughtful expression settled on Jessop's bovine features.

'Very well,' he said at last. 'But it's the beginning of November already and with Thanksgiving in less than a month I hope you can make it work, because if your volunteer GIs make a mess of it for the kiddies the whole US Army will be on Santa's naughty list.'

'How are the ropes your end, Maeve?' Alice shouted across at her friend through the rainwater dripping off her sou'wester.

Turning, Maeve gave her the thumbs-up. 'What about yours?'

'I've tightened the front near side, but the rest are okay,' Alice called back, as a gust of wind blew rain and wet leaves across the circular concrete bed of the balloon.

She looked at her watch. 'Dolly and Rose should be out to relieve us soon.'

Although it was almost four o'clock, before the war, when the sun at this time of year would almost have dipped below the western horizon, the sun was still above the warehouses. This was due to the government's daylight-saving directive of Double Summer Time, when the clocks were put forward two hours ahead of Greenwich Mean Time so that when they were turned back in the autumn they still remained one hour in front of GMT.

Both cloaked in their long waterproof overcoats and bucket-like headgear, she and Maeve had just completed their two-hourly patrol to check on Bessie, who was floating 50 feet above them, tethered to her concrete moorings by the ropes and all the other equipment of number 3 1 2 balloon site.

'Let's give the fuel and coal bunker one last check before we hand over,' said Alice, as she and Maeve regrouped in the relative shelter beneath the belly of the barrage balloon.

Rainwater dripping into her face, Maeve nodded.

Turning her head into the wind and with Maeve behind, Alice headed towards the brick-built bunker with its corrugated tin roof, where the site's diesel and coal were stored.

As they stepped inside the damp enclosure, both girls took their torches from their pockets and switched them on.

'This looks fine,' said Maeve, tapping the gauge on the side of the diesel tank. 'What about the coal?'

Alice shook the padlock on the top cover, then, crouching down, she grasped the second padlock securing the square trap at the front and tested that.

'They both look okay,' said Alice.

Maeve nodded. 'Is that Lily?'

Alice turned and spotted a figure, wrapped up against the elements, coming out of the on-duty hut door and hurrying back to the dry of the Maid of Norway.

'Looks like it,' said Alice.

'That's a bit of a turn-up for the books, seeing Lily on the site on her day off,' said Maeve.

'Especially as she barely shows her face when she's *on* duty,' Alice agreed. 'Here come Dolly and Rose.'

'Nice weather for ducks,' said Dolly, as she and Rose came to a halt in front of them.

'Never mind, Millie's lot are taking over in a couple of hours and we can get out of this blasted weather,' said Maeve.

'Any problems?' asked Rose.

Alice shook her head, flicking drops of rain. 'Other than the rain has almost soaked through to my knickers.'

'Was that Lily we've just seen scurrying away, or were my eyes playing tricks on me?' asked Maeve.

'Yes, that was our dear darling corporal,' said Rose. 'She came over to post the Christmas rota.'

'Hurrah!' said Alice.

'I wouldn't get too excited,' said Dolly. 'You haven't seen it.'

Leaving their two friends to take over the last patrol of the day, Alice and Maeve trudged through the muddy puddles towards the hut. They pushed open the door and walked in, to find Nell and Peggy slouched glumly on the sofa, George standing by the window, cigarette in hand as she glared through it, and Gwen washing up in the sink, looking as if she was about to burst into tears.

Without taking off her coat, Alice marched across and peered at the list of duties Lily had pinned up.

As her gaze skimmed down the dates and names, her temper started to rise.

'For the love of Mary,' said Maeve, looking over Alice's shoulder.

'It's not fair,' said Gwen, taking a towel and drying her hands. 'Sergeant Munroe said we were to have two days' leave before Christmas so we could visit our families.'

'But they're supposed to be two days off together before Christmas,' said Peggy. 'And Lily's given us two all right, one day one week and another day the following week. Other than Nell, none of us can get home and back in a day.'

'It will break my mum's heart, it will, not to see me at Christmas,' said Gwen, a fat tear rolling slowly down her cheek. 'Can't we tell Sergeant Munroe?'

George took a long drag on her cigarette.

'We're not in school, Gwen,' she said, turning back into the room and blowing a stream of smoke towards the light bulb dangling above. 'We can't just tell teacher.'

'I'm surprised you didn't say something, George,' said Maeve.

'I most certainly did,' George replied. 'I told her she was a...'

She let out a string of descriptive obscenities that would have made a sailor blush.

Thinking that probably wasn't the most helpful way of getting the rota changed, Alice studied the newly posted duties again.

Gwen blew her nose noisily. 'Isn't there something you can do to get it changed, Alice?'

Pressing her lips together, Alice turned and looked at her friends. 'I can't promise, but I'll try.'

She jammed her still-wet sou'wester back on her head and wrapped her scarf round her neck again, then marched across to the door and back out into the rain.

'So, I'm pleased to say, Aunt Florrie, that I have had at least a dozen GIs sign up to link with you gals in the Shadwell WVS who want some help putting a smile on the faces of the neighbourhood kiddies,' said Brogan.

He was sitting in his aunt's comfortable fireside chair, with Sam curled up at his feet and a mug of hot sweet Nescafé coffee in his hand.

He'd brought the tin with him along with a bar of soap, a can of pineapple and another of peaches, and three packs of playing cards for the Maid of Norway's customers. He'd also brought Florrie a pair of nylons, which were fast becoming a prized object to almost every woman in England. In return, he'd received an effusive welcome, a huge bear hug and a pleasant hour with his aunt in her cosy back parlour as he told her his idea about GIs lending a hand with making this year's Christmas for the children of bomb-damaged, blitzed London a merry one.

'Well, I don't rightly know if most of us can be described as girls,' she said and laughed. 'But when I had a letter from the WVS London headquarters telling me about the American army's Office of War Information and Public Relations Christmas initiative I never dreamed you'd be the brains behind it. And I'm sure our Christmas party and concert will give you something jolly to put in your next newspaper piece.'

Brogan raised his drink to his lips and drained the last of his coffee, then put the mug on the occasional table.

'It's swell seeing you again, Aunt Florrie,' he said, standing up.

'You too, Brogan, and this good boy,' she added, making a fuss of Sam, who, sensing something was happening, was on his feet with his ears up.

'He is a good boy,' said Brogan, stroking the dog's head. 'But although I'd be happy to sit by your fire a little longer, I've got to get back and you've got a pub to run.'

'True enough,' said Florrie, struggling to her feet. 'As soon as the five o'clock hooter goes, they'll be banging on the door.'

Brogan took his overcoat from the hook on the wall and shrugged it on.

'Thanks again for the coffee and things,' said Florrie, as he fastened the buttons. 'They really do help. Even with the rationing I haven't had my full four ounces of tea or ounce of cheese for the past two weeks.'

Making a mental note to see if the PX had tea for his next visit, Brogan picked up his cap. He stepped aside and Florrie led him out of the parlour and into the small hallway leading from her private quarters to the pub's main bar.

'Looks like it still raining,' she said. 'I hope you don't get too wet driving back.'

'Should be okay if I roll the side canvases down,' Brogan replied. 'And it's only a few miles—'

The public house's side door swung open and what at first glance was a cone plastered in mud staggered in. However, as a pair of grey eyes beneath the floppy brim fixed on him Brogan realised exactly who the mud-man – or more correctly woman – actually was. So did Sam. He trotted over and sat beside her.

'Alice!' gasped Florrie, staring at her in utter disbelief. 'What in the blue blazes happened to you?'

Shifting her attention onto her landlady, Alice cleared her throat. 'I accidentally fell in the bomb-shelter trench.'

'Are you hurt?' asked Florrie.

'A bit bruised, that's all,' said Alice, as the dog nuzzled her hand.

'How on earth did you do it?' asked Florrie.

'I was in a hurry to speak to Lily,' Alice replied, embarrassment tinting the cheeks, just visible beneath the streaks of mud.

'Well, you're out of luck. She and her mate went out ten minutes ago. But never mind about Lily, young lady,' said Florrie, brusquely. 'Get those boots off and then give me your hat and coat. They can dry out in the scullery, and you can brush off the mud later.'

Standing on one leg, Alice tried to kick off one wellington boot, but started wobbling about.

Brogan offered his hand and after a second or two of hesitation she took it.

An odd sensation stole over Brogan, very like the one he'd had when they shook hands the previous Sunday. He'd not thought much about it then, but...

Holding the mud-laden coat in front of her, Florrie marched back into the parlour, leaving Brogan and Alice, who was intently studying the wallpaper behind him, standing in the hallway.

'It's still raining then?' said Brogan, after an uncomfortable moment.

'Evidently.' Alice gave him a glacial look as she stroked Sam's head. 'I suppose you think me falling in a trench and getting caked in mud is funny.'

Brogan couldn't deny that her appearance was comical, but he found suddenly that he was actually thinking something quite different. Standing in a too-large boiler suit, in her thick woolly socks, with mud streaked across her face and in her hair, she did look funny, but she also looked adorable. So much so that the urge to take her in his arms and kiss her, mud and all, swept over him.

Reminding himself that she was a married woman, Brogan forcibly suppressed the impulse and grinned.

As she tucked a lock of damp hair back behind her ear, a faint hint of a smile hovered on Alice's lips for a moment, but then she frowned.

Florrie returned. 'I've hung them up by the boiler, so they should dry out before you go on duty tomorrow.'

'Thanks, Florrie,' said Alice. 'What would we do without you?'

'Catch your deaths and starve, most like,' said Florrie, giving the damp WAAF a fond look. 'Now you get yourself upstairs and in a hot bath,' she added, setting Brogan's imagination on a rather pleasant train of thought. 'And I'll bring supper up in a while. Oh, and before you go, Alice, I've got some good news about the Christmas party. Brogan and a few of his GI mates are going to pitch in and help.'

'That's very good of you,' Alice said, looking at him in a way he'd never seen before.

'Just being a good neighbour to our allies and contributing to the Christmas spirit,' said Brogan. 'So I'm afraid you're gonna see quite a lot of me, Aircraftwoman Starling, in the next few weeks.'

An emotion that Brogan couldn't interpret flicked across Alice's face for an instant and then vanished.

'Right, enough of this chatter – up you get and get yourself out of those wet clothes, Alice, before you go down with some'ink nasty,' said Florrie.

Giving him a last glance, Alice headed off up the stairs, with Brogan's gaze following her until she disappeared at the top.

'Barring a couple I could name, all my WAAFs are lovely girls,' said Florrie. 'But I have to say I'm particularly fond of Alice. She's so kind and caring and spends most of her time off helping with the children at the relief centre. To my way of thinking the top brass should have promoted her to corporal.'

'Why didn't they?' asked Brogan.

His aunt told him about Effie's predicament when her fiancé went missing in action.

'... so because she stood by her friend,' concluded his aunt, 'the blooming RAF top brass passed her over. I tell you, Brogan, Alice is like the daughter I never 'ad. Shame about her 'usband.'

Brogan's head snapped round. 'What about him?'

'She don't talk about 'im much,' said Florrie. 'But as far as I can make out he stopped a German bullet at Dunkirk.'

His heart ached for Alice, a young bride who had cruelly become a widow so young. But as much as he sincerely lamented the passing of a fellow soldier in battle, truthfully Brogan's view of life shifted onto a different plane as he felt a glimmer of hope that perhaps one day the emotions Alice felt towards him would be the polar opposite to the ones she had now.

~

'Are you decent?' called Effie through Alice's bedroom door.

'Just about,' Alice called back, rubbing her hair with the towel.

The door opened and her friend walked in carrying two mugs, her stomach straining against the fabric of her navy-blue maternity dress.

The six o'clock pips sounded out from the Bakelite wireless in the WAAFs' communal lounge as Alice came out of the bathroom, an hour after her muddy adventure at the bottom of the air raid trench. Now, swathed in her dressing gown and with the single-bar electric fire in the grate warming the bedroom, she was sitting propped up against the headboard with her legs stretched out in front of her.

'I thought you could do with a cuppa,' Effie said, closing the door behind her with her foot.

'I certainly could,' Alice replied, picking up her hairbrush.

Effie placed Alice's cup on the bedside table, then, setting the springs bonging, she made herself comfortable and rested back against the footboard.

'You must have been freezing by the time you got back,' she said, stretching her legs out next to Alice's.

'To the marrow,' Alice agreed. 'In fact, I could barely feel my feet in my wellies, despite having two pairs of socks on.'

'I bet you feel better after a soak,' said Effie.

'Well, I'd hardly call lying in six inches of water a soak,' Alice replied.

Her friend sighed. 'Well, there is a war on, you know.'

Working out a tangle in her hair, Alice gave a short laugh.

Effie glanced around the bedroom and a sentimental expression spread across her face. 'This is just like old times, isn't it?'

Alice smiled and nodded. 'Yes, how many times have you and me sat in this room sitting top to tail on the bed with a cup of tea in our hands?'

'Dozens,' Effie replied.

Satisfied she'd brushed all the knots out, Alice put her hairbrush down and picked up her tea.

'Have you heard from Nathan?' she asked, taking a sip.

Effie nodded. 'I had a letter in the afternoon post. It sounds like he's been busy, as always, training new pilots, but he has put in for leave over Christmas.' Looking down, she smoothed her hand over her stomach. 'Hopefully, he'll be here when this one makes an appearance.'

'Well, from your lips to God's ears, as Florrie is fond of saying,' Alice replied. 'Plus, if he's not you'll have plenty of company, thanks to the way Lily's done the Christmas rota. Split everyone's days off so, other than Nell, who's just a half-hour bus ride away from her family, none of the crew can get home at all leading up to Christmas. Oh, of course she's given herself and Maureen a seventy-two-hour pass from Christmas Eve, but everyone else will be stuck on site.'

'Nell mentioned it,' said Effie. 'And I heard about George's response.'

'Actually, I was so annoyed for the crew perhaps it's just as well I didn't catch her when I dashed back,' said Alice.

'So,' said Effie, resting her mug on what was left of her lap. 'How *did* you fall in the air-raid shelter trench?'

'It was stupid really, especially as I blooming well know where it is,' Alice replied. 'But I was so mad at Lily I just stormed across the site to see if I could reason with her about the Christmas rota.'

'Nell told me about it when I saw her downstairs,' said Effie.

'But the trench is four and a half feet deep – you were lucky you didn't break something.'

'Actually, I didn't exactly fall in the trench, I slid into it,' said Alice, remembering her undignified stumble downward. 'I was too near the top step and lost my balance and sort of staggered down and slid along the side of the trench to the bottom.'

Effie laughed. 'Hence the state of your coat. Florrie said you'd looked like you'd been rolling around in the Thames mud.'

Alice smiled. 'Well, I pretty much had as there was at least six inches of it at the bottom. But you know what was worst? Walking through the door and straight into Lieutenant blooming Rafferty.' Brogan's handsome face loomed back into Alice's mind. 'He could hardly keep a straight face.'

'Well, I'm not sure I'd have kept a straight face myself, if I'd seen you covered in mud,' said Effie.

'But I bet he'll have a good laugh telling all his flashy GI buddies about this stupid WAAF who fell down a hole. For goodness' sake,' Alice muttered, looking blindly at the patchwork bedspread they were sitting on. 'Why of all the hundreds of American soldiers posted in London did *Lieutenant-ruddy-Rafferty* have to be Florrie's nephew?'

With her cup poised a few inches from her lip, Effie studied Alice over the rim.

'What do you mean, Alice?' she asked.

Alice forced an innocent expression onto her face. 'Nothing.'

'Come on,' Effie replied, giving her a sceptical look. 'I wasn't born yesterday. I could see when Brogan came to Sunday dinner last week you had the hump with him about something as soon as he walked in the door. On top of which you almost rubbed the pattern off the plate you were washing when he went over to help you by drying up – so what is it you've got against the man?'

'Well – and you mustn't tell the others, I wouldn't want them to say something by mistake to Florrie as it would really upset her,' said Alice.

'My lips are sealed,' said Effie.

Alice took a deep breath.

'Lieutenant Rafferty was the American officer who assumed I was one of the drunken girls trying to hook up with GIs just to get stuff out of them,' she said. 'It was him who I had a stand-up argument with for implying I was a gold digger.'

'My goodness,' said Effie, still holding her mug before her. 'I'm guessing he's apologised.'

'Yes, he has,' Alice conceded. 'A couple of times in fact.'

'Well, you'll have to accept it was just a misunderstanding,' said Effie. 'Especially as he's pitching in with the WVS Christmas party and concert.'

'Oh, Florrie told you about that,' said Alice.

'She did,' said Effie. 'And she also told me that not only is he helping us at the Shadwell, but he's set up an initiative for American service personnel to volunteer to link up with other relief centres all over London, which is very big-hearted of him. And I'm sure there'll be lots of children who have had pretty miserable Christmases for the past three years who would agree.'

Actually, annoyingly, Alice did too.

Having dreamed of a large family, the main reason she'd got involved with Florrie and her team at the relief centre, instead of being 'adopted' by a local family as the other members of the crew had, was the joy of the children. As a childless widow, other people's children were the nearest thing to a family she might ever have.

'After all, it's not as if you'll be able to avoid him,' her friend said, cutting across Alice's sad thoughts. 'I'll say it again: the best thing you can do is accept Brogan's apology and turn the page. Who knows, Alice, you might actually find you grow to like him...'

CHAPTER 11

'Well hello there, Lieutenant Rafferty,' said a woman's voice as Brogan, hands in pockets and cap at a rakish angle, stepped through the plush curtains.

Brogan turned and found himself looking into a heavily made-up pair of eyes.

He smiled. 'Hello, Patsy.'

The young woman's scarlet lips formed themselves into a pout. 'I thought you'd deserted us.'

He was in the Blue Fountain nightclub. It was situated in one of the many alleyways between Regent Street and Shaftesbury Avenue.

The establishment was situated in the basement of the building, which was just as well as the air-raid siren had gone off as he'd arrived at the venue. He'd felt a rumble as he descended, and the overhead lights in the entrance had danced a bit, but it seemed that tonight the Luftwaffe's attention was on Westminster and Whitehall, which was a mile to the south of them.

Before him, arranged around the dancefloor, were a couple of dozen tables and, as always, the clientele consisted mainly of smartly dressed Americans with their girls, a couple of English army types sprinkled among them. On stage the five-piece band was blasting out a quickstep, while on the minute dancefloor a dozen or more GIs, each with girls in their arms, glided around.

Smiling at the waitress, who was dressed in a rather fetching black uniform with a short skirt, Brogan placed his right hand over his heart. 'Never.'

She raised an eyebrow. 'I bet you say that to all the girls.'

'Never!' he replied, looking mortified. 'My usual table, I hope.'

She nodded. 'And your date's waiting at it.'

Brogan pulled down the front of his uniform jacket, trotted down the couple of steps to the main part of the establishment, then strolled over to the table on the right edge of the dancefloor.

The strawberry-blonde, wearing a black cocktail dress and a forlorn look on her face, turned as Brogan approached.

'Sorry, Gloria,' he said, summoning up his most remorseful expression.

She frowned. 'You said nine.'

'I know,' said Brogan.

'And it's half past now,' she added.

'What can I say,' he replied. 'There's a war on.' Reaching out, he took her hand. 'Come on, honey, forgive the poor lonesome Yank and...' Bending forward, Brogan kissed her fingertips. 'Let's make up for the fun we've missed.'

Gloria's disgruntled expression remained for a few seconds, then her scarlet lips quivered.

Taking the seat beside her, Brogan drew her onto his knee and her arms wound round his neck.

'If you weren't such a bloody handsome devil, Brogan, I'd—'

He kissed her and she melted into him. He held her for a moment, then raised his hand.

A waitress hurried over and Brogan looked at Gloria.

'A double martini,' she said, throwing back the last of her drink.

'And a Scotch on the rocks,' said Brogan.

'Certainly, sir. Anything else?' she asked, giving him a lavish sidewards look from beneath her lashes.

'No, that's all for now, thank you,' Brogan replied.

Gloria's eyes narrowed as she watched the waitress sashay back to the bar for a moment, then her attention returned to Brogan.

'So why did you leave me sitting here alone for half an hour?' she asked.

'There was an unexploded bomb in Cheapside, so I had to drive up to the City Road to get back,' Brogan replied.

'Where on earth had you been?

'A place alongside the river called Shadwell,' Brogan replied.

She looked horrified. 'What on earth were you doing in East London?'

'Visiting my aunt,' Brogan replied, as the waitress returned with their drinks. 'She's my ma's younger sister and runs a pub right by the river and...' Accompanied by the odd interruption from German armaments crashing to earth, Brogan gave Gloria a short account of his afternoon with his aunt.

An explosion nearby had the barman grabbing the bottles and glasses on the bar while customers covered their drinks with their hands to prevent dislodged grit and dust from above falling into them. The band paused as the lights flickered off and on for a moment, then the music resumed.

'To be honest,' he continued, 'since I arrived in London a few months ago I've pretty much spent my time around Mayfair, Piccadilly or Soho. Although I'd heard Ed Murrow radio broadcasts about the devastation caused by the London Blitz, I was shocked when I actually saw it for himself.'

As if to illustrate his point, a bomb landed somewhere

nearby and set the overhead lights jigging in their sockets. The Americans in the club whooped and shouted abuse at the Luftwaffe planes flying overhead, while their companions looked fearfully at the ceiling.

'The folks living by the London Docks have had a real tough time of it,' Brogan added, as the band resumed playing.

Gloria gave a little shrug and, taking another sip of her drink, turned to watch the dancers.

Annoyed at her dismissive attitude, Brogan studied her clean-cut profile for a moment, then, swallowing another mouthful of Scotch, he too turned his attention to the dancers. A young woman in the arms of an RAF officer in an air force-blue uniform whirled past him, and Brogan's mind drifted back to his encounter with mud-splattered Alice that afternoon.

Somehow, discovering she was a widow had shifted something in Brogan, but to be honest he wasn't at all sure what.

'I said, the band's good, aren't they?'

Brogan dragged his thoughts back to the here and now.

'Sorry,' he said. 'My mind was wandering.'

'Well as long as it wasn't wandering to that flirty cocktail waitress who gave you the eye,' she replied, her painted nails gripping her cocktail glass.

'How could I, sweetheart,' Brogan smiled, 'When I only have eyes for you.'

In the flickering light of the Tiffany-style lamp between them Gloria's immaculately made-up face softened.

'I suppose I can't blame her for making a pass at you.' Reaching below the table, she placed her hand on his knee. 'My flatmate is visiting her parents for a few days, so perhaps when you've finished your drink we can head off to the flat.'

Running her hand up a few inches, she squeezed his thigh.

Brogan grinned and threw back the last of his drink, then stood up and offered her his hand. 'Let's find a cab.'

. . .

Half an hour later, Brogan helped Gloria out of the cab.

'Top floor. I'll leave the door open, so don't be long, darling,' she said, huskily.

She pressed her lips on his briefly, then trotted up a couple of steps to the front door of an elegant Edwardian townhouse with sandbags covering the ground-floor windows.

The house sat one side of a square ornamental garden that had lost its iron railings to the war effort. There was an air-raid warden's hut on one side, painted white so as to be visible in the blackout. It had a blackboard fixed alongside it with a clock showing the blackout times. He guessed that the vegetable patch that took up the rest of the enclosure's space was what was left of the peaceful oasis of flowers and shrubs that had previously been there.

Brogan pulled out his wallet. 'How—?'

The low wail of the all-clear cut across his words.

'Two bob, mate,' said the craggy-faced driver, the roll-up stuck to his lower lip bobbing as he spoke. 'And I bet those 'round the docks will be 'appy to hear that tune at last. They've had it bad down there tonight.'

Brogan pulled out a brown ten-shilling note and handed it over.

The cab driver rummaged around for a moment, then handed Brogan a few coins. Turning on his pencil torch, he inspected the collection of silver in his palm.

'Bad luck, *mate*, I'm one of those Yanks who understands your money,' he said, holding his change out beneath the sliver of light.

Giving him a resentful look, the cab driver added the missing shilling, flipped up his *For Hire* sign and sped off.

Brogan pocketed his change and followed Gloria up the steps and into the house. He took the stairs two at a time, then walked into her apartment at the top of the four-storey house.

Gloria's head appeared round the door at the end of the room 'Make yourself at home.'

Her head disappeared back where it had come from.

'You'll have your warden after you, for not having your curtains drawn,' he said, strolling across to the large window.

'I doubt the light can be seen from the street, let alone by a pilot flying a plane overhead,' she called back.

As Gloria clattered about in the kitchen, Brogan looked across the rooftops at the fiery red glow to the east.

The memory of his Aunt Florrie and her snug little parlour in the Maid of Norway formed itself and then added in Alice Starling.

Brogan frowned.

'Coffee,' said Gloria, emerging out of the kitchen carrying a small tray with two mugs on it. 'Percolated, just as you Americans like it.'

Pushing thoughts of Alice aside, Brogan left his study of the night sky and ambled over to the sofa. She handed him his drink and he took a sip.

'Good?'

'Very,' he replied, as the strong taste rolled down his throat.

'I get the beans from a little Turkish café around the corner,' she explained, as Brogan made himself comfortable. 'It's all under the counter, of course, but one must have one's luxuries even in wartime.'

Brogan frowned slightly. Florrie's coffee might be near on tasteless, but at least she came by it honestly.

Sitting down next to him, Gloria snuggled up, and all thoughts of coffee and the black market evaporated from Brogan's mind.

Putting his drink down, he took her in his arms and drew her closer. She tilted her face upwards, and Brogan pressed his lips to hers. But strangely, as she kissed him back Brogan's enthusiasm faltered as he caught himself wondering what Alice Starling would feel like in his arms.

'Your aunt,' said Gloria, cutting across his thoughts. 'If her husband's dead and sons have both been called up, is she running the pub by herself?'

Brogan shook his head. 'She's got an old chap who does most of the heavy work and a young barmaid,' he replied. 'And of course, there's the WAAFs.'

Gloria sat up and looked at him. 'WAAFs?'

'Yes,' Brogan replied. 'They're the crew manning the barrage balloon on the playing field opposite and they are billeted in my aunt's pub.'

'Well, poor them,' Gloria said.

The image of Alice and her friends grappling with a barrage balloon four miles away, as bombs falling around them, flashed across Brogan's mind.

'Yes, it must be hell for them tonight,' he said.

Gloria gave a tinkling laugh. 'No silly. I mean being posted to the East End. The whole place is full of squalid little houses and ugly factories, plus it's awash with spivs and loud-mouthed women, so better the Germans bombs fall there than Knightsbridge or Hampstead. I wouldn't visit the place if you paid me.' She gave him a mocking look. 'You were lucky you still had four tyres on your jeep when you came out of the pub.'

From what he'd seen as he drove through the riverside neighbourhoods east of the City she was right, but then much the same could be said about New York's Bowery district, where he was born and raised.

Gloria put down her cup, swivelled round and sat on his lap. Grasping his hair with her painted nails, she pulled him towards her and pressed her lips to his.

With a beautiful woman on his lap, Brogan expected to feel his desire rise. But surprisingly, as Gloria kissed him, nothing stirred. Well, nothing except the memory of Alice plastered in mud.

'Now, handsome,' she said, and her hands went to the Windsor knot at his throat. 'Why don't we—'

'You know, Gloria,' he said, shifting his head away. 'I think I'm going to head off and get an early night.'

Putting her off his lap, Brogan rose to his feet.

A sour expression spread across Gloria's face. 'It's a quarter past one in the morning so it's a bit late to have an early night, Brogan.'

Brogan picked up his cup, downed the last mouthful of his drink, then put it back on the tray.

'Thanks for the coffee.'

'Will I see you again?' she asked as he headed for the door.

'I'll call you,' he replied, over his shoulder.

The ponderous-looking grandfather clock struck two as Brogan walked into the Jules' main lobby and let out a low whistle.

From behind the reception desk a ball of black-and-tan fur darted out, and belted across the black-and-white-tiles towards him. With his tail wagging ten to the dozen, Sam's huge paws landed on Brogan's shoulders, and he proceeded to welcome Brogan home by licking his right ear.

Tom Rawlins, the night clerk, snoozing on the reception desk, snapped awake.

'Lieutenant Rafferty,' he said. He was a slender youth growing his first moustache. He rubbed his eyes. 'Mr Harris said not to expect you back until the morning.'

To be honest, when he set out six hours earlier to meet Gloria, Brogan hadn't expected to be back before dawn either.

'I fancied an early night. Has he been behaving himself?' he asked, as the dog circled round his legs wagging his tail.

'As always,' Tom replied. 'The head barman took him for a

walk before he went off duty at eleven and I was going to let him in the yard in a while.'

'It's all right,' said Brogan, tapping his thigh to bring Sam to heel. 'I'll give him a quick walk round the block before I turn in.'

With Sam trotting along beside him, Brogan turned left out of the hotel, and within a few minutes he was in Grosvenor Square. The old Regency square with the American Embassy on its north side looked more like a US Army base than a tranquil oasis where uniformed nannies once pushed their infant charges around in prams. Not only were there at least two dozen jeeps lined up along the kerb but there were manned checkpoints on the road leading into the square. Hardly surprising really given that Eisenhower, the Supreme Commander of Allied Forces and the American army's top brass had their headquarters around the square.

Acknowledging the sentries as he passed and still mulling over his uncharacteristic response to Gloria's advances earlier, Brogan strolled round the perimeter of the small garden once before heading back to the Jules and his room. He unlocked the door and, confident that the hotel's maid would have pulled the curtains when the blackout started, walked in and switched on the light.

The room was one of the large ones on the second floor, overlooking the small town garden at the back of the establishment. It was simply furnished with a double wardrobe, dressing table, a leather-topped desk with a typewriter so old Moses could have typed the Ten Commandments on it. There was a comfortable fireside chair on one side of the cast-iron grate and an upright office chair by the window. The drapes were plush velvet, heavy and with a deep fringing along the bottom, as was fashionable at the turn of the century. However, the diagonal cross of gummed tape on the glass panes and the bucket of water and stirrup pump in the corner gave the room a more contemporary look. It also had a bathroom with sink, toilet and a shower, an invention that the Brits had not quite embraced as yet, preferring soaking in the tub.

Sam settled himself in his basket at the foot of the bed, but despite the late hour Brogan wasn't yet ready for his bed. He stripped off his jacket and tie and hung them on the back of the chair, then unbuttoned his collar. He grabbed the decanter of Scotch sitting on a silver tray next to his inkwell, poured himself a drink, then took his notepad from the desk's top drawer. He pulled a sheet of paper with an American eagle across the top from the stationery rack on the corner of the desk and threaded it around the typewriter's carriage.

In May 1940 he was one of the American journalists who was fully behind Roosevelt's support of Britain's determination to continue the fight. He'd written at least a dozen opinion pieces in the *New York Herald* saying as much, and when America finally entered the fight it was just at the point when he was starting to catch the eye of the countrywide nationals like the *New York Times* and *Post*. However, his urge to contribute to the defeat of fascism was stronger than his career ambitions, and he had enlisted to do his duty. In addition to contributing to the *Stars and Stripes*, Brogan had regularly submitted non-military pieces to newsrooms back home about life in England in order to keep his name fresh in the newsrooms, and had had an encouraging number of articles printed.

Swallowing a large mouthful of his drink, Brogan opened his notebook and, after glancing at his notes, started typing his latest piece. However, when he got to his scribbled line about the relationships between GIs and the British female population, he paused as he rested back.

As it seemed to do on an increasingly regular basis, Brogan's brain conjured up the image of Alice, sitting next to him in that very fetching blue jumper. He wouldn't be a red-blooded man if he didn't appreciate her slender yet womanly figure, but it was her lovely eyes and warm smile that his mind and emotions focused on.

As he stared unseeing at the flowery wallpaper, understanding enfolded Brogan like a warm blanket as he realised to his utter astonishment that, without trying, Alice Starling had captured his heart. Of course, thanks to their rocky first meeting, what she felt about him was quite another matter.

CHAPTER 12

'Five little ducks went swimming one day,' sang Alice, making waving movements with her hands.

The dozen or so pre-school children sitting cross-legged and wide-eyed on the floor in front of her copied her actions.

'Mummy duck said quack, quack, quack,' she continued, making two beaks with her finger and thumb, as the children did the same. 'But only four' – she held up the appropriate number of fingers – 'little ducks came back. Four little ducks went...'

It was just after eleven on Tuesday morning, and she was seated on a child-sized nursery chair in what had been the committee room of the Congregation Hall but was now the WVS nursery.

Although she wasn't on duty until six, Alice was dressed in her WAAF uniform with her shirt and tie beneath. Since the introduction of clothes rationing just over a year ago almost everyone, be they in the armed services or a volunteer in ARP, wore their uniform even when not on duty. The reason for this was, no matter how ill-fitting or unflattering it was, a uniform was free, whereas civilian clothes cost both money and coupons, so people saved both for essentials.

She was at one end of the high-ceilinged room with the under-fives while at the far end, behind a couple of hospital screens, members of the WVS in their distinct forest green uniforms were tending to the newborns and infants in the dozen or so cots.

'... And *all* five little ducks came back,' sang Alice, waving her hands and beaming a happy smile at her small charges.

Bobbing up and down, the children waved their chubby hands and laughed with her.

The door opened and Ida Wilson, vicar's wife and founder member of the Shadwell WVS committee, peered in.

She gave Alice a smile of appreciation over her metal-rimmed spectacles, then turned her attention to the children.

'Well now, children. Have you had fun with Auntie Alice, then?' she asked.

'Yes, Auntie Ida,' chorused the youngsters sitting at her feet.

'So what do we say?'

'Fank you, Auntie Alice,' the children shouted.

Ida turned to her. 'So good of you to hold the fort like this.'

'My pleasure,' said Alice. 'Is Mrs Munday all right?'

Ida nodded. 'She just got a bit upset, that's all. They're doing liver and onion for dinner, and apparently it was her husband's favourite.'

'Grief has a way of rearing its head when you least expect it,' said Alice.

Ida placed a sympathetic hand on Alice's arm. 'I'm sorry, I forgot about your husband. Dunkirk, wasn't it?'

Alice nodded.

'Well, I'm sure you know exactly how dear Mary feels,' said Ida. 'But at least you haven't got to explain to three children why Daddy isn't coming home.'

'No, I haven't,' said Alice, feeling the familiar ache in her heart. 'Is there anything else you need me to help with?'

'Not at the moment,' Ida replied. 'Actually, while I have you here, I wonder if I could ask how you're getting on organising the relief centre's Christmas spectacular.'

'Ask away,' Alice laughed. 'We're already saving our sweet rations and up to our eyes in knitted teddies and sewing dollies' dresses in our lounge in the Maid of Norway and there's still several weeks to go.'

The vicar's wife's round face lifted in a smile. 'You balloon girls are absolute angels.'

'Well, I don't know about that,' said Alice. 'But it's the least we can do for the cakes you send up each week, plus it gives us a chance to enjoy a proper Christmas even though we're away from home.'

'Well, I wondered if I could impose on your good nature a little more?' asked Ida.

'Go on,' said Alice. 'I'll help if I can.'

'As you're so good with the children, I wondered if you wouldn't mind helping me to organise the children's nativity play?' said Ida. 'Duty permitting, of course.'

'Of course,' said Alice. 'I'd love to.'

'Wonderful,' said Ida, beaming at her. 'Will I see you on Sunday?'

'I'm on duty at eleven, so I'll be at early communion,' Alice replied.

'Splendid,' Ida said. 'Now why don't you just grab yourself some tea before the midday rush?'

Alice hooked her handbag over her shoulder, left the vicar's wife organising the nursery and returned to the main hall.

Built in the middle of the last century, the solid Victorian structure sat like a fat toad on the Highway. This thoroughfare was the main riverside route for traffic and stretched from the Royal Docks in the East through to St Katharine Docks in the west. South of it were the waterway, wharves and docks, where tons of cargo were offloaded daily. To the north of it were the streets of terraced houses where those who humped crates and sacks up from the ships' holds lived. The Congregational Hall and dozens of other missions, chapels and churches had been founded in the previous century by well-meaning philanthropists to bring succour to the poor. However, like the Congregational Hall, many were now the first port of call for those who, after a night in an air-raid shelter, arrived home to discover a pile of rubble where their house had once been.

As always, the centre was a hive of activity, with mothers and children dropping in for a cuppa after a morning's shopping and some weary-looking members of the ARP heavy rescue crew in their hard hats, cradling mugs in their hands. There were even a couple of soldiers with the bomb disposal insignia on their shoulders, lounging around by the stage.

At the far end was the canteen area, from where a faint smell of hotpot drifted across. Behind the serving hatch, half a dozen WVS volunteers were preparing the midday meal for families and workers alike, helped in their endeavours by popular songs of the day belting out from the massive Bush wireless in the corner. The rest of the hall was taken up by the dozen or so rows of camp beds with striped ticking mattresses. On each was a neatly folded grey blanket with a pillow on top, ready for the next unfortunate occupant. However, after weeks of cold clear nights allowing the Luftwaffe to use the reflection from the Thames to navigate into London, a band of fog had descended on the capital, so hopefully the emergency beds wouldn't be needed for a few days.

Skirting past a member of the St John Ambulance crew showing a couple of office girls how to apply a tourniquet, Alice made her way across to the serving hatch. After collecting two cups of tea from the motherly grey-haired woman on the other side, she made her way towards the second-hand clothing section at the back corner of the main hall, where Effie was unpacking a bundle of donated clothes and hanging them on a clothes rack.

'I thought you could do with this,' said Alice as she reached her.

Placing her hands in the small of her back, Effie straightened up. 'I certainly can – I've been at it all morning.'

Taking the cup from Alice, she sat down on one of the two chairs in front of a table piled high with men's trousers and shirts.

'You survived story time then,' her friend said as Alice took the other chair.

'Yes, I read a couple of nursery rhymes and then we did some singing,' Alice replied.

'You have a real way with children, Alice,' said Effie.

'I've never really thought about it, but I suppose I do,' Alice said, her gaze drifting across to where a young mother was cradling her sleeping baby while her toddler played at her feet. 'I'm one of four and my brother and older sister have eight between them, and my other sister, Martha has three and is expecting another around Easter, so I've always had children around me. That's one reason why I expected to have a family by now, too. But it wasn't to be, so' – looking back at her friend, Alice forced a bright smile – 'I'll just have to be the generous auntie who spoils her nieces and nephews rotten.'

Effie gave her a sympathetic look and opened her mouth to speak, but, knowing what her friend was probably going to say, Alice got in first.

'Shouldn't there be two of you manning the clothing exchange?' she asked.

Effie nodded. 'Lena Cohen should be here but her sister's still poorly after being bombed out last week, so she's gone up to Stoke Newington to look after her children.'

'Where are all these boxes from?' asked Alice.

'A couple from the Salvation Army but the rest are from the American Red Cross,' Effie replied, nodding towards four stout boxes with USA and a red cross stamped on the side.

Alice took a slurp of tea, put her mug on the floor beside her and rubbed her hands together. 'Right, where shall I start?'

'I think that box is all children's clothes, so start with them,' Effie replied, indicating the nearest carton filled with donated clothes.

Alice rose from her seat, went over and opened the top.

'Talking of Americans,' said Effie as Alice removed a pair of boy's shorts. 'Look who's just walked in.'

Alice looked round to see Brogan Rafferty stroll into the hall with his hands in his pockets. The low chatter of female voices quietened as women in the hall turned in his direction. Although she was loath to admit it, Alice didn't blame them.

Dressed in his olive-green jacket, with his fawn trousers fitting snugly around his long legs and his cap sitting at a jaunty angle on his black curls, he looked good enough to eat. At his heel, looking adoringly up at his master, was Sam.

'Don't forget to ask him for the tickets,' said Effie under her breath.

'Tickets?' asked Alice in the same hushed tone.

'Yes, to the Thanksgiving dance that George hasn't stopped talking about,' explained Effie.

He stopped a few steps into the hall and looked around until his eyes rested on Alice. His gaze locked with hers for a moment, then he headed across the hall towards her, and annoyingly Alice felt her heart do a little double-step.

'Think of Florrie and be nice,' whispered Effie through her smile.

Mutely, Alice nodded.

Actually, as Brogan Rafferty sauntered across the hall towards her, Alice found she couldn't think of Florrie, or anything else for that matter – her mind had gone completely blank.

'Morning, ladies,' he said, giving them that easy smile of his as he stopped in front of them.

'Morning, Lieutenant Rafferty,' said Effie, smiling up at him.

'How are you, Mrs Fitzgerald?' he asked.

'Very well thank you, and it's Effie,' she replied.

Brogan's attention shifted on to Alice.

'Morning,' she echoed. 'This is a surprise.'

His smile widened. 'A pleasant one, I hope.'

'I see you've got your shadow with you,' said Alice, indicating the dog sitting obediently at Brogan's side.

Looking down at Sam, Brogan's expression softened.

'He's the only GI who obeys every command and never gets drunk,' he replied, stroking the dog's head. 'Say hello, Sam.'

Sam left his side, came over and nuzzled Alice's hand, then laid his head on her lap.

'You've got a new admirer, Alice,' said Effie, as Alice tickled behind the dog's ear.

'She sure has,' said Brogan, in a low, rumbling voice and looking squarely at Alice.

An odd something rolled around in Alice's stomach, making her feel unexpectedly light-headed.

'So, what are you doing down this way, Brogan?' asked Effie, bringing Alice's mind back from its wandering.

'Aunt Florrie was going to put together a list of things she would need for the party, so I thought I'd drop by to see if she'd done it yet.' Brogan looked around the hall again and Alice's gaze traced along the angle of his jawline. 'Is she around?'

'Somewhere,' Effie said. 'With the new Red Cross canteen in Piccadilly opening in a few days, I'm surprised to see you today.'

'I was passing,' Brogan replied. 'I'm popping in on my way

back. There's always a few teething problems but I'm pretty certain, once word gets around, the whole place will be buzzing each night. The tickets for the Thanksgiving dance are already flying out the door like hot cakes.'

'Didn't you want to ask Lieutenant Rafferty about the Thanksgiving dance, Alice?' said Effie, giving her a wide-eyed innocent look.

Brogan's gaze shifted back to Alice.

'Yes, well,' she said, feeling an odd ripple run through her with his brown eyes looking into hers. 'I wa— a few of us were wondering, as we've heard so much about it, if we could have tickets for the dance. I mean, we'd understand if it was too diffi-cult or—'

'Of course you can,' Brogan cut in. 'You can be my invited guests. How many of you are there?'

'Five,' said Effie.

'Five it is,' said Brogan, beaming at them. 'I'll need your names and WAAF service numbers so I can...' He paused and looked behind him with a smile as a little boy patted the backs of his legs. Reaching down, he picked him up.

'Hey, soldier,' he said, settling the toddler on his arm. 'What regiment are you from?'

The child looked up at him wide-eyed.

Pulling a funny face, Brogan gave him a comical salute. The little boy laughed and copied him, then thrust the ragged teddy he was clutching at him.

'And who's this, then?' Brogan asked, taking the soft toy from him.

The child mumbled something, then caught sight of the brass insignia on Brogan's hat. Reaching up, he took hold of the brim.

'You wanna see how it fits, do you, general?' Brogan said, taking it off and putting it on the little boy's bright curls.

'There you are, Sydney,' called a young woman with a

colourful scarf turban on her head and an anxious look on her face as she hurried over.

'I'm so sorry,' she said as she reached them and took the toddler off Brogan. 'I just turned my back for a moment to pay for our dinner and he was gone.'

'No problem,' Brogan said, smiling warmly down at her. 'They're like lighting at this age.' He smiled at the child. 'Can I have my hat back, general?'

The boy hesitated for a moment, then pulled Brogan's cap off and offered it to him.

'You got kids yourself?' asked the young mother.

Brogan shook his head, dislodging a lock of black hair onto his forehead. 'Not yet, ma'am. But I'm aiming to one day. For now, I'm just the kindly uncle who spoils his nieces and nephews something rotten.'

They all laughed.

'Thank you for catching him, again,' said the young mother.

Holding her son on her hip, she headed back to the refectory area, Brogan and the little boy waving at each other.

'You're very good with children, Lieutenant,' said Effie.

Running his fingers through his thick hair, he grinned.

'Probably because, according to my ma, I'm a big kid myself at heart,' he said, replacing his cap.

The door leading into the corridor swung open and Florrie, wearing her WVS uniform, marched in. She spotted the three of them and her eyes lit up.

'Brogan!' she cried, hurrying across, and enveloped him in her arms.

He hugged her back, with Sam circling them wagging his tail.

'Hi, there, Aunt Florrie,' Brogan said, freeing himself from her embrace. 'I thought I'd pop by to see if you've managed to get together that list of supplies.'

'I did it last night,' said Florrie. 'It's in the office. Follow me.'

She set off back across the hall and Brogan turned to face them.

'Nice to see you both again,' he said.

'And you,' said Effie.

Brogan's gaze focused on Alice for a long moment, then, touching the peak of his cap, he sauntered off after his aunt, with Sam trotting along at his side.

As he disappeared from sight, Effie turned and gave Alice a wide-eyed look.

'What?' said Alice.

'What do you mean, what?' asked her friend. 'Didn't you see the way he looked at you?'

Alice forced a laugh. 'Don't be daft.'

Turning, she resumed unpacking the box next to her.

'You can deny it all you like,' said Effie, putting a flowery blouse on a hanger, 'but anyone with eyes could have seen Brogan Rafferty's smitten with you.'

'Smitten?' Despite the sudden fluttering in her chest, Alice gave her friend a sceptical look. 'Don't be daft.'

'You may scoff,' said Effie. 'And before you say it, yes, perhaps I do read too many Mills and Boon romances, but I wouldn't be at all surprised if you suddenly find yourself swept off your feet by a tall, broad-shouldered, handsome man after all...'

'Careful with those pictures,' shouted Brogan at the two workmen carrying a copy of *Washington Crossing the Delaware* up the stairs. 'And you.' He pointed at the private smoking by the entrance to the cinema. 'Go and see if the transport lorry from the catering warehouse has arrived yet, will you?'

It was Wednesday and he was standing in the passage leading to the Hometown coffee bar at the rear of the building.

As always, Sam was by his side, watching the proceedings with his usual calm patience. On the other hand, Brogan was a few points short of exploding.

With just over forty-eight hours until Rainbow Corner officially opened, the whole damned place still looked like it had been hit by a hurricane.

Although, thankfully, the last of the flooring had been laid the previous Friday, there were still the coffee bar stools to be unwrapped, crates of pictures waiting to be hung on the wall and boxes of books, donated from all over the States, to be unpacked in the library.

Forcing himself to concentrate on the matter at hand rather than the Rainbow Corner not being ready, Brogan cast his eyes around again.

'Are the pool tables set up?' he asked a private who had just come down the basement stairs.

'Sure have, sir,' the soldier replied, in a slow drawl straight from the Mississippi delta.

'Where you wants this, Lieutenant?'

Brogan turned to see a wiry private with curly black hair and a lean face coming towards him with a signpost over his shoulder.

'At last,' said Brogan with a sigh of relief. 'Follow me.'

With Sam trotting along at heel, he marched off towards the main entrance, with the corporal a few paces behind. Weaving his way between the decorators putting a final dab of paint on the doors and electricians fixing chandeliers overhead, he strode through to the main foyer.

'Are you free?' he asked a couple of British workmen leaning against the wall next to the reception desk smoking.

'Yer, mate, wot you need doing?' said the older fella of the group, studying Brogan from beneath a battered cloth cap.

'This signpost needs to go there.' He pointed at the bracket on the floor next to the main staircase's support column.

'Right you are,' the workman said, pinching out his roll-up and stowing it behind his ear. 'Charlie.'

'Yes, Des.'

'You take one end, and Wilf, you take the other,' the foreman replied.

They peeled themselves off the wall, ambled over, took the signpost from the GI carrying it and upended it, then set about fixing it into the brackets.

Brogan noticed the sword and key, wheel and laurels insignia on the soldier's epaulettes.

'I didn't know the Quartermasters Corps were doing their own deliveries now,' he said.

The GI chuckled. 'I saw there was a delivery to the club, so I jumped on board so as to have a little look-see for myself, like.'

He hunkered down and smiled at Sam, who had taken up his usual position sitting by Brogan's left leg.

'Hello, boy,' the GI said, stroking the dog's head.

Sam's tail thumped on the floor in response to the attention.

'Lower East Side?' asked Brogan.

'Franklin Street,' said the GI, straightening up. 'You?'

'Orchard Street,' Brogan replied.

The GI chuckled. 'I'm Mikey Spiro, by the way.'

'Brogan Rafferty,' Brogan replied. 'Well, Mikey, what do you think?'

'*Di eccellenza*,' Mikey replied.

Brogan raised an eyebrow. 'I'm not sure it qualifies as excellent just yet.'

The lieutenant looked impressed. 'You speak Italian?'

'I had a crush on an Italian girl in ninth grade, so I learned a bit,' Brogan replied.

Mikey chuckled again, then his eyebrows rose.

'Rafferty,' he said, clicking his fingers. 'Aren't you the lieutenant asking for GIs to help with the kiddies' Christmas party?'

'I am,' said Rafferty, absentmindedly tickling behind his dog's ear.

'Well, count me in,' said Mikey. 'In fact, you've saved my legs cos I was going to take a trot round from South Audley Street to Chesterfield Gardens when I'd finished my shift to sign up.'

'You're attached to the PX?' said Brogan.

'For my sins,' Mikey replied. 'I was hoping to, you know, get into the Marines or Commando unit, but the recruiting fellas saw I was in the supply business back home so stuck me in the Quartermaster Corps.'

'We've all got our part to play, Corporal,' said Brogan, giving his usual reply to recruits disappointed at not being assigned to combat units. 'And our boys sure do appreciate being able to have home comforts while they're away from their families.'

Mikey nodded sagely. 'I guess you're right, and I suppose it might mean I'll be able to help you put a smile on some kiddies' faces at Christmas.'

'As long as it's signed off fair and square by Sergeant Greenstein, that's fine by me,' said Brogan. 'He's given me a dressing-down before for not getting the paperwork right.'

'Where are you planning on bringing a bit of Christmas cheer?' asked Mikey.

'Shadwell,' said Brogan. 'It's the neighbourhood alongside the London Docks.'

He briefly told Mikey about his aunt and her plans for the WVS Christmas party.

'So, it made sense to me to jump in to help out,' he concluded.

Mikey sucked his bottom lip. 'I've heard that's the rough end of town.'

'So they tell me.' Brogan grinned. 'But not too tough for a boy from the Bowery.'

'Well, as we're both from the wrong side of Canal Street

you can put me down as one of Santa's helpers down in Shadwell.'

'Where are you billeted?' Brogan asked.

'In the Albion,' Mikey replied.

'I'll send over details,' said Brogan.

Mikey gave him the thumbs-up, then pulled a packet of Chesterfields from his top pocket and offered one to Brogan, who declined.

Mikey returned them to where they'd come from and retrieved his lighter from his trouser pocket. He flicked the top to ignite it and lit his cigarette.

He noticed Brogan studying it and held it up.

'A twenty-first-birthday present from my mother. She spoils me.' Mikey blew a stream of smoke towards the plastered ceiling. 'I'd better get on before Greenstein thinks I've gone AWOL.'

He saluted, and Brogan returned it.

Although he was sure Florrie and her team of women, working hard to give the people of Shadwell the best Christmas party, would welcome a generous donation from the US Army's PX stores, Brogan decided he would have to check any paperwork from Mikey.

Of course, he couldn't be sure, but the lighter Mikey Spiro had pulled out of his pocket wasn't the usual Zippo carried by most GIs, but a stylised Dunhill. Therefore, Brogan deduced that either Spiro's mother did indeed spoil him, or the corporal in charge of the thousands of dollars' worth of American goods shipped across for the US Army had another source of income.

'And as you can see,' said Brogan, indicating the rows of floor-to-ceiling shelves behind him filled with books, 'thanks to the generosity of the folks back home, GIs who visit Rainbow

Corner library can study anything from Classical Rome through to wildlife in the Arctic.'

The small crowd standing in a semicircle around him in the newly refurbished room nodded and looked impressed.

It was now just after three in the afternoon and he was entertaining a dozen or so representatives from London's civilian authorities. Lady Biddeford was there, next to the newspaper stand, which held both US daily broadsheets and individual states' ones. With her were Mrs Farley and two other members of the London Community Liaison Committee. Chief Inspector Crosby and his counterpart from D Division, which adjoined Crosby's patch, were by the half a dozen desks set up to enable soldiers to write home.

However, after word got out about his brainwave of putting on a tour of Rainbow Corner Brogan's list had almost doubled to include a superintendent from the City of London police force, the MP for Westminster and a couple of other local big shots who he didn't know.

'And that, ladies and gentlemen, concludes our tour of Rainbow Corner, the American Red Cross's soon-to-be-opened canteen. I hope you enjoyed it,' concluded Brogan, smiling broadly at them.

There was a small ripple of applause.

'Thank you for taking the time to come,' he continued. 'And as promised, there's hot dogs, doughnuts and Coca-Cola, so if you would like to follow me...'

Brogan led them downstairs to the snack bar, which was decorated to resemble a small-town diner, where the chief and his assistants were standing ready. Pretty soon, most of the guests were clutching freshly made hot dogs smothered in ketchup or licking doughnut sugar off their lips. As Brogan had hoped, everyone seemed to be relaxed and enjoying the experience – everyone that is except a portly middle-aged woman standing by one of the tables clutching a glass of Coca-Cola.

He'd noticed her during the tour, not just for her tightly permed hair or her expensive suit but because, while he'd even managed to get a smile out of the dour Reverend Waverly, the stuffy-looking woman had laughed at not one of his jokes. Determined that he would at least raise a smile from her before she left, Brogan made his way over.

'How are you liking it, ma'am?' he asked, glancing at the drink she was holding.

'It's very sweet,' she replied.

'It sure is,' said Brogan.

'I'm not very fond of sweet things,' she said, the expression on her face confirming her words.

Brogan formed his features into his most charming smile. 'I don't think we've met before.'

'Mrs Starling,' she said. 'Widow of the late Colonel Starling of the King's Own Royal Lancers.'

'Well, it's a real pleasure to meet you, Mrs Starling, and my condolences on the passing of your husband. Was it recent?'

'No, he died at Ypres, doing his duty,' she replied. 'Two months after my darling son was born. And you are quite correct, Lieutenant. We have not met before, although we should have because I'm the magistrate at Horseferry Road court. Thanks to this iniquitous agreement between your high command and our government, any American serviceman who breaks the law, instead of having to face justice in our courts, is handed over to you and receives a slap on the wrist, no doubt.'

Brogan's light-hearted expression changed to a serious one. 'I can assure you, Mrs Starling, that the American army takes any crime committed by our soldiers against our friends and allies very seriously.'

She gave him a sceptical look, so Brogan decided it would be wise to move the conversation onto safer ground.

'Whereabouts in London do you live, Mrs Starling?' he asked.

'Hampstead, with my sister,' she replied. 'After living in the south coast's restricted zone, where you can't go five miles down the road without a member of the Home Guard demanding to see your identity card, I left Thatcher, our steward, to run our estate outside Eastbourne and joined my sister.'

'Eastbourne?' said Brogan, looking incredulously at her.

'Yes, it's a town on the coast,' she told him.

'Ma'am, you don't happen to be related to an Aircraft-woman Alice Starling, do you?' he asked.

Her sour expression returned. 'She is my daughter-in-law. That's to say she was, until my sweet boy Arthur died at Dunkirk, doing his duty like his father before him. How do you know her?'

'Her WAAF balloon crew is billeted in my aunt's public house in Shadwell,' Brogan replied. 'My aunt introduced us. Yes, she must have told you all about life in the East End in her letters.'

'We are not in correspondence, Lieutenant,' she replied tartly. 'But I do have a few people I know well keeping an eye on her, just to ensure she doesn't do anything to bring the family's good name into disrepute.'

The image of Alice, in her boiler suit and heavy waterproof coat plastered in mud, filled Brogan's mind.

'I hardly think that's likely,' he replied. 'Not when she spends hours in all weathers and during air raids manhandling a barrage balloon.'

'All very commendable, I'm sure,' said Mrs Starling in a tone that indicated otherwise.

'It certainly is,' agreed Brogan. 'Alice is a credit to her WAAF uniform. On top of which, in her spare time she helps out with the children at the WVS relief centre.'

'Does she?'

'She does,' Brogan replied, feeling affronted on Alice's behalf at her mother-in-law's sneering tone. 'And my aunt tells me that all the children love her because she has a natural way with them. And on top of her arduous duties she is helping my aunt organise a Christmas party for the local children.'

'It sounds as if you know my daughter-in-law quite well.' A supercilious expression slid across Mrs Starling's fleshy face. 'Well enough, it seems, to refer to her as Alice.'

Brogan didn't reply.

'And judging by your tone I'd even go as far as to say you're in fact quite fond of my widowed daughter-in-law,' she added.

Brogan held the woman's venomous stare.

'As I said, Alice is a credit to her WAAF uniform. In fact, Mrs Starling, I would have thought that, as she is doing her duty like your husband and son, you would have been proud to have her as your daughter-in-law.'

Although Brogan hardly thought it possible, Mrs Starling's expression turned even sourer. Thrusting her barely touched glass of Coca-Cola into his hand, she ran her gaze disdainfully over him, then turned and marched out of the diner.

'Blooming tatas out there,' said Nell as she stomped into the WAAFs' lounge, bringing a gust of cold air with her. The sun had started disappearing behind the houses to the west, taking the mercury in the thermometer with it.

'I know, that's why I'm wearing my long johns and two vests,' Alice replied, picking up her greatcoat, which she'd thrown over the back of the sofa.

It was now just after half five and she was on duty at six so she was trying not to think about the bitter cold she would be stepping out into soon.

'Well, it is only six weeks until Christmas,' Alice added. 'Florrie's already talking about putting up the Christmas decorations in the bar, so I thought we might put some up in here too.'

'Sounds like a grand idea,' said Maeve, who had walked in after Nell. 'If we can find any.'

'We can make our own,' said Alice. 'There's a double-page spread in *Woman and Home* this week with suggestions.'

'Have you spoken to Lily about changing the Christmas rota?' asked Nell, unwinding her scarf.

Alice shook her head. 'Not yet, but she's on with me tonight so I'll tackle her then. But if she does, at least your family only live a twenty-minute bus ride away in Whitechapel, Nell, so you'll be able to pop over see them.'

Nell gave her a baleful look. 'You wouldn't say that if you knew them.'

'We just passed George, Rose and Peggy,' said Maeve. 'Who else is on duty tonight?'

'Just me and Lily,' Alice replied, wrapping her scarf round her.

'When she arrives,' said Maeve.

Nell raised an eyebrow. 'And the top brass thought it would take ten of us to handle a balloon.'

'Poor you, having Lily on your back all night,' said Maeve, going over to the glowing fire in the hearth and taking her gloves off.

'I doubt we will,' said Alice. 'She'll do what she usually does and show her face for an hour to do first patrol, then disappear back to the Maid for the rest of the night.'

'Goodness, she always did take liberties, but since she's been made up to corporal she's been lording it over all of us,' said Maeve.

'Not to mention her and her gobby mate Maureen seem to 'ave become allergic to any kind of work,' added Nell.

Alice unhooked her cap from the coat stand and set it on her head.

'Where is she anyway?' asked Maeve.

'She's already gone over,' Alice replied, straightening the peak in the overmantel mirror.

'Good,' said Nell. 'With a bit of luck she'll take the wrong turn and end up in the river.'

'I'm off,' said Alice, fastening the last button of her coat. 'The kettle boiled about five minutes ago and there's some cake I brought back from the centre.'

'Have a good night,' said Maeve.

'And we'll think of you when we're hugging our hot-water bottles in bed,' added Nell.

Alice opened the door and made her way downstairs.

With just over half an hour until blackout, the Maid of Norway's shutters were firmly in place. The end-of-day hooters from the nearby factories had started a little while before, and the saloon bar was filling up with workers and dockers having a well-deserved pint or two before heading off home. There were also a number of ARP personnel fortifying themselves with a Scotch or brandy ready for another night-time onslaught from the Luftwaffe.

As Alice reached the bottom of the flight of stairs she spotted George in the hallway below. She, like Alice, was wrapped in her overcoat with her scarf wound round her neck and her WAAF cap pulled down over her ears. She also had the Maid of Norway's telephone receiver pressed to her ear and her hand cupped round the mouthpiece.

'Must go, darling,' George said, her impeccably made-up green eyes flickering over Alice. 'Yes, Saturday. Promise.' There was a pause. 'Yes. I'll be counting the hours, too. Bye.'

She dropped the receiver back in the cradle.

Resisting the urge to ask whether the officer George was

knocking around with was army, navy or air force, Alice turned her collar up round her ears.

'Ready?' she asked.

'Lead on, Macduff,' said George.

Giving Florrie a cheery wave as they passed, Alice pushed open the public house's side door and stepped out into the gloom.

'I can barely see across the street so it should be a you-know-what night,' said George, mindful not to say 'quiet' knowing that was the best way of ensuring the opposite.

With the fog rising from the river swirling around them and pointing the weak beam of their torches at their feet, the two women stopped at the kerb. Alice was about to step off when she spotted someone half hidden in the side entrance to Dobson & Millers warehouse.

'Is that Lily?' asked Alice, pointing along the street.

'It certainly is,' George replied. 'But who's that with her?'

Alice squinted into the gloom at the figure standing very close to Lily with one hand on the wall just above her shoulder.

'Some bloke after a bit of slap and tickle, no doubt,' George replied.

'Doesn't he look a bit familiar?' asked Alice, studying the slender young man with a cocky air, beefy stance and a mop of almost-black hair, Alice scrabbled around in her brain for the memory that was eluding her – and then, just when she was about to shrug it off, the chap canoodling with Lily in the shadows stepped out of the shadow and into the fading light.

Like almost every other working man he wore rough cords, a collarless shirt, a waistcoat and boots, but in contrast to his workmanlike clothing a gold fob chain dangled from his waistcoat pocket to the middle buttonhole.

He glanced around, then, setting his pork-pie hat at an acute angle on his head, he shoved his hands in his pockets and strolled off down the street.

'It's Charlie Mulligan!' said Alice, watching his rolling gait as he disappeared into the fog rising from the river.

'Who?'

'You know, that flashy, smooth-talking chap who's always got a "little something special" in his bag,' said Alice as they carried on across the road.

'Oh, you mean that fella who used to be able to supply that delicious Italian coffee,' said George.

'You mean the black-marketeer the police came round looking for a couple of months back,' said Alice, as they walked into the park.

'Oh, yes, that too,' said George.

'He's also the man who, for reasons we've yet to discover, Nell left standing at the altar,' added Alice.

'Do you think we should tell her that her erstwhile fiancé is having a bit of hanky-panky with Lily?' asked George.

Alice shook her head. 'I don't want to upset her, and we don't know how she'll take it.'

'You're absolutely right,' George agreed. 'After all, the crew's already one WAAF down, so we don't want another arrested and carted off for murder. Besides, being seen in a doorway together isn't quite the same as being caught *in flagrante*, but' – a smile spread across her clear-skinned, high-cheekboned features – 'we could certainly use it to our advantage...'

Some ten minutes later, Alice and George pushed open the door and strolled into the on duty hut, and met Rose and Peggy wrapped up against the elements and about to take the first two-hour stint on patrol.

'Isn't Lily supposed to be on tonight?' said Rose, pulling on her gloves.

'She'll be here in a moment or two,' said Alice. 'But we'll give you the wink once she's buggered off back to the billet.'

'Ta, Alice,' said Peggy. 'Any news about the Christmas rota?'

'Don't worry. The matter is in hand,' George replied, raising an eyebrow as she gave Alice a pointed look. 'You just pop off and take a quick turn round the ground and we'll see you both later.'

Letting in a blast of freezing air and tendrils of fog, Rose and Peggy opened the door and left the hut.

'Cocoa?' said Alice, heading across to the hut's kitchen area.

'Please,' said George, flopping on the sofa.

After filling the kettle under the tap, Alice put it on the Primus stove to boil, then took down a couple of mugs from their hooks and added two heaped spoons of cocoa powder to each. As the first wisps of steam threaded their way out of the kettle's spout the hut door opened again, and Lily strolled in.

'So glad you could make it,' said George, eyeing her coolly.

'I was held up,' Lily replied, stripping off her gloves and shoving them in her pocket. 'I'll have one.' She indicated the steaming mugs of cocoa.

'The water's just boiled,' said Alice, carrying the two drinks across to the sofa and sitting next to her friend.

'About the Christmas rota,' she went on.

'What about it?' asked Lily as she spooned cocoa into a mug.

'We want you to change it,' said Alice.

Carrying her drink, Lily crossed to the threadbare sofa opposite Alice and George and sat down.

'Do you, now?' she said, blowing across the top of her mug.

'Yes, we most certainly do,' said George.

'Because the way you've allocated the duties over Christmas is unfair,' said Alice. 'So, we'd like you to redo it so that, instead of just you and your chum Maureen, all the girls on the crew get their two days Christmas leave together, as per the HQ directive.'

Lily shook her head. 'No can do.'

'The thing is, Lily,' said George. 'We're not actually *asking* you to change the Christmas rota, we're *telling* you.'

A flush coloured Lily's cheeks. 'In case you've forgotten' – she tapped the two chevrons on her sleeve – 'I'm the one in charge here, so both of you can sod off.'

Putting her feet up on the upturned fruit crate that served as the hut's coffee table, she pulled out a copy of *Picturegoer* and flipped it open.

'You do know, don't you, Lily, that once upon a time Nell and Charlie Mulligan were all set to get married?' said Alice.

Lily's head snapped up. 'Were they?'

'Apparently so,' said George. 'I can't possibly tell you why they didn't get hitched but what I can tell you is she wouldn't be very pleased to hear that we saw you and him canoodling in a doorway.'

'Of course, we wouldn't dream of mentioning it,' said Alice.

'Or telling Sergeant Munroe that the WAAF she promoted is keeping company with a convicted underworld fence and black-marketeer,' added George.

Alice rose to her feet, crossed to the noticeboard, unpinned the WAAFs' Christmas rota and then walked across to where Lily was sitting.

'Because if we did, Sergeant Munroe might call the RAF police down to search our billet, including that locked kitchen cupboard of yours.' Alice thrust the duty rota at her. 'Two days together for the whole crew starting from the first of December.'

'And make sure you don't mess with Alice's request so she can help out at the relief centre's children's party on Christmas Eve,' added George.

A sour expression slid across Lily's face and her close-set eyes narrowed as she snatched the sheet from Alice's hands.

Giving Lily a sweet smile, Alice returned to her seat beside George, and, picking up her cocoa, she took a satisfying sip.

CHAPTER 13

'How we doing back there?' asked Brogan, looking across the pristine counter at the chef wearing an equally immaculate white apron.

'I'm all set to start flipping burgers as soon as the first GI walks through the door, sir,' the man in charge replied, raising a brand-new spatula to illustrate the point.

His three assistants who were sporting the same attire, nodded their agreement.

It was just before half past six in the evening on Friday the thirteenth of November and Brogan was standing in the basement of what had been Del Monico's restaurant but was now the newly refurbished snack bar of the soon-to-be-opened Rainbow Corner.

The joint itself had high stools along the counter and red-benched booths around the walls, along with six dozen square tables all with chequered Formica tops, four chairs tucked in round them and women wearing white waitress uniforms standing beside them ready to take orders.

The diner served all the American eatery staples such as burgers, fries, hot dogs, waffles, milkshakes and doughnuts. Like all the other Red Cross Clubs, Rainbow Corner had no alcohol licence, but a wide selection of sodas including sarsaparilla, Seven Up and Coca-Cola.

Giving the room a last glance, Brogan signalled okay. 'Good luck.'

'You too,' the chef called after him as Brogan headed for the door.

Stopping only to straighten a crooked portrait of Paul Revere along the way, Brogan marched along the short passageway into the games room.

'Well done,' he said to the decorating team, who'd barely slept a wink the previous night.

On heading across the hall into the recreation room, Brogan found three of the GIs from the US maintenance services completing their last adjustments to the pinball machines to ensure they were straight.

'Everything working?' asked Brogan.

'Sure is, chief,' said a redheaded soldier, giving him the thumbs-up.

Brogan breathed a sigh of relief, understandably as, when he'd arrived that morning at eight, he'd found that somehow the fuse box powering the whole of the ground floor in the Lyons Corner House part of the establishment had blown overnight.

Mercifully, the electricians were on site within half an hour of Brogan summoning them and, after they'd rewired the circuit, the lights and plug points were up and running. Of course, it meant he had to check the electrics in the rest of the establishment were ready for the hordes of hungry, homesick GIs to pour through Rainbow Corner's door. Having sorted out the electrics he helped the frazzled young librarian to unpack and shelve three crates of books in the library, before directing the workmen where to fix the last few portraits of America's founding fathers before checking with the projectionist in charge of the club's cinema that all the reels for this week's film showing had arrived.

His last job was supervising putting up the signpost in the lobby. that pointed GIs towards Rainbow Corner's many facilities, plus Leicester Square just a few yards away, and two others with *Berlin 500 miles* and *New York 3271 miles*, pointing in opposite directions.

Brogan strolled across to the jukebox alongside the pool table at the end of the room and glanced down the menu before taking a nickel from his pocket. He pushed it into the slot and pressed one of the buttons. The arm sprang into life and, having anchored a record in its tentacle grip, deposited it on the turntable. There was a brief pause, then a trumpet blasted out the strident opening bars of 'Chattanooga Choo Choo'.

Leaving the army technicians to finish their tasks, Brogan headed back the way he had come until he reached the stairs, then, taking them two at a time, he returned to the ground floor and hurried through to the lobby.

Along with a handful of GIs who had been detailed to assist with getting the club ready, and who snapped to attention and saluted, there were also half a dozen young women dressed in blue dresses, lined up in the entrance hall. They were just some of the two hundred women who had passed the strict vetting process to be employed as waitresses, cleaners and hostesses to give the homesick GIs some female company.

Brogan smiled at Rainbow Corner's staff. 'Are we all ready?'

'Yes, sir,' they replied, smiling excitedly back at him.

Checking the clock above the doors again, Brogan beckoned one of the soldiers over.

'Hasn't General Novak arrived yet, Chesman?' he asked.

Private Chesman shook his head. 'Sorry, sir.'

'But it's almost seven.'

Brogan pressed his lips together tightly for a brief moment, glanced at the clock again, then, delving into his pocket, pulled out a large key.

'Aren't you going to wait for Major Novak, sir?' asked Chesterton.

'I can't,' Brogan replied. 'I mean, who knows how long he'll be, and if we don't open on time the GIs waiting outside will end up blocking the street and then I'll have the cops belly-aching to me about it along with everything else.'

Brogan marched across the welcome rug to the double doors, studied the closed doors for a moment, then shoved the key in the lock and twisted it, hearing the barrels inside click into place.

Having extracted the key, he handed it to Chesman. 'As Rainbow Corner will now be open twenty-four seven, I won't need this, so throw it away,' he joked.

Half-turning, he smiled at those waiting in the lobby.

'I hope you are ready,' he said. 'Because when I open this door, we'll be knocked off our feet by ravenous GIs.'

The women laughed while the soldiers whooped and whistled.

Grasping both handles, Brogan yanked open the heavy doors; and came face to face with, not a horde of cold and hungry American soldiers, but an almost impenetrably thick blanket of London fog.

He stepped back.

'Don't panic,' he said, feeling the exact opposite emotion in his chest. 'I'm sure we'll have them streaming in soon.'

Thinking of the hundreds of posters he'd pinned on billet noticeboards and announcements he'd made in the *Star and Stripes* since the start of October, Brogan stood there peering through the open doors into the thick grey-green gloom of one of the capital's legendary pea-soupers.

After he had stood there for what seemed like an eternity but was probably a little more than five minutes, suddenly the fog parted and General Novak, a square-shaped individual, short legs and an even shorter temper, marched in.

Thankfully, Brogan didn't have to deal with him very often, but as Major Jessop had suggested Brogan ask him to open the new Red Cross Club he had had to do just that.

With the smog swirling around him the pugnacious general, with his slender fair-haired driver in tow, planted his size-tens on the welcome rug.

'Damn British weather,' he bellowed. 'If it ain't the damn rain it's damn fog. And if that ain't enough to make a man lose his damn temper then having a fool for a driver who can't tell one damn London street from another...' He glared at the private, who visibly shrank under the onslaught.

Having expressed his displeasure at the British climate, Novak's eyes scanned around the near-empty lobby, then he turned his attention on Brogan.

'Well, Lieutenant, where are they?' he barked. 'Where are our brave boys I was promised would be rushing into this place as soon as the doors opened? Hundreds, I think you said, didn't you say, Tafferty?'

Brogan forced a laugh. 'We've only been open twenty minutes, General, and actually it's Rafferty, sir.'

Novak's bushy eyebrows drew tightly together. 'Tafferty! Hafferty! Or whatever you're damn well called, doesn't explain why you've wasted my damn time getting me down here to open a club that I find is already open.'

'Yes sir,' said Brogan.

'And for hundreds of damn soldiers who haven't shown up, have they, Lieutenant?' bellowed the general.

'No, sir,' said Brogan. 'I'm sorry, sir.'

'You damn well will be.' From beneath his low brow, he glared ominously at Brogan. 'I hear Eighth need personnel for their long-range aircraft bases in Scotland.'

Giving Brogan a last withering look, the general turned on his heels.

'The Dorchester,' he yelled at his driver. 'And get the right damn turn this time.'

With arms hanging limply at his sides and images of desolate Scottish moorland and driving snow looming large in Brogan's imagination, he watched his career in the US Army disappear into the fog behind General Novak.

'Lieutenant Rafferty!'

Brogan looked round to see one of the waitresses from the restaurant at the rear of the building standing by the entrance signpost.

'I'm sorry,' she said, giving him a pitying look. 'Chef sent me to fetch you because we've got a big problem in Jefferson Restaurant...'

'Hello, Auntie Alice,' a child called behind her.

Alice turned and saw five-year-old Judy Turner, wrapped up like a knitted parcel against the frosty morning air. She was perched on the toddler's seat on top of the Silver Cross pram, being pushed by her mother Violet.

'Hello, Judy,' Alice replied, her breath escaping in little puffs into the freezing air. 'Where have you and Mummy been?'

'Watney Street,' Violet replied. 'Managed to get a nice bit of scrag end for dinner tomorrow before the butcher shut up shop at midday. What about you?'

'Just popped to the dairy to get a couple of pints of milk,' Alice replied, indicating the wicker shopping basket hooked over her arm. 'How's Sidney doing?'

'See for yourself,' said Violet.

Leaning over, Alice looked down into the body of the pram and found four-month-old Sidney Turner, wearing a blue pixie hat and swaddled in blankets, looking back at her with his baby-blue eyes. As it always did, Alice's heart squeezed, and then it squeezed again when he smiled.

Judy and Sidney were just two of the thirty or so children who attended the WVS nursery. Violet, who had worked as a machinist since she left school at thirteen, had once spent long hours bending over a sewing machine in one of the many Whitechapel sweatshops making expensive evening wear. Now, as part of the war effort, she spent the same long hours over the same sewing machine, but making uniforms for the army.

'I've been learning the words to the Jesus Christmas song, Auntie Alice,' said Judy, as they started walking down Glamis Street towards the Highway.

'Well done,' Alice replied.

'I can't tell you how excited all the children at the nursery are about the Christmas party,' said Violet.

'Me too,' said Alice. 'I doubt there'll be a dry eye in the place.'

'Yes, we'd better get our hankies ready. And the kids aren't the only ones eager,' she added, raising a knowing eyebrow. 'There are a few mums who'll be putting on their glad rags and breaking out the lipstick now that there's some Americans joining us. 'Andsome buggers those GI are and no mistake.'

Alice thought of Brogan. It was the day after the American Red Cross's new servicemen's club that he was involved with had opened. Despite telling herself that she wasn't interested, all day she'd found herself wondering how the opening yesterday evening had gone.

Alice yawned.

'Sorry,' she said. 'I was on last night and only got up an hour ago.'

'Heavy night?' said Violet, giving her a sympathetic look.

Alice glanced at the black column of smoke filling the sky behind the young mother and nodded. 'A bit.'

The fog that had blanketed the area earlier in the evening had lifted at midnight and the air-raid sirens went off an hour later, so Alice, George, Peggy and Gwen had spent the rest of the night in their air-raid shelter trench keeping an eye on Bessie to make sure she was doing her bit to ward off enemy aircraft.

'Well, this is me,' said Violet, as they reached the corner of Juniper Street. 'Are you coming down to the centre this week?'

'Tuesday afternoon,' Alice replied.

'We'll see you then,' said Violet. 'Say bye-bye to Auntie Alice, Judy.'

The little girl waved, and Alice waved back as Violet turned towards her home halfway down the street. Dodging between the lorries loaded with crates and sacks trundling along the Highway from the dock, Alice crossed the main riverside thoroughfare to the Maid of Norway.

In normal times the public house would have been open for half an hour already. However, because the docks were vital to the war effort the local magistrates had reduced the licensing hours of public houses within a mile of the docks by an hour, forcing them to open at twelve thirty, just fifteen minutes before the back-to-work hooter went at twelve forty-five. Although it was now just after before twelve, the Maid of Norway's doors were still firmly closed, so Alice headed for the side door leading into Florrie's parlour. Pushing it open, she walked in, but before she could get more than a few steps into along the hallway Florrie came through the beaded curtains from the bar.

'Thank goodness it's you, Alice,' she said in a half-whisper, hurrying towards her.

'Why? What happened?' asked Alice in the same hushed tone.

Crooking her finger, Alice beckoned her over and then pointed towards the parlour door. '*That's* what's happened.'

Alice peered through the crack, and blinked in surprise to

see the man she'd been thinking about not five minutes previously sitting in one corner of Florrie's two-seater sofa in front of the fire, with Sam curled at his feet.

However, Brogan Rafferty wasn't quite his usual smartly turned-out self; his jacket was draped over the back of one of the dining room chair, his tie was off and the top couple of buttons of his light olive-coloured shirt were unfastened, with both cuffs rolled back.

'He arrived two hours ago,' whispered Florrie. 'He seemed a bit down in the mouth. I couldn't get out of him what was wrong, so I gave him a coffee and a slice of cake 'oping to cheer him up. I had to see to the brewery delivery a little while back and, when I came back, he'd pinched a bottle of Johnnie Walker from the bar and has been knocking it back ever since.'

'That's a bit of a cheek, isn't it?' said Alice.

'I'm not bothered about the booze,' said Florrie, waving her words aside. 'But I don't like to see 'im in wallowing like that. Will you go and talk to 'im?'

'Me?' whispered Alice, her eyes stretching wide at the suggestion.

'Yes. If you don't mind,' said Florrie. 'He likes you.'

Alice's eyes stretched even wider. 'Does he?'

Florrie nodded.

'Every time he comes to see me he asks how you are.'

The fluttering in Alice's chest that always seemed to happen at Brogan's name made its presence known.

'I still haven't checked all the pumps in the cellar and I have to open the pub doors soon, plus Daisy's not turned up yet, so do me a favour and keep 'im company until I get back,' Florrie added, oblivious to Alice's inner turmoil.

Alice peered through the door crack again at Brogan, who was now staring broodily at the burning coals in the fire grate.

'All right,' she said, taking off her overcoat and hat, hanging them on the hall stand and stowing her basket on the floor beneath. 'I'll see what I can do.'

'And be a love,' Florrie added as Alice put her hand on the latch. 'Try and stop 'im from downing any more of that whisky.'

Sam's ears pricked up as the door hinges squeaked, when Alice walked in the dog stood up and trotted over, nuzzling her hand by way of a greeting.

Now only a couple of yards from him, Alice could see more clearly that it wasn't just a couple of shirt buttons undone but four, revealing not only the top ribbing of his fawn-coloured singlet but also a plentiful amount of dark chest hair growing above it. She couldn't deny that, dressed in his impeccably fitting, sharply pressed uniform, Brogan Rafferty would turn any woman's head, but, loath as she was to admit it, in his present dishevelled state he looked even more devastatingly handsome.

The sound of Sam's tail thumping gleefully against the armchair roused Brogan from his contemplation of the dancing flames and he looked round.

As they focused on Alice, Brogan's dark eyes changed somehow as an emotion she couldn't interpret flickered across them. Then he smiled and Alice's mind went blank.

'Oh, Alice, it's you,' he said, looking up at her.

'Yes, it is. How are you, Brogan?' she said, smiling down at him.

'Terrible,' he replied. 'Actually, I'm worse than terrible. In fact I feel so terrible the words for how terrible I actually feel haven't been invented yet, but that's how I feel.'

Alice suppressed a smile. 'That terrible, eh?'

He gave a heavy-headed nod, then held up the half-drunk bottle of whisky. 'Do you want a drink?'

Alice shook her head. 'I thought that, as the new Red Cross Club in Piccadilly you've been setting up for weeks opened last night, you'd be on top of the world today.'

'So did I,' he replied.

Giving her another mournful look, Brogan started to raise the bottle to his lips.

'Why don't you tell me what happened,' she said, sitting down beside him.

Without taking a swig, Brogan rested the bottle back on his knee.

'It was a disaster,' he said as he looked across at her. 'A complete and unmitigated disaster.'

Alice looked puzzled. 'You had so many GIs that you had to turn them away? Or was there an explosion in the kitchen—'

Brogan gave a harsh laugh. 'I opened the Rainbow Corner's doors and all that came through them was the London fog.'

He raised the bottle again but only halfway before returning it to its resting place.

'The hot dogs were sizzling on the grill, the balls were racked up with the cues alongside on the pool tables, the pinball machine lights were flashing and jukebox loaded with the US top 40 records, while me and the clubs hostesses stood like chumps by the entrance waiting for hundreds of GIs to swarm in, and not one American soldier crossed the threshold.'

'Oh dear,' said Alice.

Raising an eyebrow, Brogan gave her a rueful look. 'I tell you, if I weren't such a gentleman I'd put it a hell of a lot stronger than that, Alice. And as to an explosion there certainly was one all right. Not in the kitchen but in the foyer when General Novak arrived. He got lost on the way, and then he arrived to perform the grand opening ceremony only to find that not only had I opened the club twenty minutes before but that there were no GIs in sight. After giving me a dressing-down in front of everyone, he stormed out. Then, just when I didn't think things could get any worse, I was called to one of the restaurants, where a fuse had gone in the grills.'

'Didn't any American soldiers turn up at all?' asked Alice.

'Some did arrive eventually,' admitted Brogan. 'Well not so much arrive as were dragged in. The club hostesses decided that "if the mountain won't come to Mohammed, then Mohammed must go to the mountain", so they marched out into the fog and searched out ten bemused GIs, dragged them in. They stuffed them with doughnuts and Coca-Cola, so they were happy enough, but as each restaurant can cater for two thousand at one sitting they looked a bit lost in the Woodrow Wilson eatery.'

A smile hovered over Alice's lips, so she pressed them together and frowned.

'A couple more drifted in later,' he added. 'But the place was a dead as a mortuary when I left at three in the morning.'

'I'm sure the number will pick up once word gets out about the club,' said Alice.

'From your lips to God's ears, as Aunt Florrie always says.'

Racking his long fingers through his black curls, Brogan let his head rest back against the sofa.

'Honestly, Alice,' he said, looking at the lampshade. 'After last night's fiasco, I'll be lucky if Novak doesn't send me off to spend the rest of the war chasing wild haggis over the moors in Scotland.'

Alice studied his well-defined profile.

'You do know, don't you, Brogan,' she said, as she imagined running her finger along his stubbly jaw. 'That a haggis isn't actually an animal.'

Despite himself, Brogan laughed, then, leaving his contemplation of the light fitting, he turned his head slowly and his brown eyes locked with hers.

They gazed at each other for a moment, then he smiled. 'That colour really suits you, Alice.'

Beneath her cornflower-blue jumper, Alice's heart did a little dance. 'Thank you.'

'Just saying the plain truth.' His gaze ran slowly over her and the odd emotion she'd seen before returned to his eyes. 'In fact, Alice Starling, you look rather—' He stopped mid-sentence and, grinning, held up the bottle. 'I think I've had enough.'

'I think so, too,' Alice replied.

She took it from him but as she did her fingers brushed over his, causing a strange sensation in the pit of her stomach. Gripping the whisky tightly, she rose to her feet.

'And I'd better make you some more coffee,' she said, giving him a bright smile and hoping only she could hear the slight tremor in her voice.

She placed the bottle on the sideboard and took the kettle from the stove.

'Why don't you stretch out?' she said, as she crossed to the scullery door. 'You must be exhausted.'

'Yes, ma'am,' he said, giving her an exaggerated salute.

Alice laughed and left the room.

'If you're kind enough to listen to my woes and make me coffee,' he called through from the lounge as she reached the sink, 'does that mean you've forgiven me?'

Turning on the single tap, Alice smiled.

'It means I'm considering it,' she called back, as the running water filled the kettle.

Satisfied she had sufficient for a couple of cups, she turned off the tap and, carrying the kettle, walked back into her landlady's parlour.

She opened her mouth to speak but then stopped dead in her tracks.

With his eyes closed and fingers laced together and resting across his broad chest, Brogan Rafferty was fast asleep. His feet, which were crossed at the ankles, were stretched out in front of him while his head, with a couple of cushions beneath it, was resting on the back of the sofa.

As she stood in the middle of Florrie's India rug, Alice's eyes ran slowly over his unruly black curls, strong cheekbones and square jaw, then moved down. Her gaze lingered on his open shirt front for a bit before returning to his face.

There, in his relaxed features, Alice saw a faint echo of the boy Brogan must have been, but she also saw an intelligent mind, underpinned by a solid strength. Alice also realised that not only had she forgiven him but, much against her will, he made her experience sensations she'd never ever felt before, not even with Arthur. It was like she'd half-opened a door and glimpsed something wonderful on the other side. What Alice didn't yet know was if she would ever be brave enough to walk through it.

CHAPTER 14

Several hours later, holding her needle up to the light, Alice ran the cotton between her lips and then threaded it through the eye. She'd just completed her task when the duty hut door burst open. Maeve and Gwen stomped in with rain dripping off their coats and sou'westers.

'Still raining is it?' said George, looking up from her copy of *The Lady*.

Maeve pulled a face. 'Sure it's enough to baptise you, George.'

Ripping off her headgear, she flicked it at her friend, splattering her with water.

George yelled and everyone else laughed.

It had rained non-stop for the past four days and looked set to do the same for the next four. As it was now the middle of November it was to be expected, but trying to manoeuvre a 64-foot-long balloon in a howling gale with sodden ropes or tie a sheep-hitch with frozen fingers was no fun.

It was just after seven and they had been on duty an hour, which thanks to the gloomy night and freezing rain already seemed like double that. Due to the weather, once they'd completed their daily maintenance tasks and secured the balloon into close haul – that was, floating 20 yards above the ground – they had taken refuge from the dreadful weather inside the on-duty hut.

She and Nell were sitting on one of the battered sofas with their feet resting on the lid of a sand-filled fire bucket, while Peggy and Rose sat on the other. As both sofas were occupied, George was lounging in one of the hut's threadbare and colourless deckchairs next to the table on which the squat Murphy Bakelite wireless was playing.

'Who's out next?' asked Alice.

'Me and Rose,' said Peggy, rising to her feet and picking up her raincoat, which was draped over the back of her seat.

'As Lily seems to have other engagements this afternoon, I'd say you should take a quick turn round the site and then head back here to the dry,' said George, turning to the next page.

'Where is Lily?' asked Gwen.

Hanging her coat over the back of a chair by the stove, Maeve shrugged. 'The Lord himself only knows.'

A small frown creased Gwen's brow. 'But she's the team's corporal, so shouldn't she be here, supervising or something?'

'That she should,' said Maeve, pouring herself and Gwen a hot drink.

'And getting an extra bob a week for being in charge,' added Nell.

'But that's not right,' said Gwen, her frown deepening as she took her tea from Maeve. 'I mean, what if something goes wrong? Isn't she supposed to do something?'

'She is,' said Nell. 'But as long as her and her mate Maureen keep out of our way, she can fly to the moon as far as I'm concerned.'

'But if she's shirking her duties all the time then why don't you tell Sergeant Munroe?' said Gwen.

'Because we ain't snitches,' said Nell.

'No, we leave that to Lily,' said Dolly. 'You've heard what she did to Effie?'

'Yes,' said Gwen. 'Alice told me, but leaving you to do all the work isn't fair.'

'No, it's not,' agreed Alice. 'But don't worry. Cheats never prosper and sooner or later she'll overreach herself and come a cropper. Now forget about Lily and come and join us.'

Shifting up closer to Nell, Alice patted the cushion.

Cradling her mug, Gwen did just that and rested her head back.

The orchestral music on the radio drew to a close and the seven o'clock pips sounded.

And now we have a short intermission before Professor McCree, Head of Classical Studies at Trinity College Oxford, talks to us about the rise of the Etruscan Empire in the fifth and fourth centuries BC, said the plummy voice of the BBC announcer.

'Oh, for the love of God,' said Maeve. 'Isn't there something a bit jollier we can listen to?'

Nell crossed to the dome-shaped Bakelite wireless on the shelf and twiddled the knobs around until a brass section blasted out 'Sing, Sing, Sing'.

'That's better,' said Nell, jumping up. 'Come on, Alice.'

Grabbing her hand, she pulled her out of the chair and swung her round.

Laughing, Alice picked up the beat as she and her friend danced around on the bare boards of the duty hut. The other WAAFs started singing along and clapping.

'It's not easy in this clobber,' Alice said as she and Nell swung apart.

'Certainly not in RAF-issue gumboots,' agreed Nell.

Maeve jumped up and grabbed Gwen.

'Oh, no, I'm not much of a dancer,' she protested.

'Well, you'd better get some practice in,' Nell called across as Maeve dragged Gwen up. 'For when we go up west for Brogan's Thanksgiving dance.'

Laughing, Gwen stood up, and Maeve swung her round a couple of times, then the tune finished.

'Come on, George, shake a leg,' Alice said, beckoning to her.

'Sorry chaps, no can do,' George said, smiling coolly across. 'I only dance with officers.'

Alice stuck her tongue out and George gave her a two-finger gesture in reply.

'Brogan Rafferty is such a brilliant dancer,' said Gwen, as that annoyingly love-struck expression spread across her face. 'If he can get us some tickets for the Thanksgiving dance, it'll be just dreamy being swirled around the dancefloor in his arms.'

Infuriatingly, an image of doing just that with Brogan Rafferty flashed through Alice's head.

The rain lashed at the window for a moment, then the opening bars of 'Chattanooga Choo Choo' blared out. Letting go of Alice, Nell grabbed a torch from the table.

Holding it like a microphone Nell started singing and Alice took up the other flashlight and Maeve grabbed a soup ladle, hooking her arm through Gwen's and they joined in with the chorus, with Dolly harmonising. Dressed in their work overalls and wellington boots, the girls lined up, Andrews Sisters style, and sang into their improvised microphones.

With the rain lashing against the windows, they hung, in harmony, on to the last note, then collapsed laughing.

The opening strains of 'Tangerine' drifted out of the wireless's metal grille and the girls sat down again.

'You know, I've got a good idea,' said Gwen. 'Why don't we do a couple of songs for the relief centre's Christmas party?'

'What, sing?' asked Dolly, resuming her seat after relighting the gas under the kettle.

Gwen nodded. 'Florrie was saying they're looking for few more people to do a turn.'

'We could, I suppose,' said Nell. 'It might be a bit of a laugh.'

'What are we going to call ourselves, then?' asked Maeve.

'I don't know,' said Gwen.

'What about the Mudlarks?' suggested Maeve. 'Sure, we're plastered with the blasted stuff most days.'

'It's not very glamorous, is it?' said Gwen. 'What about the Balloon Sisters or the Balloon Singers?'

'What about the Balloonatics,' said George, flipping another page of her magazine. 'It's certainly a better description of you lot.'

'That's perfect,' Alice said, her eyes lighting up. 'The Balloonatics.'

The band on the wireless changed again as the band struck up 'Deep in the Heart of Texas'.

After the opening Alice and her friends launched into, 'The stars at night are—'

The strident bell of the black telephone fixed to the hut wall cut across their words.

Maeve, who was making the tea, reached across and picked up the receiver.

'Aircraftwoman Lynch speaking,' she said.

With their eyes fixed on their friend, Alice and other girls waited.

'Right away, sir.' Maeve put the phone down.

'Bandits heading our way' she said, as she picked up the waterproof coat she'd hadn't long taken off. 'So we have orders to raise Bessie to three thousand feet.'

With grumbles of 'bloody Germans', no. 3 crew stood up and headed toward the row of pegs where their wet-weather kit was hanging.

'Right, girls, you heard,' said Alice, shoving her right arm through the sleeve as the rest of the crew shrugged on their outerwear. 'Let's get to it.'

CHAPTER 15

'Now, boys, remember, when Janice steps up on the chair, you all have to look scared,' said Alice, pulling a frightened face to illustrate her point. 'Do you understand?'

The seven-year-old Flannagan twins nodded, but Micky Robinson, who was a year older, looked sceptical.

'But she's a girl,' said Micky, sniffing disdainfully. 'And I ain't afraid of no girl.'

It was late Monday afternoon and Alice, who had volunteered to organise the nativity, was in the Shadwell Relief Centre stage with the pint-sized cast of the nativity play. They'd just begun running through the story and the three boys sitting cross-legged in front of her clutching knitted sheep were the shepherds. Behind them was eight-year-old Janice Cullington, plus a dozen other little girls who were her heavenly hosts, a misnomer if ever there was one. There'd already been two squabbles about who was standing in the front row before they'd even started. Plus, one of the so-called angels had pushed golden-haired Janice off her chair as Alice was getting the shepherds into place.

The three kings, alias Harry Peach, Charlie Willis and

David McFarland, were standing alongside Mary and Joseph – Susan Eccles and Arthur Lamb – in the wings. Alice had made a point of including all the children who regularly attended the centre for the after-school and Saturday clubs, so there were a dozen more children taking part, but as they played the animals in the stable and extra sheep they didn't have to come to rehearsals until a bit nearer the time.

As the children's costumes were still in the process of being made by mothers and grandmothers, the children were in their ordinary clothes, which, thanks to the dwindling clothing rations, had all seen better days.

With just a few weeks to go until the Christmas party, the women of the Shadwell Relief Centre were already preparing for the event. Although a little early, they had already strung up some paperchains made from strips cut from women's magazines and stars punched out of milk bottles dangling from cotton thread from the hall's metal rafters. Adding to the festive feel were a collection of the centre's daily teatime club's children's paintings, full of jolly snowmen, decorated Christmas trees and Father Christmases riding in their sledges. Sadly, but not surprisingly given the times the children were living through, sprinkled among the galloping reindeer were soaring Spitfires and searchlights criss-crossing the winter sky.

On a more practical note, Florrie and her valiant team were continuing their quest to provide a blow-out buffet at the party and, in addition to the growing mountain of tins of fruit and ham, had stockpiles of sugar, powdered eggs and flour squirrelled away.

Alice had decided to gather the dozen or so participants for a rehearsal after school this Monday.

'You're just pretending, Micky,' Alice explained. 'Because Janice is the Archangel Gabriel and she and the other angels have just appeared out of nowhere.'

'All right,' said Micky, giving a gangster-like shrug. 'As long as no one finks I'm turning soft.'

'I'm sure they won't,' said Alice, suppressing a smile. 'Now shall we run through the scene?' Clutching their sheep, the boys nodded. 'Ready, Janice?'

'Yes, miss,' said the golden-haired archangel, ringlets bobbing as she nodded.

'Right,' said Alice, smiling at the children on the stage. 'Everyone in position.'

The children shuffled around, and Janice took her place next to the infant-sized chair as her angels gathered around her and crouched down.

'Remember, angels,' said Alice, as they started to giggle. 'On the night you will be behind the screen, so until it's time for you to all jump up you must be very quiet.'

She put her finger to her lips and the tittering ceased.

'Narrator,' she said, nodding at ten-year-old Robert Naylor, who, script in hand, was standing to the left on the edge of the stage.

'There were shepherds in the fields looking after their sheep—'

'Sorry, Robert,' said Alice. 'Patrick!'

One of the shepherds looked up.

'You're supposed to be tending your sheep,' she continued. 'Not pulling its head off.'

'Sorry, miss,' Patrick replied, putting his sheep back on the floor.

'Carry on, Robert,' said Alice.

'And suddenly an angel appeared...' Robert paused as Janice stepped up onto the chair. 'And said—'

'There's Brogan and Sam,' shouted Micky, as he leapt up and dashed towards the stairs at the side. 'Per'aps 'e's got sweets!'

The two other shepherds jumped to their feet and dashed

after him, closely followed by most of the angels, the three kings and the holy family, leaving Janice atop her chair, with Robert and Alice on the stage.

Annoyance flared in Alice but when she turned, and her eyes rested on Brogan, it vanished in an instant.

Although she was used to having her pulse skip a beat at the sight of him, seeing him surrounded by happy girls and boys was something more. And the longing she'd suppressed for years seeped through her.

A smile lifted the corner of Alice's lips as she watched him, like a big kid himself, laughing and joking with the excited children as he handed out sweets, chewing gum and American comics while Sam danced around them all, furiously wagging his tail.

However, as Brogan raised his eyes and they locked with hers, a very different set of emotions coursed through Alice. The colours around her seemed to fade away as the realisation dawned on her that each morning she'd woken up and wondered if she'd see him that day.

Having held his hands up in mock surrender and freed himself from his junior admirers, Brogan strolled towards the stage, with Sam close on his heels.

Alice helped the abandoned archangel off her perch and then left the stage, but as she reached the last-but-one step her heel caught on a loose board and she tipped forward.

However, as the ground loomed up to meet her, a pair of strong arms caught her and set her upright. Alice planted her hands on Brogan's hard chest to regain her balance. Finding herself suddenly held in his embrace, she looked up into his kind face. Something exciting and quite unsettling flashed through his eyes, then he frowned.

'Are you okay?' he asked, his voice reverberating under her fingertips.

Actually, she really wasn't. In fact, she'd never felt less okay in her life. Not only did she feel light-headed but she had the almost overwhelming urge to throw her arms round his neck and press her lips onto his.

Thankfully, before she could give in to the impulse, Brogan released her. Getting a grip on herself, Alice scraped together a nonchalant smile.

'Yes, I'm fine,' she said. 'And I'm so sorry for crashing into you like that.'

'Don't apologise,' he said, giving her that brilliant smile of his. 'It certainly beats the more conventional way of greeting someone.'

Feeling her cheeks start to glow, Alice straightened the bottom of her jumper and brushed down her slacks. 'Well, this is a surprise.'

'A pleasant one, I hope,' he said, his brown eyes warm as they looked down at her.

'A disruptive one.' She indicated the children huddled together as they pored over the cartoons. 'We were rehearsing for the nativity.'

'Oops.' He gave her a charmingly embarrassed look. 'I'm sorry if I messed up.'

'You did,' said Alice. 'But I'll let you off.'

Placing his large hand on his chest, Brogan looked heavenwards. 'Thank goodness. But please. Let me make it up to you by buying you a, what do you call it? A bacon buttoney?'

'I think you mean a bacon butty,' Alice corrected him. 'But as my holy cast are otherwise engaged and it is almost midday, I'd love one.'

'After you, ma'am,' he said, sweeping his arm cavalier-fashion.

Aware of Brogan's tall presence beside her, Alice led him across the hall towards the WVS canteen at the far end. Brogan found an empty table in the corner and pulled out a chair.

'Can I get you a tea?' he asked as Alice sat down.

'Please, but I don't need sugar,' she said.

A twinkle flashed in Brogan's brown eyes. 'You most certainly don't.'

Leaving Alice making a fuss of Sam in an attempt to calm the fluttering in her stomach, he sauntered across to the counter, with more than one pair of female eyes following him all the way.

Taking his place in the queue, he chatted to those around him while he waited, then after setting the two matrons into a girly flutter he ambled back with their drinks and lunch.

'I'm surprised you're not having lunch in the pub with Florrie,' said Alice, as he placed her sandwich and drink on the table in front of her.

'I did drop in, but she was busy with her midday customers,' Brogan replied, sitting in the chair opposite. 'So when she mentioned you were over here, I thought I'd come over and say hi. Is it your day off?'

Feeling oddly pleased at his words Alice shook her head.

'I'm in the middle of a six-day stint of nights but I was on a twilight last night, so I got up at nine. I go on at six,' she explained. 'And if nothing happens I book off at three tomorrow morning. Of course, if the Luftwaffe come visiting it's all hands on deck, but as it's not official it works fine – as long as the sergeant doesn't arrive unexpectedly. So, as I had a few hours to spare I thought I'd organise for the children taking part in the nativity to rehearse.'

'Say, are they making Christmas decorations?' he said, nodding towards the table, where a number of women were cutting up and gluing crêpe paper.

'Yes,' said Alice. 'You can't buy decorations in the shops for love nor money due to the war restrictions on paper, so Florrie and the team have had to get creative, as you can see.' She pointed to the strings of paperchains. 'Of course, the big problem is the Christmas tree.'

'Well, if you need it set up, I'll be happy to fix it up for you,' said Brogan, slipping Sam a sliver of bacon from his sandwich.

'It's not getting it into place but finding one we can afford,' Alice replied. 'And Florrie's real worry is the food. Everyone is keeping a keen eye out for bargains but, with the number of points needed for luxuries going up and down like a yo-yo every week and the shortages in the shops, I know poor Florrie's awake half the night worrying about it.'

'Well, I'm hoping I'll be able to help,' said Brogan. 'One of the privates working in the PX has set up a children's Christmas donation box in the South Audley Street store and it's already half full. I've been trying to get back here for the past week but well' – his quirky smile reappeared – 'you could say, I've been doing a bit of twilighting myself, as I haven't left Rainbow Corner much before one in the morning since it opened.'

'How's it going?' Alice asked, giving Sam a curly length of rind.

Wiping his mouth with the paper serviette, Brogan leant back in the chair. 'Well, you were right, Alice. Despite the disastrous opening last week, word has got around to such an extent that by yesterday evening both canteens were full – as were the games room and library – plus we've dozens of GIs already signed up for the weekly lectures that are starting next month.' Amusement played across his lips. 'So you won't come home and find me clutching onto a whisky bottle in Florrie's parlour again.'

'I should hope not.' Alice laughed.

Brogan's dark eyes ran over her for a moment, then he sighed and glanced at his watch. 'The early rush in the pub should be over by now, so I'd better head back. On top of which, I have to be back for a meeting in Grosvenor Square at seven before heading off to Rainbow Corner.' Downing the last of his coffee, he stood up and, pricking up his ears, Sam followed suit.

'Oh, and when you and your friends arrive at the Rainbow

Corner's Thanksgiving dance next Friday, just tell the young lady on the reception desk you're on my special guest list. '

'We're all looking forward to it,' said Alice. 'And seeing the club we've heard so much about.'

'I'll give you a conducted tour,' said Brogan.

'Thanks for my lunch,' said Alice. 'It's been, as you say, swell.'

As he set his cap at his usual debonair angle, a smile spread across Brogan's handsome face.

'My pleasure,' he said, his brown eyes holding hers. 'Although next time, Alice, perhaps I can buy you dinner.'

Captured as she was in Brogan's intense gaze, Alice's brain took flight, taking her words with it, so with her heart beating ten to the dozen she just stared at him open-mouthed as he strolled across the hall and disappeared through the main door.

'Look at you, sitting there with a look on your face like the cat who's got the cream,' said a familiar voice.

'I really don't know what you mean, Effie,' said Alice, as her friend took the seat Brogan had just vacated.

'Yes, you blooming well do,' Effie laughed. 'I saw you fall into his arms.'

Alice tried to hold her confused expression for a little longer, then a smile lifted her cheeks. 'I didn't fall into his arms, I accidentally tripped.'

'I think there's a few young women in the centre who wish they'd thought of that ruse to end up in Brogan Rafferty's embrace,' said Effie. 'And from the way you were flirting with him over lunch I'm guessing you've forgiven Florrie's handsome nephew for your first meeting.'

'More or less,' said Alice. 'Especially as he's so good with the children.'

'He is. He'll make a wonderful father—' Effie's eyes darted across at Alice and then she pressed her lips together.

Alice forced a tight smile.

Effie was right. Brogan would be a wonderful father. And she couldn't deny that in the past couple of weeks her mind had sometimes conjured the fantasy images of a life and children with him. But then hadn't she done the same as a new bride ten years before, only to have her hopes of motherhood dashed each month? Truthfully, before she gave her heart away again to anyone Alice had to be sure it was worth the risk of suffering such bitter disappointment again.

CHAPTER 16

'Good evening, sir,' said the La Bonaire maître d'hôtel as Brogan stopped in front of his tall lectern in the restaurant's small foyer.

'Good evening,' Brogan replied, turning down his collar and taking off his coat.

The restaurant's dinner-suited head waiter was a clean-shaven middle-aged man with oiled hair, who looked about a decade older and several stones lighter than Brogan. He signalled at a young lad, who dashed over and took Brogan's greatcoat.

'It's little nippy tonight, wouldn't you say, sir?' he said. 'Cold enough for snow, I shouldn't wonder.'

'Indeed it is,' said Brogan, pulling off his leather gloves and handing them and his cap to the youth.

'Do you have a reservation, sir?' the maître d' continued.

'Yes, for two in the name of Lieutenant Brogan. I'm a tad late.'

A smile spread across the man's face. 'Urgent war business, no doubt, but the lady is already seated, so if you'd follow me.'

'Actually, if you don't mind,' said Brogan, 'I'll make my own way.'

'Very good, sir,' said the maître d'. 'Your waiter will be with you shortly.'

Leaving the master of the house at his post, Brogan strolled into the main part of the restaurant.

Situated in Dover Street a stone's throw from the Ritz, La Bonaire was an upmarket establishment, so although there was a small band playing on an equally small raised platform it was classical rather than dance music. The rest of the restaurant's floor space was given over to tables covered with pristine table-cloths and with candelabra in the centre.

Brogan slowly cast his gaze around the room until he spotted Gloria, sitting with a cocktail in her hand and an annoyed expression on her face. Taking a deep breath, he walked across the marble-tiled floor. She spotted him approaching and, frowning, looked at her watch.

'I'm sorry,' he said when he stopped at the table. 'But I was caught up with—'

'I know. War stuff,' she cut in, giving him a hard look.

'I was actually about to say Rainbow Corner,' said Brogan. 'And I am, truly, sorry.'

Actually, both things were true. He had been at Rainbow Corner nearly all day and he was truly sorry he was late, as what he intended to say to Gloria over dinner would have been difficult enough without starting off the evening on a bum note.

Gloria's eyes ran slowly over him and her disgruntled expression softened. 'Well, I suppose I should forgive you seeing as how you've brought me to this swanky place, and you look rather dashing in that uniform.'

Closing her eyes, she tilted her face to him and puckered up her red lips as an invitation. Bending down, Brogan gave her a quick peck on the cheek, and then, pulling out the chair oppo-site, sat down.

Looking slightly put out not to receive the passionate kiss she'd been anticipating, Gloria swallowed the last mouthful of her drink. Brogan called over the waiter, who brought their menus.

'Another gin and tonic for the lady, and I'll have a lager if you have it or a Guinness if you haven't,' Brogan said as he opened his menu.

'And make mine a double,' Gloria called after the waiter as he hurried away.

They sat in silence perusing the dishes on offer until their drinks arrived.

'So how are things at Rainbow Corner?' she asked after the waiter had taken their orders and left.

Brogan recounted a very much shortened version of what he'd told Alice the day before until their soup arrived. Then, lapsing into silence, he feigned interest as Gloria described a great review in the *Daily Mirror* for her new cabaret set of Hollywood film songs.

Over their main course, roast beef with red-wine sauce, dauphine potatoes and carrots, he listened while Gloria talked about the debonair French marquise who had just moved into the apartment opposite hers. Brogan rounded off his meal with a baked apple while Gloria gave him an overlong update on her ongoing squabble with the Blue Fountain's manager about her billing at the club.

'You're very quiet tonight, Brogan,' she said, after the waiter had removed their dessert bowls and brought their coffee.

'Am I?' Brogan replied as he stirred in a spoonful of sugar, feigning surprise.

'You are,' she said. 'Which is surprising, given I haven't seen or heard from you for almost two weeks.'

'I know and I'm sorry for not being in touch, but the truth is, Gloria, having to deal with getting Rainbow Corner off the ground alongside the rest of my duties has kept me pretty busy well into late evening most days.' He gave her a regretful smile. 'I'm afraid I won't be around much from now on.'

She looked puzzled. 'But surely you have some time off.'

'I do, but most of it is taken up with getting GIs linked up with churches and ARP relief centre for Christmas,' Brogan continued. 'And any spare time I have I'm down at my aunt's pub helping her with the Shadwell WVS party for the kiddies and a Christmas concert they are planning to put on.' He forced a laugh. 'So, I'm sorry to say—'

'Your aunt's putting on a Christmas concert?' Gloria cut in.

'Yes, she is,' said Brogan. 'It's nothing big, just a chance for everyone to have a few laughs and with a couple of people putting on a turn, so I'm afraid—'

'I'll come,' she said, her eyes lighting up.

Brogan looked alarmed. 'What do you mean?'

'I'll come along and sing a couple of numbers,' Gloria said. 'No offence, and I'm sure the locals will do their best, but, well...' A condescending expression spread across her powdered face. 'It would be a good opportunity to meet this aunt of yours.'

Despite the alarm bells ringing in his head, Brogan somehow managed to muster an amiable smile. 'That's very generous of you but the concert's Christmas Eve and didn't you tell me you were topping the bill for the club's Christmas cabaret night?'

Gloria laughed. 'Yes, but that doesn't start until ten thirty so I'll have plenty of time, on top of which if he complains I'll tell the Blue Fountain's old humbug manager that I'm doing a concert in aid of the war effort. I'd have to be the headline act, of course. You know.' She raised her hands to sketch an invisible arch in the air. "Acclaimed West End cabaret artist, Gloria Chalmers, singing at..."' In the candlelight Gloria's eyes sparkled as she beamed across the table at him. 'I'm sure your aunt will be thrilled to have a star entertainer like me.' She smiled brightly. 'Drink up or your coffee will get cold.'

• • •

'Lieutenant Rafferty,' said Tom, who was at his usual station behind the Jules Hotel's mahogany reception desk. 'Another early night, I see.'

Brogan gave him a wan smile in reply.

On seeing his master, Sam, who had been curled up under the hallway's long table, came bounding along the hallway. Brogan gave the dog a quick fuss, then made his way back out into the street and, with Sam at his heel, headed towards Piccadilly.

It was now just before twelve and some thirty minutes since he'd left La Bonaire, making his excuses to Gloria as to why he had to head back to his billet rather than her apartment.

As always at any time of the day or night the broad thoroughfare that ran from Piccadilly Circus to Hyde Park Corner was awash with American servicemen.

After sidestepping a gang of soldiers careering down the street and passing two burly military police officers who had an unconscious GI slung between them, Brogan crossed the road into Green Park.

Shining his dimmed torch on the floor in front of him with Sam padding along beside him, he strolled along the pathway towards Buckingham Palace. When he reached the wedding cake-style memorial to Queen Victoria in front of the royal residence, he climbed up the two flights to the platform and perched next to one of the carved dolphins on the surrounding wall, leaving Sam to sniff around. As he rested his head back against the marble, Brogan's gaze drifted down the Mall.

After arriving in the capital Brogan had learned that, although there was bomb damage in Mayfair, nine times out of ten an air-raid warning that sounded at this end of town was a false alarm. An air-raid siren had sounded as he'd set out from the Jules Club that evening and another while he'd been in the restaurant, but both had come to nothing. However, although the West End of the capital slept soundly in their beds, judging by the searchlights criss-crossing the black sky and the red glow over Admiralty Arch, he guessed the same couldn't be said about those in the East End.

In the quiet stillness of the night, with Sam sniffing around, Brogan's thoughts returned to Alice, as they did a hundred times a day. However, for once it wasn't just her trim figure, lovely eyes and soft smile his mind's eye conjured up but the nightmare of Gloria, swanning into the Maid of Norway and introducing herself to Alice as his special lady friend.

CHAPTER 17

'Evening girls, lovely weather, isn't it?' said Ted Thompson, the area ARP warden, as he strolled up to them.

'Yes, for ducks.' Alice replied, through the rainwater dripping off her sou'wester.

'Still, Dolly and Rose should be out to relieve us soon,' said Nell, who was standing beside her.

Both cloaked in their long waterproof overcoats and bucket-like headgear, she and Nell had just completed their hourly check of Bessie, who was floating 50 feet above the ground and securely tethered to her concrete moorings.

Like them, Ted, a wiry individual with a walrus moustache, was dressed for the weather in a waterproof mac that nearly scraped the pavement.

He and his wife Lena ran a corner shop in Cannon Street Road and, although they were in their sixties, as soon as hostilities were declared both had rolled up their sleeves and pitched in for the home front war effort, him as a warden and Lena alongside Florrie in the WVS.

'And at least we've had a you-know-what night so far,'

added Alice, trying to ignore the damp seeping through the seams of her waterproof.

'Let's 'ope it stays that way,' said Ted.

Rainwater dripping into her face, Nell nodded. 'From your lips to God's ears, Ted.'

'My Lena tells me as 'ow you girls have got yourselves a ticket to a dance at this new Yank club up west everyone's talking about,' said Ted.

'Yes, thanks to Florrie's nephew, Brogan,' said Nell.

On hearing his name Alice's heart did its usual little double-step.

'I met him last week when he dropped into the relief centre,' said Ted, as the image of Brogan laughing and surrounded by children formed in Alice's mind. 'Nice bloke. Still, I'd better push on.' He touched the edge of his black tin hat. 'Keep safe.'

'You too, Ted,' said Alice.

'And give our regards to Lena,' Nell added, as the warden sauntered off down the darkened road.

Alice took out her pencil torch and looked at her watch. 'Almost time for handover, so let's head back and meet Dolly and Rose halfway.'

'Good idea,' said Nell. 'Let's hope someone's put the kettle on ready.'

'Ted's right,' said Nell, as they sloshed through the muddy puddles of the former playing field. 'Florrie's nephew is a nice bloke. And' – looking at Alice, she winked – 'he's sweet on you.'

'Don't be daft,' said Alice.

'He is, anyone with half an eye could see it,' said Nell as they stopped beneath the balloon to shelter.

'And anyway,' said Alice, in what she hoped was a light tone. 'I'm surprised you haven't set your sights on him – I believe you said you were going to snap up a tall, dark, handsome American.'

'I am, and Brogan would certainly fit the bill, but he's only got eyes for you,' Nell replied. 'You didn't see him but, when he walked into the centre last week, he stood for a full minute watching you rehearse the children for the nativity.'

As Alice was trying to make sense of her friend's words, the sound of the hut door squeaking open cut across her jumbled thoughts.

Looking round, she saw two slivers of light appear as Rose and Dolly switched on their muted torches.

'Everything checked and as it should be,' said Alice, as the two WAAFs stopped in front of her.

'Thanks,' said Dolly. 'Fingers crossed it stays that way. We'll see you in two hours.'

'Don't get washed into the river,' Nell called over her shoulder as they walked away.

They reached the door of the hut a few minutes later and after stepping round the blackout screen walked thankfully into the warm interior. George was stretched out, her cheeks lathered with face cream, pink frilly shade covering her eyes and fake fur earmuffs, on the top bunk at the far end of the hut. Gwen, who was stretched out on one of the sofas flipping through a copy of *Picturegoer*, sat up as Alice and Nell walked in.

Of course, Lily was on duty too, but instead of resting in the hut between patrols, like the rest of the crew, she always hightailed it back to the Maid of Norway, for which they were all very thankful.

'Cocoa?' Gwen whispered.

Alice and Nell nodded as they shook out their wet coats where they stood on the rubber doormat.

Gwen stood and padded over to the stove in the kitchen area in her thick woolly socks, and relit the Primus under the kettle. Sitting side by side on the other sofa, Alice and Nell unlaced their boots and eased them off.

Standing up, Alice picked up hers and Nell's boots, then

tiptoed across to the hut's pipe stove in the corner, set them on top to dry and returned to her seat as Gwen brought their hot drinks.

'Thanks,' said Alice, wrapping her fingers round the mug in an attempt to get the feeling back into them.

'What's on at the flicks then?' said Nell, indicating Gwen's discarded magazine.

'Well, I quite fancied the new Will Hay one. I think it's showing at the Troxy,' Gwen replied. 'But the romantic comedy starring Ginger Rogers sounds good too, so I've not decided. I'll worry about it next week because all I can think about at the moment is seeing Brogan on Thursday.'

Alice's heart gave an uncomfortable thump as the memory of Brogan swirling Gwen around in Florrie's parlour came back to her.

'At the Rainbow Corner dance,' Gwen explained, seeing her bemused expression.

'Sorry.' Alice laughed awkwardly. 'My brain went completely blank for a moment.'

'Don't worry, Alice, mine does that all the time,' said Gwen. 'But I was reading in the paper that the American canteens serve hamburgers and hot dogs, whatever they are, plus doughnuts, ice-cream and that fizzy drink Coca-Cola that everyone is talking about. I'm so excited,' she continued. 'I honestly don't think I'll sleep a wink until Friday. Brogan is such a brilliant dancer.' Clasping her hands together and with a starry look in her eyes, the young WAAF gazed heavenwards. 'And he's just so dreamy.'

Alice certainly could not argue with that.

She raised her cup to her lips and was just about to take a sip when the harsh sound of the black telephone on the wall jarred in her ears.

'I'll get it,' she said, placing her mug on the fruit crate coffee table and rising to her feet.

'If that's the palace, tell the king I'm not in,' said George from beneath her eyeshades.

Alice crossed the hut and picked up the receiver. 'Balloon site 312. Aircraftwoman Starling speaking.'

'Number three command here,' the tinny voice replied. 'Bandits sighted over Deal heading your way ETA forty minutes. So, balloon up three thousand.'

'Copy.' Alice replaced the handset, grabbed her boots from their drying place and marched back to the sofa.

'Sorry, girls,' she said, shoving her feet into her still-damp footwear and lacing them up. 'But it's going to get a bit hairy in half an hour.' She grabbed her coat and put it on. 'So shake a leg and start hoisting Bessie up to the first six hundred and steady, and I'll be back in five.'

'Where are you off to?' asked George as she jumped down from her bunk.

'To fetch Lily,' said Alice, buttoning up her oilskin.

She wrapped her scarf round her neck tightly, yanked her sou'wester off the peg, squashed it onto her head and marched out.

She passed on HQ's orders to Dolly and Rose as she tramped past them, and a few moments later arrived at the side door of the Maid of Norway. She opened it with her key and made her way through the silent pub and up the stairs to the top floor.

Lily's room was at the far end overlooking the yard at the rear of the building. Alice stopped in front of the door and knocked.

'Who is it?' Lily called from the other side of the door.

'Alice,' she replied.

There was some movement on the other side of the door, then it opened a couple of inches and Lily, her eyes clogged with sleep and make-up, peered round it. As she did Alice saw, reflected in the dressing-table mirror, a hairy male leg poking out from beneath Lily's crumpled bedclothes.

'What do you want?' snapped Lily.

'We're to raise the balloon,' said Alice, forcing her gaze to remain on the woman in the doorway.

'What, now?' Lily replied, as the man shifted and revealed his arm and bare upper torso.

'Well, they don't mean a week next Wednesday, do they, Lily?' Alice snapped. 'Unless, of course, you want me to ring HQ and—'

'All right, all right,' Lily cut in, giving Alice a hateful look. 'I'll come.'

She turned to close the door, but as she did she inadvertently opened the door an extra inch and Alice glimpsed who the man was.

Alice stared at the closed door for a second, then the two-tone wail of the air-raid siren on the roof of the East London Hospital for Children brought her back to the here and now. Alice turned and, with her mind whirling, hurried back downstairs.

After stirring the tea in the pot a couple of times Alice poured herself a cup and then, cradling her drink in her hands, left the kitchen. Through the Maid of Norway's window Bessie glistened silver in the winter sunlight as the sound of 'Jingle Bells' being played on the saloon bar piano below drifted up.

It was just before eleven thirty and, although the winter sun cut through the public house's shutters in sharp slivers of light, the temperature outside in the street hovered around freezing, hardly surprising as it wasn't long now until December.

Alice took a sip of her tea, studied it for a few moments, then went downstairs to the pub below. As Florrie's lounge door was open, she went in, and found Effie sitting at the table with the account books in front of her. She looked up as Alice walked in, and smiled.

'I thought I'd join you for a cuppa?' Alice said, indicating the cup of hot tea at Effie's elbow.

'Please do,' said Effie, putting her pen down and straightening up. 'I'm just about finished.'

'Is that George playing?' asked Alice, as she sat on the chair beside her friend.

Picking up her mug, Effie nodded. 'She's practising for the concert. You're up early considering I heard you come in well past midnight.'

'I couldn't sleep,' said Alice.

'I'm not surprised with the racket Lily and Maureen made when they came in earlier,' said Effie. 'But at least you've finished nights now.'

It was true Lily and her chum had made enough noise to wake the dead that morning, but that wasn't the reason for Alice's lack of sleep.

'But you're not the only one.' Placing her hands on her swelling stomach, Effie arched her back. 'Goodness, this baby's either going to be a Tiller Girl or the centre forward for West Ham United.'

Alice gave a wan smile and took a sip of her tea.

'There was a letter on the hall table for you. Did you see it?' asked Effie.

'I picked it up on my way through,' Alice replied.

Effie looked puzzled. 'I thought you had one from your sister yesterday.'

'I did.' Diving her hand into her pocket, Alice pulled out an expensive envelope, and held it up. 'This one is from Arthur's mother. She's asked me – or should I say she's commanded me – to meet her at the Beaumont in Bloomsbury at three next Wednesday.'

Effie's eyebrows rose in surprise. 'Oh. You don't look very thrilled at the prospect.'

'I'm not,' Alice said. 'Especially as I haven't heard from her for over two years and then it was only to tell me she'd had the steward take the last things of mine from her house to my sister.'

'Does she say why she wants to meet you?' asked Effie.

Alice shook her head.

'Well, perhaps it won't be as bad as you think,' said her friend.

Alice forced a smile.

No, she thought, it would probably be ten times worse.

The opening bars of 'White Christmas' drifted through from the saloon bar.

'George is very good, isn't she?' said Alice, pushing all thoughts of her acerbic mother-in-law aside.

'She is,' Effie agreed. 'She was playing a classical piece a while back that even made the pub's old upright sound like a Steinway.'

Alice chewed her lip.

'What's the matter?' asked Effie.

'I'm in a bit of a quandary about Nell,' Alice replied.

Effie looked worried. 'What's wrong with Nell?'

'Nothing,' said Alice. 'It's not her but the chap she was supposed to have married before the war, Charlie Mulligan.'

'What about him?'

'Before last night's raid started, HQ rang...'

Alice told her what had happened when she came back to the Maid of Norway to fetch Lily the previous night.

'Are you sure it was him?' asked Effie when she'd finished. 'After all, it was the middle of the night.'

'Lily's bedside lamp was on, so I know it was definitely him,' said Alice. 'On top of which, when George and I were going on duty a couple of weeks ago we saw them canoodling in a doorway. And I'd put money on the fact that behind that locked cupboard door of hers you'd find all sorts of illicit goodies. So that's my predicament – should I say something or not?'

'What, to Sergeant Munroe?'

'No, to Nell,' said Alice.

'As she joined the WAAFs as soon as war broke out, like I did, then whatever did happen between them happened over three years ago,' said Effie. 'And judging by the fun she's been having for the past year, I'd say whatever it was that stopped her marrying him is well and truly in the past, so I'd keep mum if I were you.'

Alice sighed. 'You're right. There's no point stirring up trouble. It's bad enough with Lily as it is without giving her another excuse to hate us more than she does already.'

Looking over the rim of her cup, Effie scrutinised Alice's face. 'You look tired, Alice.'

Alice forced a smile. 'We had a pretty lively night last night.'

'I know,' said Effie. 'But you've looked as if you could sleep standing up for days and it's not like you. What's wrong?'

Alice looked at her for a moment, then let out a long sigh. 'I don't know, Effie. After a night duty I used to fall into bed and sleep like a log till well past midday, but recently I sleep for an hour or two and then I'm wide awake. It's the same at night. No matter how tired I am after a shift, when I turn in for the night I just lie there for hours on end with my mind racing, and when I do finally drop off' – she gave Effie a sheepish look – 'I have... dreams.'

Effie looked puzzled. 'What, like you're trapped under rubble or can't escape from a burning build—'

'No, nothing like that,' cut in Alice. 'They are much more, sort of personal, dreams.' She drew in a deep breath. 'The truth is, Effie, as soon as I close my eyes I start having wild, vivid dreams about... about Brogan Rafferty.'

Amusement spread across Effie's face. 'And I'm guessing in these "wild vivid dreams", it's not a building that's on fire but you and him.'

Several nocturnal images of Brogan in various stages of undress flashed through Alice's mind, setting off the familiar squirmy feeling below her navel.

'Although to be honest, Alice, I'm not surprised,' continued Effie. 'Especially as I've seen the hungry way you look at him.'

Alice bristled 'I don't.'

Her friend raised a knowing eyebrow.

'All right, all right, perhaps I do,' conceded Alice, as the memory of him catching her as she fell down the stage steps and the feeling of his arms round her returned. 'But well... it's quite... quite unsettling, especially as I can't ever remember it happening before, when I was with Arthur.'

'You were very young when you and Arthur started courting, so you didn't know about what men and women got up to under the sheets,' said Effie.

Alice gave her friend a rueful look. 'That's for sure. All my mother did to prepare me for my wedding night was to tell me to turn out the light and do what my husband said.'

Effie gave a low laugh. 'My mother didn't even say that much. Barrack-room chatter when I joined the WAAFs filled in some of the gaps about the birds and the bees, but it wasn't until I met Nathan that I understood how wonderful being with the man you love can be. But as you were married, you now know that, too.'

Old memories of Arthur's gentle but infrequent lovemaking drifted into Alice's mind but were instantly replaced with pulse-racing thoughts of doing things, intimate things, with and to Brogan that had never even crossed her mind during nine years of marriage.

'But I'm guessing from your expression, Alice, that perhaps I'm wrong about that,' said Effie softly.

'I feel awful saying it, even to you, Effie,' admitted Alice. 'I loved Arthur, I really did, but I never felt breathless and light-headed when he looked at me or got goosebumps when we touched, but just thinking about Brogan makes me tingle all over and I don't understand why.'

'Well, Alice, there's really a very simple explanation,' said Effie. 'Of course you loved Arthur, but perhaps you weren't *in* love with him.' A languid expression slid across Effie's face. 'And believe me, there's a whole world of difference.'

'I'm beginning to realise that,' said Alice. 'But I'm not sure what I should do about it, if anything.'

'From what I've seen, even when you were being horrible to him when he first arrived it didn't put him off, so I'd say Brogan clearly likes you,' said Effie.

'I suppose he might,' said Alice. 'I mean, it could have been a throwaway remark, but I think he sort of asked me to dinner when he dropped into the relief centre.'

'Well, there you are,' said Effie. 'And, as I've said before, you're too young and beautiful not to find happiness again, and as this is 1942, not 1842, you should take matters into your own hands. You're going to the Thanksgiving dance at Rainbow Corner, aren't you?'

Alice nodded. 'Although I'm not sure what to wear.'

'I don't think which dress you wear will matter because, even if you turned up in a potato sack, I'd bet a pound to a penny that Brogan would ask you to dance as soon as you walked through the door,' said Effie. 'So perhaps give him a bit of encouragement and, who knows...' She winked.

The final chords of 'Kiss Me Goodnight, Sergeant Major' faded and there was a pause, then George ran through the intro of 'You Made Me Love You'.

'I think George is playing your song,' said Effie.

Alice laughed. 'Yes, very appropriate because here I am, a

twenty-seven-year-old woman who was married for nine years, behaving like a daft girl having her first crush.'

'You're not, Alice,' said her friend. 'You've just fallen in love.'

'Hi, Lieutenant, swell job you've done here,' shouted a GI as he and a handful of his friends passed Brogan.

'Thank you, soldier,' Brogan replied, raising his hand in acknowledgement. 'Glad you like it.'

The young serviceman grinned, then disappeared into the crowd of revellers in Rainbow Corner's ballroom.

It was almost five past eight in the evening on Thanksgiving Day and Brogan was tucked away behind one of the pillars just to the side of the stage, on which a seven-piece band was blasting out dance tunes from the current Billboard hits.

The room, with Doric columns supporting the plaster ceiling with its classical architraves, was filled with a hundred plus American soldiers and a sprinkling of US naval personnel.

The numbers of American servicemen visiting Rainbow Corner had risen a hundred-fold each day from its rather inauspicious opening two weeks before. In fact, to accommodate the number of GIs who wanted to celebrate their country's founding fathers in the traditional way the Rainbow's two canteens had been serving the traditional turkey dinner with all the trimmings since nine o'clock that morning, and still had a queue outside when he went past them an hour before.

Some of tonight's visitors were on the dancefloor, some at the bar getting a soda and others relaxing round tables. However, no matter what they were doing nearly all of them had a girl by their side, something Brogan was hoping for himself, which was the reason why he was standing across from the ballroom's double doors.

'So, this is where you are.'

Brogan turned and saw Todd standing beside him holding two bottles of Coca-Cola.

'Hi, Todd,' said Brogan. 'I thought you would have been here a bit earlier.'

'I was,' said Todd, handing him a drink. 'I arrived half an hour ago to take a look round the place.'

'Well, what do you think?' asked Brogan.

'I'd say it all looks pretty good,' said Todd. 'The games room is packed and there's a long queue for the pool tables, not to mention in the basement diner where the guy's flipping burgers, which is why, with so much going on tonight I find you here, hiding in the corner.'

'I'm not hiding,' said Brogan. 'Just keeping an eye out for someone.'

'Gloria?' asked Todd.

Brogan shook his head.

'Then it must be that civvy typist in the duties office, you know, the blonde one with the—'

'I'm not waiting for any of them,' said Brogan. 'In fact, if you must know I'm not looking to meet up with any of them again.'

Todd looked surprised. 'Not even Gloria?'

'Actually, Gloria's a bit more complicated,' Brogan replied, remembering their conversation over dinner a few weeks before. 'But... well just let's just say I've got other things on my mind.'

'By things I take it you mean Aircraftwoman Starling,' said Todd.

Brogan looked puzzled. 'How did you know?'

'Well, apart from the fact that you couldn't take your eyes off of her when we had dinner with your aunt two weeks back,' said Todd, 'her name seems to crop up in every conversation since.'

Brogan opened his mouth to deny it, then gave a heavy sigh. 'You're right. I thought she would have arrived by now – it's almost eight thirty.'

'It's just ten past,' said Todd. 'I heard they found an unexploded bomb in Aldgate, so she's probably having trouble getting through the city.'

A flash of colour among the olive green of American uniforms snagged Brogan's eyes and he held his breath, only to let it out when he realised the young woman wearing it wasn't Alice.

Brogan's heart sank and his attention returned to his friend.

'There were reports that the East End has had some heavy bombing for the last couple of nights, so perhaps she's been called back on duty, or perhaps she's ill or injured or' – a thought loomed into Brogan's mind and he caught his breath – 'perhaps she's out with some fella. What?' he asked, noticing Todd's amused expression.

'You.' His friend chuckled.

'What about me?' said Brogan.

'What was it you told me you were going to do in London? Ah yes, I remember. Wine, women and song, or perhaps it should have been wine, song and women, because you've certainly had your fair share in the last few months. And now look at you. Totally smitten.'

Brogan gave his friend a wry look. 'You're enjoying my agony, aren't you?'

'Immensely,' said Todd.

'It's all right for you,' said Brogan. 'At least you know that the woman you adore feels the same, whereas—'

Out of the corner of his eye he caught a flurry of movement at the entrance as a group of partygoers entered. He turned and his heart leapt into his throat.

Standing just in front of the ballroom's entrance was the woman he had quite suddenly found himself in love with – Alice Starling.

She wasn't alone – alongside her were her four friends – but Brogan's eyes were filled with Alice. She was wearing a rather snazzy cherry-red satin cocktail dress with tight-fitting bodice, puffy sleeves and flared skirt, which highlighted her slender yet shapely figure, but she would still have been the most beautiful woman in the world if she'd been standing there in her boiler suit with a mud-streaked face.

'Happy now?' asked Todd, from what sounded like a long way away.

Not able to speak, Brogan nodded.

'I'll leave you to it then,' his friend added as he slipped away.

As she hadn't seen him yet, Brogan gave himself the pleasure of observing her unnoticed for a few moments, then, probably sensing his eyes on her, she turned and looked straight at him, and their gazes locked together.

For what could have been a couple of seconds or a couple of hours or perhaps eternity they stared through the dancefloor's smoky atmosphere at each other, then Brogan peeled himself off the wall.

He walked towards her, but he'd only taken a couple of steps when Major Jessop loomed in front of him.

'Ah, Lieutenant Hafferty,' he bellowed, his eyes boring into Brogan. 'I want a word with you.'

Resisting the urge to shove his very senior officer out of the way, Brogan straightened up and smiled. 'Yes, sir. Of course.'

~

'Isn't it, Alice,' said Gwen, her voice seemingly coming from some far-off place.

'Sorry, Gwen,' she replied. 'I—'

'She said, isn't it wonderful?' said George.

Alice just nodded, as whatever it was that had stopped her mind from working had taken over her voice as well.

Actually, she was lying, because Alice knew exactly what had taken over her consciousness and it was called Brogan. As soon as his eyes captured hers across the crowded room everything around her stilled as all colour in the room faded.

'Wheee,' squealed Gwen, clasping her hands together. 'Brogan's over there,' she said, gazing adoringly across the room. 'Doesn't he look handsome?'

The balloon crew's youngest WAAF wasn't wrong.

With his hair slightly ruffled and his sharply pressed uniform fitting him like a glove, he'd never looked so good.

To be truthful, although she'd spent all day schooling herself to be cool, calm and collected when she saw him, she had been quite thankful when the bear-like general blocked his path because, as Brogan started walking towards her, she felt breathless and slightly dizzy.

Dragging herself back to the present, Alice looked around at her four companions. They were all dressed up to the nines, which for Nell and Maeve meant stylish cocktail dresses in navy and green respectively, George was sheathed in a cream chiffon number, while Gwen had dressed for the occasion in a navy dress with a white sailor's collar and flared skirt.

'Why don't you three nab us a table, Nell, while me and George fetch us all some drinks,' said Alice.

'Good idea,' Nell replied. 'I can see one over the other side of the dancefloor.'

Leaving their friends heading across the room, George and

Alice made their way to the bar and squeezed their way between a mountain of boisterous GIs to the counter.

'What's your poison, ladies?' said the barman, who was dressed like he worked in an American diner.

'Five Coca-Colas, please, my good man,' said George.

As the barman went off to get their order, the GI next to them turned round.

'Gee, lady, I just love your accent,' he said, his fair, freckled face looking down at her in wonder.

George's aristocratic features lifted in a friendly smile. 'Why, thank you.'

'Tell me, ma'am, do you know the king?' he asked.

'Of course,' said George. 'Lovely man.'

Their drinks arrived with straws poking out of them.

'Here, let me get those,' said the soldier, diving into his trouser pocket. He handed the barman a brown ten-bob note.

'You're very kind,' said George, as she picked up two of the bottles and Alice the other three.

'Perhaps I'll see you later,' said the GI.

George gave him a cool smile. 'Perhaps.'

Leaving the crowded bar area, they headed back to the main part of the hall.

'Do you really know the king?' asked Alice, as they navigated their way between the crowded tables.

'He's been to the family pile a couple of times,' George replied. 'I knew his brother better.'

'You mean the Duke of Windsor?' said Alice.

George nodded. 'Awful man. Kept banging on about how brilliant Hitler was. He was bad enough but that American woman he'd latched onto was even worse. The Bahamas are welcome to them. Here you are,' she said, as she and Alice placed the drinks on the table. 'Where are Maeve and Nell?'

'Where do you think?' said Gwen, nodding at their two friends, who were energetically jitterbugging with a couple of

American servicemen on the dancefloor. 'And that blooming general is *still* talking to Brogan.'

Alice glanced across at Brogan, and yearning rose up in her chest.

A red-haired young GI appeared alongside Gwen and stood to attention.

'Excuse me, ma'am,' he said, in a voice that hadn't quite lost its youthful wobble. 'But would you like to dance?'

Gwen squealed again and, jumping up, followed her dance partner onto the floor.

'Bloody hell!' said George. 'What's that bastard doing here?'

Alice's gaze followed her friend's eyeline and she saw an RAF officer standing with an American major and captain on the other side of the room. It took her a minute or two before she realised who he was.

'Isn't that the wing commander who took our passing-out parade last March?' said Alice.

With her lips pulled into a tight line, George nodded. 'It is indeed. Wing Commander Percy Cuthbertson. Damn him!'

Whipping the straw out of the top of her soda bottle, George opened her evening bag and took out a silver flask. She flipped the top off, poured a full measure from it into the top of the Coca-Cola, then knocked back a large mouthful of her doctored drink.

'Scotch and Coke. Not bad,' she said, and raised the bottle to her lips again.

'What on earth are you doing?' asked Alice, her eyes wide with horror.

'Fortifying myself before I go over and speak to the lying bastard,' George replied. And, with an expression of grim determination on her face, George stood up and marched off across the floor.

The dance finished and when the band struck up again

Nell, Maeve and Gwen just paused for a moment before they picked up the tempo for the next dance.

Alice took another sip of her drink and surreptitiously glanced across to where she'd last seen Brogan, only to find that his place by the pillar had been taken by a couple of American sailors.

'Good evening, Alice,' said a deep voice.

She looked round and her heart caught in her throat as she stood up.

'Hello,' she replied, gazing up at him. 'I see you've not got your four-legged shadow with you.'

'Sam's not much of a dancer.' Brogan laughed. 'I'm sorry I haven't come over to say hello sooner, but General Novack waylaid me.'

'I saw,' said Alice. 'He looked like he was giving you a dressing-down.'

Brogan shook his head. 'He talks to everyone like he's on a parade ground but actually he was saying what a success the place was.'

'Well, judging by tonight I'd say he's right,' said Alice. 'And my friends obviously agree.'

She indicated to where Maeve and Nell were being swirled around the dancefloor by a couple of energetic GIs.

'Brogan!'

Alice looked round and saw Gwen barrelling towards them.

'Brogan,' she repeated, skidding to a stop in front of them. 'I've been looking everywhere for you.'

'Well, now you've found me,' he said, smiling down at her. 'Are you enjoying yourself?'

'Oh, yes,' she replied. 'I said I thought it was wonderful, didn't I, Alice?'

'Yes, you did,' Alice agreed, damping down a niggle of irritation at the interruption.

The band blasted out the last chords of the piece they were

playing and the dancers paused. They clapped along with everyone on the dancefloor, then the band leader counted his troupe into the next number.

'Is this a rumba?' asked Gwen.

'No,' Brogan replied. 'It's a samba.'

Gwen frowned. 'I don't know that one, will you teach me?'

Brogan gave her a regretful smile. 'I'd love to, Gwen, but I asked Alice just before you arrived.'

His dark eyes returned to Alice and he held out his hand.

With her heart thumping uncomfortably in her chest, Alice took it. Brogan led her out onto the dancefloor. They faced each other for a moment, then Brogan took her in his arms. He held her for a couple of beats and then they stepped off.

'I hope you'll forgive me,' he said, as he guided her through a spin. 'Forcing you to dance with me.'

'You've done worse,' she replied.

Brogan gave that quirky smile of his and laughed.

To be honest, with her hand in his and his arm encircling her waist, Alice would have forgiven him almost anything.

They circled around a few couples, then without a pause the band slowed the tempo and started to play 'You Made Me Love You'.

Drawing her into his embrace, Brogan changed into a slow foxtrot without missing a beat and set off a very much quicker one in Alice's heart. She couldn't quite work out why, but with his arms round her something changed between them.

Was it the strong feeling of his shoulder muscles under her fingertips or the hardness of his chest against hers? Alice didn't know but she did know that she liked it. She liked it very much indeed.

Brogan spoke again. 'You look very lovely tonight, Alice,' he said, in a low, resonant voice.

Looking up, Alice saw his words reflected in his eyes.

'Thank you,' she whispered.

Brogan's arm round her waist tightened ever so slightly. 'In fact, to me you always look very lovely.'

Alice stared wordlessly up at him and her feelings for him, which had been simmering for the last few weeks, suddenly came to the boil.

'Oh, Brogan,' she whispered as the last bars of the music faded.

They came to a stop on the other side of the room from her friends. Still holding her hands, Brogan drew her off the dance-floor and behind one of the pillars.

'It's a pity about our first meeting,' he said, looking deep into her eyes. 'Because, Alice, we might have got to know each other a whole lot sooner.'

His arm tightened round her and with her hands on his chest Alice tilted her head back, in readiness for his lips pressing onto hers.

He dipped his head and, with anticipation trembling through her, Alice closed her eyes...

'There you are, Brogan!'

Alice looked round and saw a woman tottering towards them on impossibly high heels, with her blonde hair piled high on her head and wearing a skin-tight, gold-sequinned dress with a very plunging neckline.

'Surprise!' she shouted, flinging her arms wide.

'Gloria!' Brogan said. 'What on earth are you doing here?'

He released Alice, who took half-step back, catching a whiff of alcohol as the woman pushed between them.

Laughing, she threw her arms round Brogan and gave him a noisy kiss on the lips.

Swaying slightly, she gave another tinkling laugh and pressed her lips to his cheek, leaving bright red lipstick behind. 'What a silly question to ask your girlfriend.'

Alice's heart sank.

Brogan untangled himself from her, so she slipped her arm

possessively through his. Her eyes narrowed and they snaked over Alice.

'Aren't you going to introduce me?' she asked, dragging on his arm.

Brogan swallowed. 'Alice,' he said, looking into her eyes. 'This is Gloria Chalmers; she's a singer at the Blue Fountain Club.'

'Charmed I'm sure,' said Gloria, her tone indicating otherwise.

'Gloria,' Brogan continued. 'This is Alice Starling.'

'Are you one of the little hostesses who work here?' Gloria asked, swaying unsteadily for a moment.

'No,' said Alice. 'I'm a WAAF attached to 906 Balloon Squadron Auxiliary Air Force.'

'Alice is one of the balloon girls billeted with my aunt, the ones I told you about,' said Brogan, trying unsuccessfully to free himself from Gloria's grip.

'Really.' Gloria's eyes flickered over her again. 'I thought you were all beefy sorts, like sports mistresses and policewomen.'

Alice gave her a syrupy smile. 'And I thought clubs liked their cabaret singers to be young.'

Gloria's pleasant expression faltered slightly, then, tightening her hold on Brogan's arm, she looked adoringly up at him.

'Have you told her about the Christmas concert, darling?' she asked.

He looked confused. 'I'm not sure—'

'That I've volunteered to come along and sing a couple of numbers,' Gloria cut in, batting her mascaraed eyelashes at him. 'To add a bit of glamour to the proceedings.'

'No, he didn't,' said Alice, looking hard at Brogan.

'Fancy forgetting. Although I suppose' – Gloria giggled – 'it's understandable as you had other, more pleasant things on your mind.'

She winked suggestively at him and a jagged-toothed saw sliced through Alice's heart.

'Lovely to have met you, Gloria, I ought to rejoin my friends,' Alice forced out, somehow scraping together an amiable smile. 'Enjoy the rest of your evening.'

With tears pinching the corners of her eyes, she turned and hurried off.

'Alice,' Brogan called after her.

Ignoring him, she carried on across the ballroom, but then he caught her arm. Steeling herself, she turned and looked coolly up at him.

'Alice, please, let me explain—'

'There's really no need, Brogan.' She pulled her arm free and gave him a frosty smile. 'No need at all.'

Watching the woman he loved walking away from him, Brogan knew it was his own stupid fault.

Hadn't he specifically taken Gloria to dinner over a week before to end their relationship? But instead of just telling her straight out that their affair was over, he'd pussy-footed stupidly around the subject until he ended up painting himself into a corner by mentioning the concert. He really was the biggest numbskull on the entire planet.

He watched Alice for a few moments more, then turned back to Gloria, who was more than a little drunk.

She flung her arms wide. 'Surprise!' she trilled again.

Brogan didn't smile or move.

Swaying slightly, Gloria jutted out her bottom lip. 'You don't seem very pleased to see me.'

'How did you get in?' asked Brogan. 'It's invitation only.'

She wobbled forward a few steps and flung her arms round his neck again.

'I told the old biddy on the door that I was with you,' she said, gin fumes wafting up as she spoke. 'I wondered why you'd not mention the dance, but then I saw you smooching that little WAAF and I knew.'

'I wasn't smooching,' Brogan replied, putting her from him yet again.

Gloria's bottom lip trembled. 'Don't tell me you wouldn't have kissed her if I hadn't arrived.'

Brogan didn't deny it.

He glanced over Gloria's head, across to the far side of the room where Alice, with two of her friends, was chatting to a couple of GIs. Even at this distance Brogan could see her smile was forced.

Cursing himself again for his utter stupidity, he turned back to Gloria.

'The truth is, Gloria, I—'

'I love this one,' cried Gloria, as the band struck up 'Begin the Beguine'. She grabbed his hand and started dragging him to the dancefloor. 'Come on, let's dance.'

'No,' he replied, planting his feet firmly on the floor.

'Why?' she said, still tugging at his arm. 'You danced with her. That mousy little thing. I saw you. All starry-eyed and lovey-dovey.' Her face crumpled. 'Why, Brogan? Why?'

Throwing herself on him again, she started sobbing on his chest and those around them started to look their way.

Brogan's mouth pulled into a hard line and, removing her arms again, he took hold of her wrist. 'Let's talk outside.'

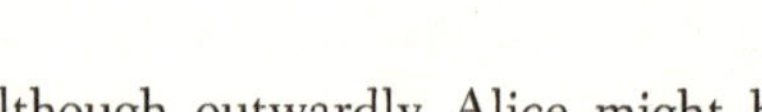

Although outwardly Alice might have looked as if she was enjoying watching the merrymakers swing back and forth to the band's lively rendition of 'Pennsylvania 6-5000', inside she was sobbing. Well, half of her was sobbing – the other half was raging at her own stupidity in thinking that Brogan, like nearly every other single GI in London, wasn't making the most of the warm welcome the capital's womenkind were extending to him.

And why wouldn't he? After all, he'd give Tyrone Powell and Errol Flynn a good run for their money in a handsomeness contest and he could charm the birds from the trees, so it wasn't surprising that he probably had a string of women, like the one who had plastered her lipstick all over his cheek just now, desperate for his company.

Although she tried to stop herself, Alice surreptitiously glanced across to where Brogan had been standing, only to find he'd gone. Off somewhere secluded and quiet, no doubt, with the glamorous Gloria, she thought, twisting the knife already embedded deep in her heart.

The tune finished and mechanically Alice clapped the band as the dancers drifted off the floor.

'Are you all right, Alice?' asked Nell, as she returned to the table carrying two bottles.

'I've got a bit of a headache, that's all,' said Alice. 'What have you got there?'

'Something called 7 Up, which tastes a bit like lemonade,' said Nell, handing her one and sitting down.

'Where's everyone else?' asked Alice.

'Well, despite the place being packed with Americans, Gwen has found herself a sergeant who's in the Welsh Guards, and Maeve is over by the bar with a chap from Oklahoma talking about dairy cows.'

'Very romantic,' said Alice, smiling despite her heavy heart. 'What about George?'

'She had a few dances but then I found her tucked in a corner with a liquor-laden Coca-Cola staring broodily at that RAF officer she noticed when we came in,' Nell replied. 'I tried to get out of her what her beef was with him, but she kept shtum, but I'd lay a pound to a penny he's done the dirty on her somewhere along the line.'

I know how she feels, thought Alice as the music paused again.

Couples drifted off to return to their seats while others took their place, as the band struck up an old-fashioned waltz. However, as the dancers set off around the dancefloor again Alice spotted Gwen, wearing an uneasy expression on her young face, hurrying towards them.

'What's up?' asked Nell as she reached them.

'It's George,' Gwen replied. 'You'd better come.'

Leaving their drinks on the table, Alice and Nell stood up, and all three of them wended their way through the GIs milling round the edge of the dancefloor to one of the small alcoves at the back. George was leaning against the wall, a bottle of Coke in her hand and a deep scowl on her face.

'What's the matter?' asked Alice, as they crowded around their friend.

George's scowl deepened and, after taking a large mouthful from the bottle, she jabbed it at a group of American officers, including Wing Commander Cuthbertson, sitting in one of the many booths round the edge of the ballroom.

'Him! That's what's wrong with me,' she slurred, glaring hatefully across at the RAF officer.

She flipped open her handbag and took out a quarter bottle of Johnnie Walker.

'Where in the name of God did you get that?' asked Maeve, as her friend poured a generous amount of it into her fizzy drink.

Giving a bleary-eyed grin, George tapped the side of her nose and raised the bottle to her lips.

'It was him,' she continued, swaying on her heels as her attention returned to Wing Commander Cuthbertson, 'who had me transferred for balloon training.'

'I thought you volunteered,' said Alice.

'I did, but it wasn't as if I had much choice once his wife arrived,' said George.

Gwen looked puzzled. 'What's his wife got to do with—'

'For goodness sake, Gwen, do you have to have it spelt out?' snapped Nell.

The young WAAF's perplexed expression remained for a second or two more, then her eyebrows almost disappeared into her hairline as the penny dropped.

After taking another swig from the bottle, George stood away from the wall. 'Perhaps I should go over to say hello.'

She staggered forward.

'Actually, George,' said Alice, slipping her arm through her friend's. 'I've got a better idea. Let's take you home.'

George pulled away. 'No, not yet. Not until I've told him what an absolute bas...'

Swaying, she took a few steps, then staggered sideways. Alice and Nell caught her and exchanged a look.

'I'll go and call a cab,' said Maeve.

Nell nodded. 'Let's get her out of the side door.'

'I agree,' said Alice. 'Best not to draw attention to ourselves and have someone query how she got drunk in an establishment with no alcohol licence.'

Supporting their friend, who was now illustrating what the term legless actually looked like, Alice and Nell, with Gwen carrying their handbags, set off.

Although she tried not to, when they got into the main dance area Alice's gaze skimmed around the room. Although the ballroom was filled with American servicemen, Brogan was not one of them. The ache in her chest returned but she brushed it aside and looked at George slung between them, who was now softly weeping.

Pushing aside the urge to burst into tears herself, Alice fixed her eyes on the ballroom's main entrance and headed towards it.

~

'I'm sorry, Gloria,' said Brogan, flatly. 'I never meant to hurt you, but it's over, so, no matter what you say, I won't be coming round from now on,' he added, just to make it crystal clear.

She looked confused. 'I don't understand.'

Brogan had finally managed to get Gloria out of Rainbow Corner.

Finally, because she'd insisted on taking a tour of every room they passed on the way to the front door. Not wanting to draw any more attention to them both than they already had, Brogan had been forced to play along.

They were now standing around the corner from the main entrance in the alleyway that ran down the side of the club. They weren't alone, as there were a dozen or so other couples who were taking advantage of the darkness between the buildings, for quite a different purpose. It wasn't the best place to have this sort of conversation but at least it was out of sight of half the American army, who were going in and out of the main door.

'The truth is, Gloria, I'm in love with Alice,' he said, enjoying finally admitting it out loud.

'Alice? You're in love with that WAAF?' said Gloria.

'I am,' he replied.

In the low light reflected up from his muted torch, Gloria stared blankly at him for a moment, then, taking a step forward, she laughed. 'You're telling me that you, Brogan Rafferty, who has a new girl on your arm practically every month, aren't going to be playing the field any more because you're in love?'

'That's about the size of it,' he replied. 'And again, I'm—'

Stepping forward, Gloria threw her arms round him, pushing him back against the wall.

'I'm sorry,' she sobbed. 'I didn't mean to make a scene back there but seeing you with her...'

Clinging to him, she tried to kiss him, but Brogan raised his head. 'Stop it, Gloria,' he said firmly.

He tried to remove her arms from round his neck but as he did a door to his right opened. Momentarily distracted, Brogan looked round and, as he did, Gloria's lips pressed onto his. Gripping her wrists firmly, he raised his head, only to find himself looking straight at Alice.

In the dimly lit alley, their gazes locked briefly, then, looking away, Alice turned and walked on towards Piccadilly with her three friends.

Prising Gloria's arms from round his neck, Brogan stepped away from her. 'I'll call you a taxi.'

Holding her arm, he guided her out of the alleyway as she wobbled along beside him on her high heels.

Although it was now almost half past eleven at night, the pavement outside Rainbow Corner was still packed with American servicemen queuing four or five deep to get in. Skirting around them, Brogan stopped at the kerb and spotted a taxi with its yellow light on. He raised his hand and the vehicle came to a halt.

'Twenty-three Lupus Street, Pimlico,' he said, and offered the cabbie a green pound note. 'And make sure she gets home safely.'

The driver touched his forehead, and Brogan opened the back door.

Gloria climbed in and sat down, but when Brogan tried to close the door she stayed it with her hand. 'Come with me,' she said and gave him an enticing smile. 'I'll make it worth your—'

'Goodbye, Gloria.' He tried to close the door, but she pushed it back again.

'I suppose you're going after her,' she snarled.

'Damn right I am,' Brogan replied.

With a sulky expression on her face, Gloria slumped in the

back seat, and Brogan slammed the taxi's door shut. He stepped
back and the vehicle sped off.

Another taxi pulled up a little way away. The passenger
door opened, and General Jessup squeezed himself out. He
spotted Brogan by the side of the road.

'Ah, Lieutenant Rafferty!' he said. Brogan's very senior officer, a British major and RAF wing commander, climbed out of
the cab behind him. 'Just the man.'

Cursing under his breath, Brogan stood to attention. 'Sir.'

'You can come with me and show my friend here around
Rainbow Corner and show them a real, all-American howdie-
doodie.'

Brogan's eyes returned to Alice as she headed off down the
street taking his heart with her, then with a heavy sigh his attention returned to his senior officer.

He forced a smile and swept his arm towards the front door.
'After you, sir.'

CHAPTER 19

Turning her collar up round her ears, Alice pushed open the Maid of Norway's side door and stepped out into the dark morning.

Judging by the sheen of ice over the puddles, the temperature was well below freezing, and the frigid air snapped Alice out of her tiredness in an instant.

It was the day after the Thanksgiving dance, and just after half five in the morning.

Although it was no more than a ten-minute walk, by the time Alice reached the door of the on-duty hut her nose was like a block of ice. Pushing open the door, she entered the welcoming warmth of the hut.

'Good of you to join us,' said Lily, giving Alice a sour look.

She was lounging on one of the sofas alongside her shadow Maureen. Opposite them on the other sofa were Nell and Maeve, while George lay supine on the lower bunk with her eyes shut and her complexion the same bleached colour as the pillow beneath her head.

'You're a fine one to talk about timekeeping, Lil,' said Maeve.

'And look, day duty don't start for another ten minutes,' said Gwen, glancing up at the clock as she brewed the team's first pot of the day at the stove.

'Yeah, so shut your trap,' added Nell.

Lily gave her a hateful look, which Nell returned.

'Are you all right, Alice?' asked Gwen.

'I've just got a bit of a headache, that's all,' Alice replied.

'I'm not surprised.' Peggy laughed. 'It must have been one hell of a night last night with all those Yanks.'

Alice gave her a wan smile.

Having got back to the pub at a few minutes past twelve and bundled a semi-conscious George into bed, Alice had collapsed into hers. However, despite being bone-weary, she had spent the rest of the night staring at the overhead light fitting and torturing herself by picturing Brogan with Gloria in his arms, with her lips on his, until her alarm clock sounded at five. So no, the reason for her headache had nothing to do with alcohol and everything to do with that sinfully handsome, smooth-talking, womanising Lieutenant Brogan Rafferty, who she'd stupidly fallen in love with.

'Do you want a cuppa, Alice?' asked Gwen, as she set out the cups.

Ignoring the pain in her chest, Alice nodded. 'That would be—'

'She ain't got time,' cut in Lily. 'Last in, first out, so don't bother taking off your gear as you're on first patrol. And you can join her, Nell.' She grinned. 'Off you go. Chop chop.'

'How are the ropes your end, Nell?' Alice shouted.

Turning, Nell gave her the thumbs-up. 'What about yours?'

'I've tightened the front near side, but the rest are okay,' Alice called back.

Despite the winter sun having crested the two-up two-down

houses to the east of them, Alice didn't imagine that the mercury on the barometer had shifted upward more than a degree. Wrapped up to the ears in their long overcoats and balaclavas, she and Nell were almost at the end of their patrol with just a few last checks to do. Bessie was floating at close haul, tethered to her concrete moorings by the ropes.

'Gawd, it's blooming freezing,' said Nell, blowing on her hands to warm them.

Angling her arm towards the first ray of sunlight lighting the eastern sky, Alice looked at her watch.

'Maeve and Gwen should be out to relieve us soon, so I'll give the fuel tank and coal bunker one last check if you go and put the kettle on,' she said, her breath visible as puffs of steam in the frosty air.

'Sounds like a fair deal to me,' said Nell.

With her hobnail boots crunching across the gravel, she headed off back to the hut.

Alice turned towards the brick-built bunker with a corrugated tin roof where the site's diesel and coal were stored.

Stepping inside the damp enclosure, she took the torch from her pocket and switched it on. She shone it on the dial and tapped the gauge on the side of the diesel tank, then, crouching down, she grasped the second padlock securing the square trap at the front and shook it. Satisfied that they were both in order, she straightened up, but as she started towards the hut a jeep screeched to a halt by the entrance of the balloon site.

Alice was rooted to the spot and her heart thumped painfully in her chest as Brogan leapt out with Sam following close behind.

Brogan paused for a moment, then, with his greatcoat flaring behind him and his dog bounding alongside, he strode towards her.

Alice turned and continued down the path to the hut.

'Alice, wait,' he shouted. 'Please.'

She stopped and, forcing a composed expression onto her face, turned to face him.

Stopping in front of her, Brogan smiled. 'Alice, thank goodness. You're here.'

Looking up into the dark brown eyes and handsome face of the man she'd foolishly given her heart to, Alice felt the band of pain that had encircled her chest since she'd seen him kissing Gloria in the alleyway tightening further.

'Non-RAF personnel aren't allowed on the site,' she said, as Sam circled round her, wagging his tail.

'I realise that, and I'm sorry for turning up like this, but I had to see you,' he replied.

'Why?'

'To explain,' he said. 'About Gloria.'

'You don't need to,' said Alice, giving him an icy look. 'Because it's quite obvious what Gloria is to you, and I bet she's not the only one.'

The truth of her words flickered across Brogan's handsome face, cutting deep into Alice's heart.

She gave him a look of distaste, then, with the tears pressing at the back of her eyes, turned and started for the hut again.

Brogan skirted round her and stood in her path. 'Alice, please. It's not—'

'"Love 'em and leave 'em,"' cut in Alice. 'That the GIs' moto, isn't it?'

'No! Well, yes, but—'

'I know you Americans have bets with each other for the number of women you can have on the go at any one time,' Alice continued. 'And I bet you score pretty high in those stakes.'

'That might have been true in the past—'

'And I know there are hundreds of women who are out to find themselves an American, but I tell you this, Brogan Rafferty,' Alice continued, as bitterness and anger churned around inside her. 'You can take your smart uniform, money-stuffed wallet and lazy New York charm elsewhere because I'm not going to be another notch in your headboard.'

'But I don't want you to be, Alice,' said Brogan. 'You're not like the others. You're special.'

Despite the ache squeezing her heart, Alice raised a cynical eyebrow. 'What a corny line.'

'I mean it,' Brogan replied. 'You're different.'

'Am I now?'

'Yes, you are,' Brogan replied. 'And I'm different now. Completely different, too, because I love you, Alice. I love you.'

With his dark eyes looking deep into hers and an earnest expression etched on his chiselled face, Alice's scepticism wavered a little. The words 'I love you too' hovered on her lips – but then her doubts and fears surged back.

Damping down her emotions and mustering every inch of resistance, she looked Brogan squarely in the eye. 'Let me pass.'

'Alice, please—'

The hut door opened.

'Alice?' Nell's voice shouted across the icy darkness.

'Just coming,' she yelled back, without taking her eyes off Brogan.

With his jawline tense and his dark eyes locked on hers, he stood looking down at her for a second longer and then stepped aside.

Squaring her shoulders, and with the blood pounding in her ears, Alice set off for the hut again.

'I love you, Alice,' he called after. 'I love you,' he repeated, as tears shimmering on her lower lashes distorted her vision.

Signalling for Sam to sit at the kerb, Brogan let the British ARP wagon roll past before he crossed the road and pushed open the Man in the Moon's saloon bar door.

Situated in the middle of the area known as Shepherd Market, the pub was very like the Maid of Norway and thousands of others up and down the land. There was a horseshoe-shaped bar, with a row of beer pump handles fixed along it and a shelf above loaded with various-sized glasses. Behind the bar, in front of a large mirror with gummed tape crisscrossing it advertising Mackeson Stout, were a row of upended bottles with their necks wedged in optics that dispensed a tot.

Now, finding himself surrounded on all sides by US Army personnel, the enterprising landlord had come to an arrangement with the army's quartermaster stores to supply bourbon, Budweiser and Blue Label, which, thanks to an antiquated refrigerator out back, he served cold.

As it was now just before six in the evening, the bar was pretty full of GIs, lounging around at the dozen or so tables playing cards or chequers or just unwinding with their buddies at the end of the day's duty.

Casting his eyes around, Brogan spotted Todd clutching a beer and reading a letter in one of the booths under the window.

With Sam following behind, Brogan headed for the bar, while Sam stuck his nose in the water bowl on the floor at the end counter.

Rita, the Man in the Moon's barmaid, who was polishing glasses at the other end of the bar, glided over to greet him.

'Lieutenant Rafferty,' she said, flipping her tea towel over her shoulder. 'What can I get you?'

'Two Ballantine, please,' said Brogan.

She reached below the counter and pulled out two bottles.

'Anything else?' she asked, popping the caps off and placing them on the mahogany counter in front of him.

Brogan rummaged in his pocket and pulled out a couple of coins. 'Not just now.'

He picked up his drinks and made his way through the busy public house to his friend.

Todd looked up as he approached.

'Man, you look like hell, Brogan,' said Todd as he picked up his drink.

Brogan took a swig of his own drink. 'I know, and, believe me, I feel ten times worse.'

'But I thought the Thanksgiving dance was a huge success,' said Todd, stroking Sam's head as the dog joined them.

'It was,' said Brogan. 'A huge success.'

'So why do you look as if you've just lost a million dollars?' asked his friend.

'Because I have lost a million dollars, metaphorically speaking,' Brogan replied.

'I guess you mean Aircraftwoman Alice Starling?' said Todd.

With the bottle halfway to his lips, Brogan nodded.

'I'm guessing you were just about to tell her how you feel and managed to louse it up somehow?'

'Not me, Gloria,' Brogan replied. 'Well, not so much her as me being a damn idiot. I had Alice in my arms and was just about to kiss her when...'

He told Todd about what had happened at Rainbow Corner the previous night.

'If Alice had come out of the door a moment earlier or a few seconds later, then...' He raked his fingers through his hair. 'I tell you, Todd, the look on Alice's face when she saw me outside the club with Gloria cut right through me.'

As if sensing his master's mood, Sam rested his head on Brogan's knee.

'So what did you do then?' said Todd.

'I bundled Gloria into a taxi and gave the driver a hefty tip to see her home safely,' said Brogan, stroking his dog's head absentmindedly. 'Then I was going to try to catch another to go after Alice but General Jessop turned up with a senior British naval officer and dragged me in to show his top brass British army guests around. It was gone two by the time I finally got away. As I could hardly go knocking on the Maid of Norway's door at that time, I went back to my room to catch some shut-eye.'

'Did you?' asked Todd.

'Not a damn wink,' Brogan replied. 'I got up at six, took Sam for a quick trot, collected a jeep from the pool and drove down to Shadwell. Luckily Alice was patrolling the site when I arrived. I tried to explain about Gloria, but she accused me of being a Don Juan—'

'Which you are,' interrupted Todd.

'I *was*, Todd, past tense,' corrected Brogan. 'But she didn't believe me, and told me to go fly a kite.'

'So what are you going to do?' asked his friend.

'There's nothing I can do other than keep telling her I love her until she believes me,' said Brogan. 'And then beg her to marry me.' He raked his fingers through his hair again. 'God damn it. What a mess.'

Taking a swig of beer, Brogan slumped back in the chair, then spotted his friend's gleeful expression.

'Go on then,' he said, raising an ironic eyebrow. 'Say it.'

Todd grinned. 'I told you so.'

Pausing on the pavement, Alice looked across the street at the entrance to the Beaumont Hotel.

The double-fronted building with classical columns and steps up to the front door had been constructed in the last days of the Regency period. It had once been the town house of a wealthy family, but had become a hotel some time in the middle of the last century. It wasn't alone in offering comfort to travellers from the Home Counties visiting the capital; there were at least half a dozen more such establishments in the street. Like them, the Beaumont was doing its bit for the war effort, as the sandbags piled up halfway up the ground-floor windows and the gummed tape criss-crossing panes of glass in the casements above showed.

Alice let an ARP ambulance and a couple of delivery lorries trundle past, then, taking a deep breath and squaring her shoulders, she marched across the road.

She trotted up the couple of steps, pushed through the revolving doors and entered the lobby.

Like the outside, the pastel and floral décor of the hotel's lobby area echoed the days before the country's first fight with Germany, when the Empire was at its height and summers were full of Pimm's, tennis and country house parties.

On seeing her enter the lobby a steward, a slender middle-aged man with oiled hair, stepped forward.

'Good afternoon, madam,' he said, smiling politely at her. 'How can I be of service?'

'I'm Mrs Starling and I'm having afternoon tea with my mother-in-law,' Alice replied.

'Very good,' he replied. 'I believe Mrs Starling senior is already here, but let me take your coat.'

'Thank you,' said Alice as she unbuttoned her heavy WAAF overcoat.

The steward snapped his fingers, and a young lad dressed in the hotel's livery sprang forward.

Alice shoved her cap in one pocket and her scarf in the other and handed it to the youngster.

'This way, Mrs Starling,' said the steward.

Straightening her hair with her fingers and pulling down

the front of her dress uniform jacket, Alice followed him down a few carpeted steps towards the tearoom.

The afternoon refreshment area was decorated with Chinese-style wallpaper, with potted palms and ferns dotted around the walls and mock bamboo tables and chairs.

Glancing around at the men and women enjoying a few hours of genteel respite from the war raging around them, Alice spotted her mother-in-law sitting at a table by one of the criss-cross-taped windows at the back of the room.

The steward handed Alice over to the waitress, who led her between the tables.

As she drew near Cybele, who had been gazing out of the window at the hotel's rear terrace, looked round.

Just a few years shy of her fiftieth birthday, Cybele Margaret Starling was wearing a russet-coloured shot-silk dress and jacket with three-quarter-length sleeves, and a mink stole draped round her shoulders. To complete the ensemble, she had a net and velvet fascinator pinned to her tightly permed grey hair.

Although she had repeatedly reminded herself throughout her hour-long journey from Wapping station that Arthur's mother no longer held sway over her, as Cybele's deep-set eyes fixed on Alice a too-familiar anxiety tightened in her chest.

'Good afternoon, Mrs Starling,' said Alice, in as even a voice as she could muster.

The waitress held the chair out and Alice, tucking her skirt under her, sat down opposite her mother-in-law.

'Tea for two,' Cybele said to the waitress. 'Indian, naturally. And make sure the sandwiches are freshly cut. The ones you tried to serve me last time I was here were curling at the edges.'

'Yes, madam.' The waitress bobbed a curtsy and shot off.

Cybele's attention returned to Alice. 'Punctuality never was your strong suit, was it, Alice?'

'There were delays on the Central Line,' Alice replied.

Cybele rolled her eyes. 'The blasted railway workers striking again. What's the point of passing a law to make strikes illegal if those who do aren't prosecuted? I blame Attlee. It's him and his communist cronies in the government who encourage such things.'

The waitress returned carrying a tray loaded with their tea. The two women sat in silence while she set the tea things on the table. As the young girl left, Cybele picked up the teapot.

'As you clearly couldn't be, I'll be mother,' she said, giving Alice a withering look.

Alice held her mother-in-law's caustic stare. 'I was rather surprised to receive your letter, especially as I haven't heard from you for over two years.'

'Well, you wouldn't have now either if it hadn't been for the fact that your name cropped up recently.' Cybele slid a cup across the table.

Alice looked surprised. 'Did it?'

'It did and in rather concerning circumstances,' Cybele continued. 'On the lips of an American. A certain Lieutenant Rafferty.'

Alice's heart thumped uncomfortably in her chest.

'He seemed to be very taken with you,' added Cybele.

'Did he?' asked Alice.

'Yes, he did, very taken indeed. Singing your praises, in fact.' Cybele's eyes fixed on her. 'Are you romantically involved with him?'

'No, I'm not,' said Alice.

'Are you sure?' asked Cybele.

'I said I'm not,' Alice said firmly, somewhat surprised to feel a twinge of regret.

'And I expect you to keep it that way,' continued her mother-in-law. 'You have brought enough disgrace to the family already without having the Starling name linked to some brash Yank.'

'Lieutenant Rafferty is not a "brash Yank", Mrs Starling, but a liaison officer with the US Army's Office of War Information and Public Relations division,' said Alice coolly.

'With a dozen girls in tow like the rest of them, no doubt,' Cybele replied. 'Honestly, the Americans have the morals of a tomcat.' She fixed her granite-hard eyes on Alice. 'I sincerely hope you haven't debased yourself and become one of this lieutenant's paramours.'

The memory of seeing Brogan kissing Gloria outside Rainbow Corner loomed back into Alice's mind.

'I have told you twice already I am not,' she said, firmly.

'Good,' said Cybele. 'As I said previously, if you were to become involved romantically with any man it would be an unforgivable slur on my son's memory. It would be particularly reprehensible if you became entangled with any American, but especially with this Lieutenant Rafferty, who had the bare-faced affrontery to tell me that I should be proud of you for being a WAAF.' Her mother-in-law's top lip curled in a sneer. 'Proud of *you*? I doubt he'd have held that view if he'd known how you failed to provide your husband with a son.'

'There are many couples who aren't blessed with children, Mrs Starling,' Alice forced out over the lump lodged in her throat.

Through her veil, Cybele's eyes narrowed. 'Remind me how many children your two sisters have?'

'Marge has four and Mary two,' Alice replied.

'And another on the way, so Thatcher tells me,' said her mother-in-law. 'And your brother?'

'Five,' Alice replied, as the memory of her brother Will's boisterous child-filled cottage flashed through her mind.

'So a dozen between them,' said Cybele, looking hard at her. 'And you couldn't manage to produce one.'

Alice held her mother-in-law's scornful gaze for a moment,

then, taking her napkin from her lap, she threw it on the half-eaten Battenberg cake on the plate and stood up.

'I'd like to say it's been a pleasure to see you, Mrs Starling,' she said, looking across the cups, teapot and sandwiches at the older woman. 'But it hasn't. I came out of courtesy this time, but I won't again.'

'That suits me perfectly.' Cybele's hard eyes bored into Alice's. 'And in deference to my dear son's memory I'd advise you to accept widowhood, especially as, once they discover that you're barren, no man, even your flashy American lieutenant, will want you.'

As her mother-in-law's often-repeated words rang in her head, the grey cloud of her fruitless marriage gathered around Alice again as pain tightened across her chest. She snatched up her handbag and, with tears threatening to fall, stumbled between the white-clothed table towards the door.

'Here we are, Florrie.' Nell, still wearing her navy boiler suit, walked through from the scullery carrying a steaming mug in either hand. 'Two hot cups of Rosie Lee.'

'Thanks, Nell,' Florrie said, taking one from her.

Nell, blonde-haired and with sapphire-blue eyes, strong cheekbones and a figure that, despite three years of rations, was best described as a pleasing armful, took the seat opposite.

It was somewhere close to five and, with her stockinged feet resting on the old leather pouffe, Florrie was sitting in her favourite fireside armchair in her lounge.

She'd closed the doors on the last midday drinker at ten minutes after last orders at three. Unfortunately, that was an hour and a half ago. Since then she'd been hard at it washing glasses and restocking the bar, and had only been able to free her aching feet from the torture of her high heels ten minutes ago, which was five minutes before Nell knocked at the door.

'I wouldn't have asked,' said Nell, sinking into the chair opposite. 'But Dolly and Rose have got their smalls soaking in the sink while they do their ironing, so I couldn't get in the kitchen, let alone boil a kettle, and I was gasping.'

'Don't be daft,' said Florrie, waving away her words. 'I'm always happy for any of you girls to pop down.' She winked. 'Well, almost any of you.'

Exchanging a knowing look, they both laughed.

Cradling the cup with both hands, Nell took a sip. 'Oh, that's better. I'm beginning to thaw out.'

'Yeah, it's right parky out there,' said Florrie.

'It's not much warmer in our duty hut,' said Nell.

'But you only had your coal ration delivery last week,' said Florrie. 'You can't be running low on coal already.'

'We are,' said Nell. 'We only put on enough nuggets to keep the chill out, so I can't think why we're almost out of this month's allocation.'

As she'd seen Lily hanging around with that chancer Charlie Mulligan, Florrie had a pretty good idea. But given Nell's history with the Whitechapel wide-boy she thought it best not to mention it.

Rocking onto one hip, Florrie felt in her pocket. 'Blast, I've left my ciggies on the bar.'

She swung her feet off the pouffe.

'I'll fetch them,' Nell said, putting down her drink and getting up from the chair.

Florrie sank back. 'You're a luv.'

Nell left the room, leaving the door ajar.

As the five o'clock pips sounded, Florrie heard the pub's side door open.

'What the bloody hell's happened?' Nell said, outside in the hall.

A woman mumbled something, then burst into tears.

The door opened and Nell came back in hugging a weeping Alice.

Florrie got up from her chair, padded across in her stockinged feet to Alice and took over from Nell in comforting duties.

'Right,' she said. 'You come and sit down while Nell gets you a nice cup of tea, and you can tell us all about it.'

Holding Alice's shaking shoulders firmly, Florrie walked her across to the fireside chair she'd just vacated while Nell scooted back to the kitchen. Sitting her down, Florrie took her clean hankie from her pocket and, perching on the pouffe in front of her, offered it to Alice.

'I... I'm so... so... sorry Fl... Florrie,' she sobbed, taking it from her. 'I pr... promised myself I... I wouldn't cry and I managed to hold it in all the way home on the bus but... sh... sh... she's just so hateful.'

'Who?' asked Nell as she returned.

'My mother-in-law,' said Alice, pressing the handkerchief beneath her eyes.

'I know you weren't keen on going. Was it as bad as you thought it would be?' asked Nell as she placed a mug of tea on the table next to her.

'Worse,' Alice replied. 'But with Christmas just round the corner I thought perhaps... well I don't know what I thought really, but after cross-examining me about my personal life she spent the rest of the time lecturing me about tarnishing the family name and dishonouring Arthur's memory by becoming romantically involved with...' Alice's gaze flickered briefly onto Florrie. 'With a... a... anyone. And then she launched into her favourite subject. What a wicked wife I was because I couldn't give my husband a child.'

Alice's expression crumpled and, burying her pretty face in her hands, she sobbed again.

Florrie exchanged a sad look with Nell, who again put her arm round her friend's shoulder and gave her an affectionate squeeze.

Alice raised her head.

'Doesn't she think I *wanted* to have a baby?' she said, looking from Florrie to Nell and back again with red-rimmed eyes. 'Doesn't she think I was bitterly disappointed and heart-broken, too?'

Feeling her heart ache for her, Florrie took the young woman's hands in hers.

'I'm sure you were, luv,' she said, softly.

'I would have given anything, Florrie, to have held my own child in my arms,' added Alice. 'Anything.'

The three of them lapsed into silence for a few moments, then Florrie squeezed Alice's hands.

'Of course,' she said, looking Alice squarely in the eye. 'And I 'ope you don't mind me saying, but perhaps it wasn't you but Arthur who couldn't have children. And if you were to marry again you might not have the same problem.'

'Florrie's right,' said Nell. 'Bette Tyler and her 'usband Bill, who lived in the flat opposite us, tried for years to have a family. 'E died and she married one of the porters from the Spitalfields market and 'ad twins the following year, followed by two more kids after that.'

A kernel of hope flickered across Alice's face and then she frowned. 'You might be right, and I know if I was offered a second chance at happiness and a family of my own a part of me would want to take that chance, but I'm just not sure my heart and sanity would take it again.'

CHAPTER 20

'Now, the British money might take you a bit of time to get used to but I'm sure you'll soon get the hang of it,' said Brogan, looking out at the sea of faces.

It was early December and he was again standing on the stage in the ballroom of the Brook Street Hotel, on the last day of the two-day Welcome to Britain orientation course. In front of him were fifty-plus newly minted GIs who had sailed across the Atlantic Ocean in the teeth of winter storms and arrived on Great Britain's shores the week before. He'd run through the usual programme and had fielded the usual questions about duties and accommodation.

'And remember, if the British seem a mite stand-offish at first, it's not because they're unfriendly, no sir, it's because they are reserved. And remember, they've been through hell these past three years, as you'll see for yourself as you travel around the capital. Now, before we finish, are there any further questions?'

A fair-haired trooper in one of the middle rows stood up. 'Private Muller, sir.'

Half-knowing what the question would be, Brogan nodded. 'Go ahead.'

'My brother is with the Mighty Eighth, stationed in some place up in Norfolk,' Muller began. 'And he wrote me to say that if you flash a few bucks and hand out a couple of pairs of nylons the gals are... well... you know, sir.'

He certainly did, and, looking across the sea of grinning GIs nudging each other, shame burned in his chest as Alice's lovely face loomed into his mind.

Brogan cleared his throat, and the sniggering subsided.

'I have three sisters back home. One in sixth grade, another in her junior year and the eldest has just got engaged,' he said, strolling slowly across the stage. 'I'm guessing that most of you have sisters, wives and sweethearts at home, too.'

All round the room heads nodded in agreement.

'Well, then perhaps you'll take a minute and consider that these British "gals" you will meet walking down the street, working in shops or serving in bars and restaurants or in dance-halls are other men's daughters, sweethearts and wives,' he said, acutely aware of the irony of his words as he turned to make his way back across the stage. 'Another man, just like you, who might be fighting the enemy in North Africa, chasing U-boats across the frozen Atlantic or braving German anti-aircraft guns on night flights over Germany.'

The overconfident posture of the GIs in the room shifted as Brogan's words sank in, and they straightened up in their seats.

'Do you get my drift, men?' he asked, looking as many of his audience square in the eye as possible as he cast his gaze over them.

'Yes, sir,' they chorused back.

'Good.'

'Yes, sir. Thank you, sir,' said Muller, looking more than a little sheepish as he resumed his seat.

'Now, are there any further questions?' asked Brogan.

No one stood up.

'Very well, but before you're dismissed, I've talked a lot today about getting to know our hosts and joining in with their everyday life. And yes, they say lift instead of elevator and tap instead of faucet, but, as you'll see for yourself soon, because of their war effort over the past years the Brits are down to the bare bones, so with that in mind and with Christmas on the horizon, I'd like to let you in on a little initiative I'm setting up...'

He explained about the WVS, the relief centre in London and what they did, then told them about his plan for GIs to link up with them to help the children have a happy Christmas and for GIs to have the opportunity to celebrate the festive season with a family.

'Now.' Picking up the clipboard from the table next to his briefcase, Brogan held it up. 'If you'd like to put a smile on the faces of some London kiddies then sign your name, rank and unit on the dotted line or leave a message for me at the Office of War Information. It's round the corner from here in Chesterfield Gardens. Other than that...' His gaze ran over the sea of clean-shaven faces again. 'Dismissed, and enjoy your evening.'

There was a scraping of wood on wood and the rumble of male voices as the men rose to their feet and made their way out of the hall while Brogan gathered his papers together.

However, against the tide of GIs heading towards the exit was a captain, who looked about Brogan's age but with a slighter build, making his way toward him.

'Lieutenant Brogan?' he said, as he made his way up the stairs to the stage.

Brogan saluted. 'Sir.'

'Captain Holland,' he said, returning the salute. 'I'm an editor at the *Stars and Stripes* and based in Lincolns Inn House.'

'I know,' said Brogan. 'I read the leader you wrote last week about how Rommel's army are faltering in North Africa. Is it about the piece I submitted about Rainbow Corner?'

The captain shook his head. 'No, no, we're printing it in this Saturday's edition. And I would have phoned, but I was in the area and, as the clerk in your office said you were here, I thought I'd pop down in person. It's about this initiative you've set up to link American personnel with this British neighbourhood's Christmas celebrations. We'd like to do a feature on it for our Christmas week edition.'

'Do you want me to write it up?' asked Brogan.

The captain gave him a sideways smile. 'Not as such. We want the angle to be allies coming together during the festive season in the face of the enemy. I'll be sending Lenny Shurbin down to interview you, some of the servicemen who've volunteered and a few of the WVS women who are organising things, and take a few pictures.' He offered Brogan a card. 'This is his number, so give him a call and sort out the details.'

'I'll ring him first thing tomorrow,' said Brogan, taking the card and saluting.

His senior officer touched his cap, then turned to leave the stage, but after a couple of steps he turned back. 'What paper did you work for in New York?'

'The *Brooklyn Eagle*, sir,' Brogan replied. 'On the crime desk mainly.'

Captain Holland nodded and marched off the stage.

Brogan stared in disbelief after him.

Lenny Shurbin, one of the most respected journalists on the *New York Herald* and senior editor on the *Stars and Stripes*, was doing a special Christmas feature on his children's Santa initiative. However, somewhat to his amazement, the thing that him pleased him the most was not the golden opportunity it might give him to further his own career when he got home but the fact that Aunt Florrie and her WVS's constant hard work and selfless sacrifice were to be featured.

'Morning, Lieutenant,' said Sergeant Greenstein, saluting Brogan as he walked up to the polished wooden counter.

'Morning,' said Brogan, returning his salute.

'So,' said Greenstein, placing his hairy, shovel-like hands on the counter. 'What are you after this fine morning?'

'My usual dailies, half a dozen Hershey bars, couple of packets of gum and a couple of Marvel comics,' Brogan replied. 'I'm off to my aunt's tomorrow and I want to take something for the kids.'

It was a few minutes before eleven on a Tuesday in mid-December and he was standing in the US Army's Mayfair Post Exchange Store.

At thirty-five, Morry Greenstein was very near the upper age limit for active service but, as he owned a general store back home in Minnesota, he was in his element in the army's Quartermaster Corps.

Brogan would have to say that, of all the army's PXs he'd ever been in, this was by far the classiest. Unsurprising really, considering the US Army had taken over what had once been a medium-sized department store sitting on the corner of South Audley Street and Tilney Street.

Set over two floors, the requisitioned late-Victorian shop had an ornate ceiling supported by neo-classical columns and a sweeping staircase with wrought iron balustrade. However, the mahogany shelves lining the walls that had once displayed fine goods from all four corners of the British Empire were now filled with American-branded soaps, shaving creams, razors and toothbrushes, along with Lucky Strike and Marlboro cigarettes and tins of instant coffee. The glass display cabinets dotted around the floor had playing cards, baseballs, gloves and boxing gear in them. There was a music section on the second floor selling portable phonograms and the US Billboard top 40 records, plus a clothing section where you could purchase among other things underwear, watches and sunglasses. In short, everything the average American soldier needed to make them feel a little less homesick.

'You don't seem very busy,' said Brogan, glancing around at the handful of soldiers browsing the elegant art nouveau store.

'There's a baseball tournament in Kensington Park today between the boys from Signal and Engineer divisions, so I expect they've all gone there. I bet you're glad that things are picking up at Rainbow Corner,' said Greenstein as he gathered Brogan's order together.

'I sure am,' Brogan replied with feeling.

Now that London's newest American Red Cross canteen was up running like clockwork he would be able to concentrate on the Christmas party in Shadwell and convince Alice that he loved her and to marry him.

'Is Private Spiro around?' Brogan asked.

'Spiro!' bellowed the sergeant.

There was a pause, then Mikey, dressed in his everyday fatigues, appeared through the open stockroom door and saw Brogan. He sauntered over and saluted.

'How are things going with the collections?' Brogan asked as he returned the greeting.

'I've got half a dozen boxes full of goodies for Shadwell WVS sitting out back ready to go,' Mickey replied.

'That's swell,' said Brogan.

Greenstein cleared his throat.

'I guess this time of year a lot of the fellas are missing their own kids a bit more than usual. I know I am,' he said, gruffly.

'Plus,' continued Mikey, handing him a docket. 'I've managed to get you some of these, Lieutenant.'

Brogan skimmed down the sheet and his eyes widened in surprise. 'Where on earth from?'

'That's what I'd like to know, Lieutenant,' said Greenstein, eyeing his subordinate suspiciously.

'I told you, Skip, they're all legit,' Mikey replied. 'I've got a cousin in the Engineers.'

Brogan turned to Greenstein. 'Any chance of the use of one of your trucks tomorrow, Sergeant, and a couple of privates, so I can relocate the goodies to Shadwell?'

'There's no deliveries on the books until Monday, so I don't see why not.' Placing a brown paper grocery bag in front of Brogan, Greenstein looked him in the eye. 'Just make sure you bring it back in one piece or, with all due respect, Lieutenant, you'll be the one telling Captain Scott why.'

Brogan grinned. 'See you at oh-nine-hundred hours, Sergeant.'

Still smiling, he picked up his purchases.

An hour or so to load up, then three-quarters of an hour to drive through the city – by his reckoning he should be at the Shadwell Relief Centre just after eleven. He just hoped that Alice would be there too.

CHAPTER 21

'Right, girls,' George called, looking at Alice across the top of the upright piano. 'Let's take it from the top.'

Running her fingers deftly over the keys, she played the introduction to 'Who's Sorry Now?' and then, as she struck the opening chord, Alice, Nell, Maeve and Gwen leant into the microphone in front of them.

It was Wednesday and just before eleven thirty in the morning and Alice, along with her fellow Balloonatics, was on the Congregational Mission Hall stage rehearsing.

With the Shadwell WVS Christmas party and concert only a week and a day away, Florrie and her team were working hard to make the austere Victorian hall as festive as possible. There was a red postbox fashioned out of cardboard and crêpe paper for the children to post their letters to Father Christmas. Those in the after-school and Saturday clubs had been decorating the window shutters with robins, snowmen and brightly wrapped parcels cut from women's magazines. Paperchains made from strips of glossy periodicals were strung between the beams and a couple of the heavy rescue crew from the Cable Street depot had constructed a fairy grotto in the far corner, with an old leather armchair for Santa when he arrived on his sleigh. There was also a box full of donated tree ornaments, but unfortunately Florrie hadn't yet found a tree that Shadwell WVS could afford to hang them on.

Taking a deep breath, Alice waited for the beat, then she and her two friends sang, in close harmony, then left George to play the closing bars.

'Well done,' said George, beaming across at them. 'If you closed your eyes, you'd think it was the Andrews Sisters themselves singing.'

'Wot, dressed like this?' said Nell, indicating the working WAAF fatigues of serge trousers and a battle jacket that they were all wearing.

They laughed.

'Which number do you want to run through next?' asked George, running her fingers up and down the keys.

'What about "Straighten Up and Fly Right"?' suggested Gwen.

Alice and her friends nodded their agreement and George shuffled through the song sheets on the music rest. She ran through the opening refrain but then, as Alice opened her mouth to sing, the hall door flew open and Florrie hurried in, followed by Brogan.

At least she assumed it was Brogan because, other than a long pair of legs wearing fawn trousers and the lower half of an olive-green uniform jacket, the rest of him was hidden behind by a huge Christmas tree.

He wasn't alone – bringing up the rear, with Sam excitedly dancing around them, were half a dozen GIs, staggering under the weight of several crates, plus another, slightly built officer with a satchel slung across his leather flight jacket, carrying a flash camara.

The activity and chattering in the hall ceased as, with all eyes on them, the party marched into the hall. Under Florrie's direction the GIs carrying the crates headed for the kitchen, while the rest followed Brogan, who was still shouldering the tree, across to the fairy grotto. Putting their burdens aside, they helped him stand the tree upright and secure it in place.

Brogan stood back to survey his work, flexed his shoulders and then turned and looked around. His gaze skimmed over those in the hall until it alighted on her. As his eyes locked with hers, Alice's heart did a little fandango in response.

'Oh, it's Brogan,' squealed Gwen, clasping her hands together as she gazing adoringly across at him. 'Isn't he just sooooo handsome?'

She was right. Brogan looked good enough to eat. Blast him!

'Let's go and see what he's brought,' Gwen went on as she sprinted off the stage.

Closing the piano lid, George stood up. 'Looks like we're taking a break.'

Feeling Brogan's eyes on her, Alice followed her four friends off the stage and towards the refectory area. Suppressing the urge to go to him, she quickened her pace, but then Sam bounded forward into her path. Wagging his tail, he circled round her, desperate for her attention.

'Hello,' said Brogan, as he caught up with her.

She gave him a frosty smile.

'How are you?' he said.

'Well enough,' she replied, stroking Sam's head.

'I heard you've recently had a couple of heavy nights of bombing,' he said.

'We're used to it,' Alice replied.

Shifting his weight back and forth, Brogan frowned. 'Look, Alice, I meant what I said the other night. I love you. I do. I really do, and—'

'Brogan!'

Alice looked behind him and saw Gwen, who had been helping in the kitchen homing in on them.

'Brogan!' the young WAAF repeated as she came to a breathless halt next to them. 'It's been over two weeks since the dance. Where have you been?'

'I wanted to come to see you all last week,' Brogan replied, without taking his eyes from Alice. 'But I was ordered down to Dorset for work.'

'Well, we've missed you, haven't we, Alice?' said Gwen.

With Brogan still gazing down at her, Alice forced a friendly smile.

'But where on earth did you get the tree?' the young WAAF added.

'The US Army's engineering corps are building the airfields for our long-range bombers in in East Anglia and they're chopping hundreds of fir trees down in the process,' Brogan replied.

'Good of you to bring us one,' said Alice. 'Now if you'd excuse me.'

She hurried past him and joined her friends, who had sat down at one of the empty tables next to the serving hatch.

'I see Gwen has captured old handsome chops,' said Nell as Alice took the empty seat opposite her.

'Lucky him,' said Maeve.

'Here we are, chaps, tea,' said George, placing four mugs on the table. 'Made with the finest Darjeeling leaves, which for your delectation have been plucked in the early-morning mist of the Himalayan foothills.'

'Don't you mean ration-book Typhoo tea leaves?' said Nell.

George raised an eyebrow but didn't comment as she sat down.

Taking the mug nearest her, Alice raised it to her lips and blew across it.

'Oi, oi, look wot the cat's dragged in,' said Nell.

Shifting her attention from Brogan, Alice followed her friend's eyeline and saw Lily. She was standing alongside the ARP information table watching Florrie and a couple of the

WVS committee unpacking the one of the crates the GIs had brought in.

'Probably seeing if she can purloin something,' said George.

'Who's that she's talking to?' asked Maeve.

Alice's attention shifted from the crew's work-shy corporal to the American she was in conversation with.

Unlike most of the other soldiers heaving crates around, he was only just over middling height, and had tanned skin and dark hair. Also rather unusually, he wore a rather expensive-looking watch on his wrist.

'Search me,' Nell replied.

'He's not bad though if you like your men dark and broody,' added Maeve.

A deep laugh rumbled across the hall, dragging Alice's eyes back to Brogan.

The unexpected arrival of so many strapping Americans had caused a flurry of excitement, and they were now all the centre of predominantly female attention. Naturally, Brogan had his fair share of this admiration, including Gwen, who, much to Alice's irritation, was practically glued to his side.

Feeling an uncomfortable gnawing in the pit of her stomach, Alice watched as Brogan laughed and joked with those around him. As if sensing her eyes on him, he raised his head, and Alice's heart cantered off again as his gaze locked with hers.

He gave her a tentative smile but, feeling the pain of seeing him holding Gloria in his arms reigniting, Alice lowered her eyes and buried her nose in her drink.

Although he smiled and joined in the fun, as his aunt introduced the reporter Lenny Shurbin to everyone in the relief centre Brogan's whole focus was actually across the other side of the room on Alice. While Florrie ran through what the WVS did and what they had planned to cheer everyone up for Christmas, he tried to think of a plausible reason for going across to talk to her. Having run through and then discounted at least a dozen, he now resigned himself to casting furtive glances across the hall at her.

Despite his aching heart, a cynical smile raised one corner of his mouth. Boy, how the tables had turned. Gone was carefree Lieutenant Brogan Rafferty, sophisticated man about town, leaving in his place a lovesick tenth-grader who mooned about all day with his head in the clouds and was awake half the night conjuring up domestic scenes of married life with Alice – alongside more earthy ones of them as lovers.

If he wasn't so despondent about the complete mess he'd made of everything, he would have found his current predicament amusing.

'And this,' said Florrie, as she brought him and Lenny to a halt in front of a wooden arch with silver and green tissue paper leaves glued all over it, 'is our fairy grotto, where Brogan will hand out the presents. Of course, it's not quite finished, but once we stick the cotton-wool snow over it'll be just as good as the one up the road in Wickhams.'

Lenny gave Brogan a curious look. 'You're Father Christmas?'

Brogan nodded. 'The chap who was supposed to be doing the job was injured in an air raid last week, so I agreed to step in,' he explained.

'And that's what we do around here,' added Florrie. 'Pitching in. And that's what everyone's done here to make it a real family Christmas.'

'Is that what the British papers call the Blitz spirit?' asked Lenny.

'It is,' Florrie agreed. 'But it's not just the locals – others like my Women's Auxiliary Air Force girls have been no end of help down here at the relief centre since they arrived and I bless the day I agreed to billet them with me in the Maid of Norway.'

'Actually, Lenny,' said Brogan, nonchalantly. 'I've just spotted a couple of them over by the serving hatch. They might give the story another angle.'

Beneath his heavy brows, Lenny's eyes lit up. 'Why didn't you say sooner? Introduce me.'

Thankful for the excuse to seek Alice out again, Brogan followed on as his Aunt Florrie led Lenny across.

Alice looked up as they approached, and her eyes met Brogan's briefly before she looked away.

'Girls, there's someone wanting to meet you,' said Florrie, stopping by their table. 'This is Lieutenant Shurbin. He's here to do a bit about our Shadwell WVS festive celebrations for the army newspaper.'

'Afternoon, ladies,' Lenny said, touching the peak of his cap briefly. 'And we're all friends and allies here, so Lenny will do. I'm a reporter on the *Stars and Stripes*, which as Mrs Granger said is the US Army's daily newspaper. It's designed to keep the troops up to date with everything from the front line of fighting through to sport, and even has some funnies – cartoons, I think you call them. But I heard about the Christmas initiative Brogan helped set up and I thought it would make a grand double spread for the paper's Christmas edition. It's what we in the trade call a human-interest story. You know, the US and our British hosts working together in a spirit of peace and goodwill to bring Christmas cheer to the children. Now I've already got a fair idea about the way things are run around here but, when Mrs Granger mentioned that we also had some lovely ladies from the British Royal Air Force helping out with the celebrations, I just had to come over and say hello.' Lenny took his dog-eared notebook from his pocket and a pencil from behind his ear and dabbed the pencil on his tongue. 'So what is it you ladies are doing for the big celebration next week?'

'What aren't they doing?' chipped in Florrie, beaming at them. 'Making the decorations for the hall and knitting all manner of toys to wrap up as presents. Not to mention donating their sweet and sugar rations so we can make biscuits and cakes.'

Scribbling, Lenny looked suitably impressed.

'To tell the truth, it's Alice who roped us in,' said Nell. 'Plus, she's the one organising the children who are doing the nativity play.'

Lenny's eyes shifted to Alice. 'Isn't that a lot of work on top of your duties manning the balloon?'

'It is. But I get a lot of pleasure helping out in the WVS nursery,' she said. 'It's traditional for the children to put on a nativity play at Christmas, so I thought I'd organise it to remind people what the Christmas message is all about.'

Her lovely grey eyes flickered fleetingly to Brogan's face before she lowered them again, but not before he saw the sadness and longing in them.

Feeling his very soul aching to enfold her in his arms and take that pain from her, Brogan was just at the point of stepping forward when a voice cut across.

'And the Balloonatics were my idea,' said Gwen.

'The Balloonatics?' asked Lenny, looking a little confused.

'It's our singing group,' explained Maeve. 'A bit like the Andrews Sisters. We're singing a couple of ditties at the concert.'

George glanced at her watch.

'Speaking of which,' she said, putting her empty mug on the table, 'as we're all on duty at six, shouldn't we be getting on with our rehearsal?'

'Right you are,' Nell said, knocking back the last of her drink and then standing up.

Maeve and Alice did the same.

'Perhaps I could get a couple of photos before you carry on

with your practice?' said Lenny. 'Perhaps one of you girls all together.'

The five WAAFs shuffling around, then lined up, hugging each other round their waists.

'Perfect,' said Lenny, raising the camera and squinting through the viewfinder. 'Cheese!'

The girls smiled and the flash popped.

'Perhaps one of you, Mrs Granger, with the girls?' said Lenny, as he changed the flashbulb.

Florrie squeezed herself into the middle. They all smiled, and the flash popped again.

'Now lastly,' said Lenny, changing the flashbulb for the second time. 'One with Mrs Granger, one of the girls and Brogan.'

Gwen stepped forward, intent on being in the line-up, but before she could, Florrie hooked her arm through Alice's. 'Brogan, stand between me and Alice.'

Stepping forward, he took up position as instructed.

Enjoying Alice's nearness, he smiled as Lenny lined up the shot. The shutter clicked and white light cut briefly through his vision.

'Thanks,' said Lenny, giving them the thumbs-up. 'Now perhaps I can get a couple of you girls singing on the stage.'

Before Brogan could say anything to her Alice hurried off to join her friends, and he stared forlornly after her.

Florrie slipped her arm into his.

'Why don't you just tell her you love her, Brogan?' his aunt said, looking sympathetically up at him.

'I have, Aunt Florrie,' Brogan replied. 'Three times, but she doesn't believe me.'

Florrie fixed him with a steely gaze very similar to the one his mother occasionally employed. 'Well, boy, I suggest you keep on telling her until she does.'

~

'So have you got everything, Alice?' asked Nell, as they stopped outside the Blind Beggar public house.

Hooking her basket over her arm, Alice took a list out of her overcoat pocket.

'More or less,' she said, her tired eyes skimming down it. 'All we need now is something a bit special for Florrie as a big thank-you from all of us.'

As this was the last Saturday before Christmas, the street market that spread out either side of Whitechapel station, known locally as the Waste, was packed with shoppers trying to get a few extra bits for the big day.

The shops facing onto the market stalls were of the usual sort you'd expect to find on any high street but, although the news from Europe was increasingly cheerful, there was even less on display by way of presents and decorations than the previous year.

However, what the shops lacked in variety they made up for in enthusiasm – cut-out paper snowflakes were pasted around the edges of every front window apart from that of the kosher butcher next to Home and Colonial grocers.

The stallholders along the market had done their best as well and had created a bit of festive cheer by stringing bunting made from magazines along their awnings, and there were bunches of holly that had probably been cut in the dead of night from bushes in Epping Forest.

'How much did you get in the end?' asked Nell.

'Four shillings,' said Alice. 'As Lily and Maureen wouldn't chip in their tanner.'

'Blooming skinflints,' said Nell.

'There seem to be plenty of practical gifts in the shops such as knitting needles, blackout torches and packets of vegetable seeds,' Alice continued, putting the list away. 'But I want to get her something a bit more special. It's the least we can do considering all she does for us.'

'Well, I saw a decent selection of toiletries on that stall just past the station, so why don't we walk back and see if we can find something there,' said Nell.

'Good idea, but let's warm ourselves up with a mid-morning cuppa first,' said Alice, nodding at Alf's café on the corner of Brady Street, where people could be seen sitting inside enjoying elevenses.

The door to the café opened as they reached it, and they let the two postmen from the sorting office opposite come out and then stepped into the warm fug, heavy with the smell of coffee and fried food.

Although the corner restaurant had the same black-and-white wall tiles as dozens of other East End eating houses, with a selection of battered copper pans fixed to the wall behind the counter and paintings of Italian-looking landscapes on the wall, Alf's café had a distinctive Continental feeling about it.

'You find us a seat and I'll get our tea,' said Nell.

Spotting an empty table in the window, Alice made her way over while her friend went to the counter to get them their drinks.

Alice unwound her scarf, unfastened her greatcoat and then, placing her basket under the chair, she sat down.

She gazed idly out of the window at the late-morning shoppers.

'There we are,' said Nell when she returned carrying two steaming mugs in one hand and a plate with the same number of cake slices in the other.

After placing them on the table, she shoved her knitted scarf into her overcoat pocket and took the seat opposite. Picking up one of the slices of cake, she sank her teeth into it.

'I thought it went well with that American reporter Brogan brought down, don't you?' she said through a mouthful of cake.

Cradling the mug in her hands to warm them, Alice nodded.

'And I bet Florrie will be tickled pink when she sees herself and her Shadwell WVS girls in print when Brogan fetches her a copy,' continued Nell.

As always, the sound of his name brought images of the man and his words of love flooding back into Alice's mind. Not that they were ever that far away, as anything from a snippet of a song on the wireless to a dog barking would fill her mind with Brogan.

Raising her cup to her lips, Alice took a sip and, as Nell munched her way through her cake, her gaze wandered out of the window and along the row of market stalls opposite. Then she spotted a familiar-looking character through the steamy glass.

'Is that Lily over by the hardware stall?' she asked.

Nell paused mid-bite and her gaze followed Alice's.

'It is,' she said. 'But who's that bloke she's with?'

'I think it's one of the Americans who came down to the relief centre with Brogan the other day,' Alice replied. 'They look deep in discussion with the stallholder.'

'That's Bill Tugman,' said Nell, flatly. 'He's one of Dutch Holland's heavy mob, so I doubt they're asking him the price of his zinc buckets. Looks like they're waiting for someone—' She stopped as her one-time fiancé, dressed with his usual extravagant flair, emerged from the crowd. 'Charlie Mulligan,' she said, sourly. 'I might have known.'

'But do you know who that is with him?' asked Alice, looking at the tall young man in a wide-lapelled Crombie overcoat bowling along beside him.

'Unfortunately I do.' Nell's mouth pulled into a hard line. 'It's my brother, Frank.'

CHAPTER 22

Holding tightly on to Sam's leash, Brogan emerged from the bright lights of Piccadilly underground station into the freezing air of the winter night, which had more than a whiff of snow about it.

A Salvation Army brass band was playing 'God Rest Ye Merry, Gentlemen' and a couple of buskers were performing tricks to amuse passers-by and earn a few pennies.

Brogan dropped a few coins in the Salvation Army tin as he passed, then cut across Piccadilly Circus and headed down the street itself.

It was a week since he'd taken Lenny Shurbin to the Shadwell Relief Centre, and he'd set off back to Dorset the following day.

Although thousands of American service personnel had arrived in England in the past ten months, other than a handful of infantry and armoured divisions that had joined the British and Commonwealth Forces in North Africa, the rest of the US Army was holed up in Britain awaiting the order to cross the Channel. However, before they could set foot on French soil they had to prepare, and Brogan's task for the past five days had been to act as a conduit between the American army's top brass and the stout-hearted people of the little village of Tyneham. Not an easy task when the message he brought them was that they would to have to leave their homes because the American army was taking over in order to prepare for liberating Europe.

Thankfully, his work down there had concluded late last night and a day early, so, after several changes of train and a two-hour wait on Reading station, he'd finally stepped off the train at Paddington forty minutes ago. Much as he'd have liked to dive into Rainbow Corner and eat, Major Jessop was attending a meeting at the Ministry of War in the morning and would need Brogan's report from his trip to the West Country to take with him.

It was the day before Christmas Eve and the relief centre's party. Once the report was on his senior officer's table, he was on furlough for two whole days, so this time tomorrow he would have a long white beard and a bright red Santa costume and be doling out presents to children in the centre. And even more important – to him at least – he would have a chance to prove to Alice that he truly meant it when he told her he loved her.

Passing the hollowed-out shell of St James's Church, courtesy of the Luftwaffe two years before, Brogan continued on.

Despite the three years of bombing and shortages Londoners had endured, the capital was doing its best to put on its Christmas face. Though the blackout meant that the shop windows along Piccadilly were devoid of twinkly Christmas lights, there were still festive displays in the shop windows visible through the glass. Brogan passed Fortnum & Mason, with its display of ration-friendly Christmas food in the window, and Burlington Arcade, bustling with GIs and well-heeled Christmas shoppers, turned into Half Moon Street and then turned again, into Curzon Street. Now he was off the busy highway, Brogan let Sam off his leash and they walked through the tight-knit community of Shepherd Market towards Chesterfield Gardens. Brogan took the half a dozen steps up to the Office of War Information's entrance two at a time, walked in, returned the salutes of a couple of privates as he passed and continued on up the imposing late-Regency staircase to the second floor, where the London Liaison section of the OWI was located. He noticed that, although Major Jessop's secretary had gone home, the light in the major's office was on.

After putting his briefcase on his desk and telling Sam to stay, Brogan knocked once on the frosted glass of his senior officer's door and walked in.

Jessop, who was sitting behind his desk writing, looked up as Brogan entered.

'Rafferty,' he said, setting aside his pen. 'I thought you'd have been back hours ago.'

'So did I,' replied Brogan. 'But there was an unexploded bomb on the line, so the train was diverted to Bristol and then held for an hour at Swindon.'

'How was it?' asked Jessop.

'Difficult,' Brogan replied. 'You'll have the full report on your desk when you arrive tomorrow, but I suspect we'll be taking another couple of trips down to Dorset before we get everything smoothed out.'

'You're probably right,' Jessop replied. 'But you won't be the one going, Rafferty, because you're being transferred.'

'Transferred?' said Brogan, feeling as if ice water had been thrown over him.

'Yes. To North Africa,' Jessop replied. 'Algiers, to be precise. Apparently, your contributions to the *Stars and Stripes* have impressed the editors, and they're setting up an edition of the paper for the American troops out there and need a journalist.'

'When?'

'Two or three weeks,' his commanding officer replied.

Alice's lovely smile filled Brogan's mind.

'I haven't got all the details,' Jessop continued, oblivious to his subordinate's inner turmoil. 'But you're to report to the CO at Lincoln's Inn House at oh-nine-hundred hours Monday, and no doubt they will brief you about everything. Oh, and you're being promoted to captain. Congratulations. That'll be all.'

Slack-jawed, Brogan stared at Jessop for a second or two, then he snapped to attention and saluted, before marching out.

Sam raised his head but, sensing they weren't going anywhere any time soon, rested it back down again, as Brogan sat at his desk. Brogan retrieved his notebook containing his jottings of the past week and pulled the clunky khaki-coloured typewriter towards him.

He sat back and stared motionless at the wall opposite for a moment or two, then his mouth pulled into a tight line.

Well then. If he only had a few short weeks until he shipped out overseas, he had to convince Alice once and for all that he loved her – and soon. And what better place to do that than at Shadwell Relief Centre's Christmas celebrations tomorrow?

CHAPTER 23

Beating time with her hand, Alice mouthed the words, *'The cattle are lowing, the baby awakes,'* to the twenty or so children standing in front of her on the Congregationalist Mission Hall stage. It was just after five on Christmas Eve and, as the blackout was about to start, the long curtains at the hall's windows had already been drawn.

For those with tickets for the Shadwell WVS Christmas party, the doors of the centre had opened at three that afternoon. Two hours later, of the plates of sandwiches, flans, sausage rolls, jam tarts, fairy cakes and mince pies that Florrie and her team had been preparing since early that morning, only crumbs remained. Along with the crumbs, ripped crackers, discarded paper hats and dirty crockery were all that was left on the trestle table in the refectory area.

After the food had been demolished, the afternoon programme had moved on to the nursery children's nativity play, which they were just concluding with a couple of carols, 'Away in a Manger' being the final one.

Despite the shortages, the ladies of the WVS had pulled out all the stops, and the whole cast, from the lowly shepherds in the fields to the holy family, had been kitted out splendidly, from cannibalised tapestry and chenille curtains for the kings to chopped-up sheets for the shepherds and Joseph, plus tea towels as headgear, and a damask tablecloth fashioned into the traditional white robe for Mary, topped off with her veil made from blue skirt lining.

Behind Alice, sitting on the half a dozen rows of chairs, were the mothers, fathers, aunts, uncles and grandparents of the children on the stage, many of whom were holding handkerchiefs to their eyes.

Not that she blamed them one bit. You'd have to have been made of stone not to have a lump in your throat watching the 1942 Shadwell WVS Relief Centre nativity play.

Alice raised and lowered her hand once again and mouthed, *'and fit us for heaven, to live with Thee there'* before signalling the end.

Then she stepped to the side of the small thespians and indicated for them to take a bow.

There was a pause as the children did as they'd practised, then the audience burst into rapturous applause and whistles.

Clapping along with the rest, Florrie, in her full grey-green WVS uniform, climbed up the side steps onto the stage.

'Thank you so much, Aircraftwoman Starling,' she said as she reached Alice. 'You've done a splendid job with the nursery children. Hasn't she, everyone?' she shouted.

There was another burst of applause.

As she smiled, Alice's eyes skimmed over the men and women sitting in the audience and then, of their own volition, on to Brogan, who was standing at the back of the hall with a dozen or so other American soldiers.

Like Alice, Brogan had dressed for the occasion in his olive-green square-shouldered uniform jacket and snugly fitting fawn trousers. He also wore a look of utter devotion on his face as he gazed across at her, which came very close to dissolving her defences.

'Now,' continued Florrie. 'If everyone can pitch in with clearing away the chairs, we'll have a couple of party games and then' – her light blue eyes looked down at the thirty or so boys and girls sitting cross-legged in front of the stage – 'we might have a very, very special visitor...'

'Father Christmas!' screamed the crowd of children, bobbing excitedly up and down.

As mums and dads collected their children from the stage and everyone in the hall started moving chairs and tables, Alice made her way off the stage and over to the far corner, where Effie was sitting on one of the chairs ranged around the wall.

'Well done, Alice,' said her friend as she took the chair next to her. 'There wasn't a dry eye in the place.'

'Considering they are so young, the children did very well, didn't they?' said Alice.

'They certainly did,' agreed Effie.

'Although I'm a bit disappointed that baby Jesus had to be played by a doll swaddled in a couple of towelling nappies and not baby Fitzgerald,' said Alice, pointedly looking at her friend's expansive middle.

'I wish I could have obliged,' said Effie, running her hand over her stomach. 'Especially as this baby's kept me awake half the night shifting back and forth. Plus, today they must be lying on a nerve – I've got blooming backache as well.'

'Poor you,' said Alice. 'Is it very bad?'

'Thankfully it comes and goes, but I could do without it. Especially as Nathan's supposed to be arriving home at any time. Looks like the crew's enjoying the afternoon too,' she went on, nodding across to where Nell and Maeve were chatting to a couple of the GIs Brogan had brought with him. 'George, too. Although I'm surprised to see her sitting with Minnie and Artie Cadwell.'

Alice glanced across at her glamorous friend drinking tea with the two elderly spinsters.

'She met them at church, a few months back,' she said.

Effie's eyebrows rose in surprise.

'She sneaks into early communion at St Matthew's from time to time,' Alice explained.

Effie grimaced and arched her back.

'Are you all right, Effie?' asked Alice.

'I'm fine, honestly,' her friend said. 'But I think I might go back to the pub and put my feet up for an hour or so.'

'Do you want me to come with you?' asked Alice.

Effie shook her head. 'It's only ten minutes away. I'll be fine once I've had forty winks.' Smiling, she slowly rose to her feet. 'And don't worry, I'll be back in time to see the Balloonatics do their turn.' Her friend's eyes shifted briefly onto something behind Alice.

Alice turned and saw Brogan heading towards her, carrying a cup and with Sam at his side.

'My advice, Alice,' Effie whispered. 'Trust your heart. Not your head.'

With her gaze fixed on Brogan and conflicting emotions crashing around in her head, Alice couldn't reply.

'Good afternoon, ladies,' he said as he reached them.

'Afternoon, Brogan,' Effie replied as Sam greeted them with a wag of his tail.

'I just thought I'd come over and say that the nativity was really swell, Alice,' said Brogan. 'And I thought you might need this.' He offered her the cup.

'Thank you.'

She took it from him and her fingers brushed against his, sending the all-too-familiar shiver up her arm.

'No sugar. As you like it,' he added.

Alice was locked on his gaze and her heart thumped wildly as she gazed up at him.

'It was a great idea of yours, linking up with your aunt's WVS group,' said Effie, bringing Alice back to the here and now. 'And it looks like they're having as good a time as the children.'

Tearing his eyes from Alice, Brogan glanced across at a couple of GIs playing tag with a group of laughing children and smiled. 'I reckon they are.' He frowned. 'I'm sorry, Mrs Fitzgerald. I should have gotten you a drink, too. I'll—'

'Thanks for the offer,' said Effie. 'But I'm just going back to the Maid of Norway to have a little lie-down before the concert. If you'd excuse me.'

Giving Alice a meaningful look, she waddled off towards the door.

Alice gave Brogan a brittle smile. 'Thank you for the tea. But I ought to go and—'

'I'm being posted,' he said, his brown eyes looking deeply into hers. 'To North Africa. In a couple of weeks.'

'Oh,' said Alice.

'I won't deny that since I've been in England I've played the field,' he continued. 'But meeting you has changed everything. I love you. I love you more than I ever thought it possible to love anyone. And I want to spend my life with you. For us to raise a family together. I'm asking you to marry me.'

The hurt she'd endured for nine long years faded a little as hope struggled to break through, but then her fear returned and she looked away.

'Why is it so hard for you to believe me when I say I love you, Alice?' he asked, in a low, vibrant voice.

'It's not that I don't believe you,' she said, raising her head and looking at him.

'What is it then?' he asked. 'If it's Gloria then—'

'No, it's not Gloria,' Alice interrupted, shaking her head.

'Then what?' he asked, confusion and pain etched deep into his handsome face.

With the pain of her nine years of disappointed hopes and crushed dreams of being a mother gripping her chest, Alice raised her gaze to meet Brogan's.

'Because I can't have children,' she said flatly.

'You don't know that for certain,' said Brogan.

'I was married for nine years, Brogan, and never once in all that time did I conceive.'

'That doesn't matter to me, Alice,' he replied, as she stared up at him. 'It's you I love and want to spend my life with. And if we can't have children of our own, we can still have a family,' he continued. 'A family full of children who have lost their parents – and believe me, there'll be plenty of them around when this war's ended.'

Deep within her a tiny spark of hope flickered, and her resolve wavered; but, as her mind started conjuring up images of her with a babe in her arms and Brogan with children perched on his knee, her mother-in-law's cutting words loomed into her mind.

'I'm sorry,' she muttered, and dashed away.

With Alice's words rolling around in his brain, Brogan stared after her as she hurried across the hall.

'Brogan!'

Suppressing the urge to go after Alice, he turned, and saw Florrie, standing by the fairy grotto and beckoning him over him.

With his heart somewhere in his boots, Brogan made his way over to where his aunt was waiting for him.

'Sorry, but it's time for Father Christmas to make an appearance,' said Florrie, grabbing his arm and pulling him through the vestry door behind the fairy grotto.

Hooked up on the wall inside was a red Santa suit complete

with hood and fur trimmings and with a long white beard hooked round the hanger.

'It been made big, so it should go over your uniform,' said Florrie, taking it down from the peg and handing it to him. 'Although I think we'll need to stuff you with a few pillows.'

'Is the jeep ready?' Brogan asked, stepping into one of the trouser legs.

Florrie nodded. 'All loaded up with presents and parked round the corner.'

A team from the US Army maintenance corps had mocked up Santa's sleigh out of packing crates, painted it and fastened it over a jeep like a giant shell.

Tightening the cord through the trouser waistband, he tied it, then took the jacket from Florrie. He walked across to the long mirror fixed on the back of the door. Bringing the rest of his costume with her, Florrie came across to join him.

'Did you get anywhere with Alice?' she asked, as he buttoned the long tunic.

Brogan shook his head.

'What do you know about Alice's husband, Aunt Florrie?' he asked.

'From what I understand they were childhood sweethearts,' said Florrie. 'Arthur didn't know his father as he died in the Great War. He was an only child, and from what Alice has said I reckon he was a bit of a mummy's boy. His family had a long tradition of serving in the British army. So Arthur volunteered as soon as war was declared and was attached to his father's old regiment. He died on the beaches at Dunkirk waiting to board a rescue boat.'

'So, you've never had the impression that she was unhappy in any way?' Brogan asked.

Florrie shook her head.

'He sounded like a sweet boy. But his mother, she sounds like a miserable old battleaxe,' his aunt said sourly.

'She certainly is,' said Brogan, as his encounter with Mrs Starling senior flashed through his mind.

Florrie's pencilled eyebrows rose in surprise.

'I met her a few weeks ago when...' He told her about the invited guests' visit to Rainbow Corner.

'Well, reading between the lines, Arthur's mother made Alice's life hell because...' Florrie pressed her lips to together.

'Because she didn't have a baby?' said Brogan.

Florrie's pencilled eyebrows rose even higher. 'How do you know?'

'She told me herself just now.' Brogan recounted the conversation he'd had not ten minutes before. 'I told her it doesn't matter to me because I love her and want to marry her no matter what, but she didn't believe me.'

Florrie put her hand on his forearm. 'She's just scared of history repeating itself, that's all. Did you tell her you were being posted?'

'I did, and, before I ship out, I have to convince her that...'

Feeling hopelessness rising up, Brogan pressed his lips together.

He felt his aunt's soft hand on his arm. 'Don't worry, son, I'm sure it will come right. I know it.'

Brogan forced a smile. 'What's the expression you use around these parts, from your lips...'

'... to God's ears,' Florrie finished.

They exchanged a fond smile, then Brogan took the false beard from her. 'Now come on, Aunt Florrie, shake a leg. There are kids out there waiting for Santa, so where are those pillows?'

~

'This is where you're hiding,' said Nell, sitting beside Alice on the top step of the stage.

Alice gave her friend a wan smile. Of course she could deny she was hiding, but that would be a lie.

She was hiding because she feared that, if Brogan told her one more time he loved her, her resolve would crumble. To be honest, half of her wanted it to while the other, the scared, hurt half, was still much too afraid.

'You've missed Father Christmas arriving,' continued Nell, oblivious of the torture tearing at Alice's heart.

'I thought I'd hold the fort in here instead of getting in the way,' Alice replied. 'And Florrie asked me to keep hold of Sam.'

She indicated the dog, who, sensing her sadness, was curled up beside her with his head resting on her lap.

'Well, you missed a real treat,' said Nell. 'The team Brogan brought along had done the jeep up as a red-and-gold sledge with painted reindeer cut out of ply-board fixed to a frame on the front. Honestly, when the kids saw it they went wild with joy. And Brogan was right there in the thick of it, ho-ho-ho-ing with the best of them.'

'Yes, I saw that when he came in,' said Alice.

How could she not? Dressed in red, carrying a sack and surrounded by excited children.

As ever, as he walked in his eyes found hers and held them for a long moment before he disappeared into the fairy grotto. That was some thirty minutes ago and since then she'd sat on the stage steps with only Sam for company, watching the queue of children waiting patiently for their turn to visit Father Christmas.

'Well, goodness only knows what Florrie and her WVS girls will do next Christmas because I can't see them ever topping this one,' said Nell. She looked at her watch. 'Half six. I reckon another half an hour and we'll be ready to wave Father Christmas on his way and start the concert. I'll give it ten minutes, then I'll get those taking part togeth—'

The scream of the air-raid siren on top of the children's hospital a few streets away cut across Nell's words.

Chairs scraped and people in the hall started shouting as they moved around in response.

Ruth Goldstein, the Shadwell air-raid warden, in her tin helmet with a white W on the front, walked up onto the stage.

'Right, everyone,' she shouted above the racket. 'That was a ten-minute warning, so there's no need to panic. Parents, collect your children, and then everyone form an orderly queue into the basement. I repeat. No need to panic.'

Alice stood up. 'You take Sam, Nell, I've got to go back to the Maid of Norway.'

Nell grabbed her arms. 'You can't. You'll never get back in time!'

'I have to,' said Alice, shaking her off. 'Effie's in the pub.'

After fighting her way through the people heading for the Congregational Hall shelter, Alice reached the Maid of Norway some five minutes later. Retrieving the key from its hiding place behind a loose brick, she opened the door, and rushed into the dark, empty pub.

'Effie!' she shouted above the scream of the siren as she ran up the stairs.

'I'm up here,' her friend called back.

Taking the steps to the first floor two at a time, Alice dashed past the pub's family quarters to Effie's room at the back of the house.

A flash of red and yellow light streaked along the hallway as a distant boom indicated the German bomber had already reached Woolwich and Bermondsey, three or four miles to the south.

Alice swung round the doorpost into her friend's room.

'Can't you hear—'

She stopped dead at the sight of her friend, who was lying on the bed, with panic in her eyes. A pool of fluid was spreading across the floorboards.

'My waters went half an hour ago,' Effie said. 'I tried to get downstairs to telephone for help, but my legs gave way in the hall—'

Alice crossed the room and knelt down next to her.

'Are you having contractions?' she asked, taking her friend's hand.

Effie nodded. 'About one every fifteen min—'

Another blast from a bomb rattled the windows as Effie gasped and clutched her stomach. Closing her eyes tight, she gripped Alice's hand until the knuckles cracked.

Looking at her watch, Alice counted the seconds until her friend's contraction subsided and then stood up.

'Right,' she said, bending over and heaving Effie into an upright position. 'Baby Fitzgerald is about to make an appearance, and we've only got a few minutes until the Luftwaffe get across the Thames to us, so let's get you to the shelter.'

Leaving Effie sitting on the edge of the bed to catch her breath, Alice picked up the basket of towels, and the pads and baby clothes Effie had packed in a knapsack ready for the hospital, and returned to her friend.

Another bomb crashed to earth, somewhere close enough to shake the pub's floor and walls. Grit from the blast peppered the glass panes of the window.

Fear surged up but Alice thrust it away.

Her mouth pulled into a determined line. 'I think it's too late to get to the shelter, so I'm taking you to the cellar.'

Alarm flashed across Effie's face. 'What about if the baby comes?'

'Better I deliver it in the pub cellar than in the street with bombs raining down, Effie,' Alice replied. 'Now, let's get a move on.'

With the light fitting dancing from another explosion, Alice shouldered Effie's weight and, holding the knapsack in her other hand, walked her slowly out of the bedroom.

'Wait,' panted Effie, stopping, after they'd walked a few yards towards the stairs.

Bracing her hand against the wall, she bent forward. In the dim light from the flickering flames outside Alice counted the seconds as, breathing heavily, Effie let another contraction pass.

'That one was stronger,' she told Alice as her pain subsided.

Taking up Effie's weight and focusing on getting them to the relative safety of the public house's basement, Alice started towards the stairs again, but she'd only taken a couple of steps when something crashed through from above, bringing shattered timbers, fragmented bricks and smashed plaster with it, and Alice's whole world went black.

CHAPTER 24

'That's right, boys and girls, no pushing,' said Brogan, as the earth shook and the strip lighting above the Congregational Hall's basement stairs flickered. 'Aunt Florrie and her friends have bags full of candies and other goodies for you, plus a special treat: bottles of Coca-Cola,' he added, smiling reassuringly at nervous children streaming down to safety.

Thankfully, he'd just given out the last couple of presents when the siren went off, so, after stripping off his Santa costume, he'd joined in the efforts to get everyone to safety before the bombing started. That was twenty minutes ago and now, with the Luftwaffe raining death and destruction down on them from above, he was squeezed into the relief centre's cellar along with a hundred other people. However, notwithstanding the overcrowded conditions, his aunt's fellow WVS members had rolled up their sleeves and were already handing out cups of tea from behind the counter of the shelter's canteen to calm people.

The ground shook again as another bomb crashed to earth nearby and sent a gush of cordite-laden wind down the stairway from above as the final few stragglers reached the bottom of the stairs, the last one being Nell, with Sam hot on her heels.

Nell stopped on the last step, and her eyes skimmed those sheltering in the basement. She frowned. 'Have you seen Alice?'

'Isn't she with you?' Brogan replied, as Sam circled round him.

Nell shook her head. 'No. When the siren went off, she went back to the pub to fetch Effie. I told her they'd be cutting it fine to get back before the raid started but I thought they'd be here by now. Perhaps Florrie's seen her.'

Brogan glanced around and spotted his aunt helping a young mother soothe a fretful baby. He and Nell went over to her.

'Alice went back to fetch Effie when the siren went off – have you seen them come down?' he asked Florrie.

'No, I...' Horror spread across his aunt's face. 'You don't think...'

Brogan's mouth pulled into a hard line.

Signalling Sam to stay, he elbowed his way back to the stairs.

With his heart beating wildly and unthinkable scenarios crashing around in his mind, he stepped out into the street. The vacuum created by a blast nearby tugged at his hair and clothes. Brogan turned his coat collar up and tucked his chin down, then ran towards the Maid of Norway, his path lit by the factories and warehouses ablaze on either side of the road.

Three or four minutes later, Brogan was in sight of his aunt's public house, but there was an ARP van parked fifty yards back from it and a rope with yellow ticker-tape strung across from a couple of bollards blocking off the road.

'What's happened?' he asked the slim-faced warden as he came to a halt in front of him.

'UXB landed in the pub, mate,' the warden replied.

Looking over the man's black steel helmet, Brogan saw a gaping hole in the roof of his aunt's public house. He went to walk past but the warden raised his hand.

'Sorry, mate, no one's allowed,' he said, the flames from the burning buildings around them reflected in his eyes. 'Or do you think we've strung the rope across for fun?'

'But there's two women trapped inside and one of them is pregnant,' said Brogan, struggling to keep a grip on his rising panic.

'That's a crying shame, it really is,' said the warden. 'But if the rescue team go in to get them and the bomb goes off then there'll be a dozen more of us who'll be turning up at the pearly gates tonight, too.'

With fear tightening Brogan's chest and churning his stomach, he gazed across at his aunt's damaged pub. Then he sprang forward and, pushing the warden out of the way, dashed towards the pub.

But four of the men unloading equipment off the back of the heavy rescue vehicle left their task and hurried across.

'No you don't, mate,' said the unshaven individual grabbing hold of Brogan's right arm.

Brogan tried to pull himself free but couldn't.

They marched him back to the rope cordon and pushed him across to the other side.

'We've got enough to do tonight wivout bloody Yanks throwing their weight around,' said the older one of the group. 'Now push off or we'll call the rozzers.'

Clenching his fists and with his lips pressed firmly together, Brogan looked across at the damaged public house, silhouetted by the red and yellow flames of the buildings blazing around it.

Imagining Alice trapped, injured, with a bomb ticking

beside her threatened Brogan's sanity for a moment, but then he took a deep breath and raised his hands in surrender.

He turned round and, feeling several pairs of eyes boring into his back, retraced his steps towards the Congregational Hall. However, once he was sure the ARP workers couldn't see him in the darkness he slipped into an alleyway between two warehouses and hurried towards the river.

'That's it, Effie,' said Alice, dabbing her friend's forehead with a wet tea towel. 'Just breathe through the pain.'

Effie, who was sitting on the floor beside her surrounded by cushions, gave a little nod and gripped Alice's hand as another contraction started to build.

Having picked herself up from the floor, Alice found that, although she had no broken bones, a splinter from one of the falling beams had sliced a nasty gash across her forehead. Although it had bled all down her right cheek it was, thankfully, just superficial, so after holding a wound pad on it for a few moments she'd been able to staunch the flow. She had more pressing worries than a flesh wound. She'd heaved Effie off the floor. Taking her into the WAAFs' lounge, she barricaded her behind the two sofas in the furthest corner from the stairs. A short investigation had revealed that the reason for their predicament was a 250-kilo unexploded bomb that now sat halfway down the bottom flight of stairs. Unfortunately, along with the stairs and their escape route, the bomb had taken out the lights. Although Alice had pulled back the blackout curtains, the only illumination they had was her service torch and the red-and-gold glow of the blazing buildings around them.

As the wave of pain released Effie, she opened her eyes. 'Have the bomb disposal team arrived?'

Alice shook her head. 'Not yet.'

An unexploded bomb in a pub would be pretty low on a bomb disposal team's list of priorities compared to those in power stations and on railway lines. In fact, sometimes it took the army's bomb disposal units days to deal with those UXBs they classified as domestic, so Alice wasn't expecting to see them any time soon.

'And that's why we're getting out of here,' she said, letting go of her friend's hand and resuming her task of tying together the sheets she'd stripped from the WAAFs' beds.

With sweat glistening on her brow, Effie looked dubiously across at her from her nest of cushions. 'I don't think I can—' Grimacing, she clenched her fists as another contraction took hold.

'Of course you can,' said Alice, brightly. 'My sister was in labour for sixteen hours, so you've got ages to go. Besides, I'm not just going to sit around here doing nothing.'

To be honest, anything was better than nothing – although, if the bomb went off, she, Effie and her unborn baby would be blown to smithereens, literally.

Giving her friend a reassuring smile, Alice tied off the last two sheets, then, put her improvised ropes aside and stood up.

'Right, hold tight,' she said, tugging at the knots to tighten them. 'I'll be back in a jiffy.'

Creeping across the floorboards and back onto the landing, Alice glanced briefly over the banister at the inert metal cylinder that had trapped them on the first floor of the public house. The deadly armament, with its four crumpled fins, lay on the stairs like a cigar shaped egg in a nest of splintered rafters and broken roof tiles.

There was a flash of light through the side window over the stairs and the public house shuddered as another bomb landed nearby.

Panic started to bubble up again, but Alice shoved it aside.

She flattened herself against the wall and, careful not to kick any of the shattered bricks and plaster underfoot down the stairwell, she edged along to Dolly and Peggy's bedroom at the far end. Dashing to the window, she looked down into the pub's backyard below, then, as fast as she dared, hurried back to the lounge.

'Right,' she said, diving behind the sofa barrier. 'What we're going to do is—'

She stopped at the sight of Effie clutching her stomach with tears running down her cheeks and a terrified expression on her face.

'What's wrong?' asked Alice.

'The baby,' gasped Effie. 'I want to push—'

She confirmed her words by curling forward and straining as an explosion rattled the windows and set the coloured paper-chains strung across the ceiling swaying back and forth.

Ignoring the blood pounding in her ears, Alice forced a calm expression onto her face as she heard the distant sound of a fire engine bell. 'Let me take a look.'

Bending down, she lifted her friend's skirt and shone the torch beneath. Effie curled forward again as another contraction took hold, and then flopped back on the cushions supporting her.

'Well?' she asked.

Despite the fear coursing through her, Alice summoned up a reassuring smile and patted her friend's hand. 'It looks like you're going to have a Christmas baby after all. I'll get the hot water and towels.'

Scrambling to her feet, she raced next door into the WAAFs' kitchen.

With her friend groaning as another contraction pulsed through her, Alice pulled out an enamel pitcher and wash-bowl from the dresser. Thankfully the water in the kettle was still warm, so after decanting it into the jug Alice searched out half a dozen clean tea towels, a ball of twine and a pair of scissors.

After placing everything on the wooden draining board she loaded it into the bowl, but then she looked out of the window, across the open expanse of the yard 20 feet below, at the ack-ack guns' fire tracing an arc of dotted light across the ink-black winter sky.

Alice rested both hands on the edge of the butler sink in front of the window. Her head fell forward, and she closed her eyes as the despair of the situation swept over her.

In the darkness, her mind conjured up the image of Brogan, in his olive and fawn uniform, steady, calm, confident. Brogan would know what to do. There was a tap on the glass, and she looked up in shock to see the face she'd just imagined in her head looking through the glass at her.

'Open the window,' he called, clinging on to the lead drainpipe.

Stretching across the sink, Alice released the catch, then pushed up the lower section of the sash window.

Open-mouthed with disbelief, she watched him as he concertinaed his six-foot-two frame and climbed through.

'Oh... oh, Bro... Brogan...' Her words failed and she started to shake.

Stepping forward, he enfolded her in his arms, and she rested her head on his chest.

'It's all right, Alice,' he said, his words reverberating through her. 'It's all right.'

She rested in his embrace until she'd steadied her nerves, then she straightened up. 'What are you doing here?'

Brogan dusted himself down, then, reaching out his hand, ran his index finger gently down her cheek. 'I'm here for you, Alice. And Effie.'

Before she could stop it, Alice's heart did a little double-step; but the red flare of flames in the window and the cups on the dresser jingling brought her back to the here and now.

She looked bewildered. 'How on earth…?'

He peered out of the window he'd just entered. 'I scaled the timber yard's wall next door, then shinned up the drainpipe.' He spotted the gash on her head and frowned. 'What happened to your head?'

'A splinter, I think,' said Alice. 'But it's fine.'

'Are you sure?' he said, peering closer. 'Do you have a headache or double vision?'

'No, I'm fine,' Alice insisted. 'Which is more than I can say for Effie.'

'Where is she?'

'In the lounge behind the sofas.' She indicated the open door. 'She was in labour when I arrived, so I made a rope from some sheets so I could lower her out of the window, but then the baby decided to arrive—'

'What – now?' he said, alarm written large on his face as he raked his fingers through his hair.

A wry smile lifted the corner of Alice's mouth. 'I don't suppose they covered delivering a baby in your first aid training.'

'Not that I recall, but I'm hoping your training did.' He removed the torch from his pocket and switched it on. 'Where's the bomb?'

'Near the bottom of the stairs,' she replied.

Tucking his torch under his arm, he sighed, then he picked up the bowl from the draining board. 'Well I suppose we'd better deliver this baby and then get the hell out of here. After you.'

With Brogan half a step behind her, Alice hurried back through to the front of the house. She hunkered down next to Effie, wedged up against the underside of the old sofa, her teeth clenched and beads of sweat glistening on her forehead.

Alice gave her a reassuring smile. 'I've brought rein-forcements.'

Effie, whose hair was plastered to her forehead and cheeks with sweat, forced a grim smile. A blast somewhere close by shook the building.

The image of the bomb below them flashed through Alice's mind and, looking deep into Brogan's eyes, with her heart hammering in her chest, she held her breath.

The moment passed and Alice let out a long breath.

With grit from the ceiling pitter-pattering down around her, Effie curled forward again, straining.

'Put the bowl there,' Alice said to Brogan as she shifted around in front of her friend. 'And put your torch next to mine on the side table.'

Doing as he was asked, with the light beam pointing in Effie's direction, Brogan stationed himself discreetly next to her.

'What else can I do?' he asked, the light from the torch high-lighting the strong planes of his face.

'Cut me a couple of eight-inch lengths of twine, then put them on one of the towels next to the torches,' Alice replied.

After doing as instructed with the ball of string, Brogan took the flannel floating in the bowl, wrung it out and dabbed it across Effie's forehead.

Effie grasped Alice's wrist in a surprisingly strong grip. 'Everything's all right, isn't it?'

'Absolutely fine, lovely,' said Alice, trying not to think of the bomb ticking away two floors below them. 'And don't worry. I've been with my sister while she had all three of her children, so I'm an old hand at this.'

Gulping in air, Effie squeezed her eyes tight, then, gritting her teeth again, curled forward and bore down.

'Right, Effie,' Alice said, as the Canning Town ack-ack guns half a mile away fired off a round skywards. 'I think the baby's about to come, so next time another couple of pushes.'

'Pass me a towel,' she asked Brogan, reaching out without taking her eyes off the emerging baby. 'Now hold her hand,' she added and, bending forward, she spread the towel on the floor.

Effie roared and curled forward again.

'Chin in, Effie,' said Alice, cupping her hands under the baby's head. 'That's it. Push! A bit more. Push!'

Breathing heavily, Effie strained harder for a moment, then the infant's head emerged. Hooking her finger round the baby's neck, Alice checked for the cord, then, supporting the head with both hands, she looked up at her exhausted friend.

'One big push—'

Effie curled forward again and as the contraction reached its peak the rest of the baby emerged.

'It's a boy, Effie,' Alice cried, beaming from ear to ear as she wrapped the newborn in a towel. 'You've got a son.'

Effie's exhaustion disappeared in an instant and she laughed joyously.

Looking somewhat stunned, Brogan smiled at Alice.

'Well done,' he said in a soft voice as he gazed at her cradling the baby.

Just to confirm that he had indeed arrived, Master Fitzgerald let out a cry.

Tucking the tiny infant firmly into the towel, Alice cradled him gently in her arms and gazed down at him.

From nowhere, tears suddenly shimmered on her lower lids as the familiar ache of years of disappointment clawed at her chest. She raised her head and found herself looking into Brogan's dark brown eyes, which had an expression in them she'd never seen before.

They stared at each other for a second or two, then the baby cried again. Red-faced and sweating, Effie reached for her son. With emotion almost overwhelming her, Alice tore her gaze from his and placed the baby in her arms.

'Congratulations, Effie,' said Brogan, rising to his feet. 'Now I think it's about time we all got out of here.'

By the time Brogan returned to the lounge Alice had cut the baby's cord and helped straighten Effie's clothing as best she could. He was carrying one of the blankets she'd stripped off Dolly's bed and as he walked in his dark brown eyes fixed on her immediately. There was a moment's pause, then he glanced briefly at Effie, who was resting back on the upturned sofa cradling her infant.

He beckoned to Alice and, giving Effie a reassuring smile, she stood up and went over.

'Will the sheets tied together do the trick?' she asked in a low voice.

Brogan nodded. 'I'll lower you first so you can help Effie and the baby down, then I'll follow.'

'Let's go,' she said, taking the blanket from him.

'Right, Effie,' she said as she hunkered down, and wrapped her friend and baby tightly in the blanket. 'We need to leave. Can you stand?'

'No need,' said Brogan.

He bent down, tucked his arms beneath Effie and scooped her up effortlessly from the floor. Holding the new mother in his arms, he looked at Alice and smiled.

'Let's get out of here.'

With Alice half a step behind him, they made their way in single file along the hallway, back to Dolly and Peggy's bedroom.

Brogan had already tied Alice's sheet rope to the cast-iron frame of Peggy's bed. Placing Effie and her baby down gently on Dolly's bed, he turned to Alice.

'Ready?'

Although she was not at all sure she was ready to swing down two storeys on sheets tied together, Alice nodded.

He handed her the end and Alice tied it tightly round her waist, then climbed onto the chest of drawers beneath the window and sat on the windowsill.

Brogan wrapped the sheets round his arms and braced his long legs against the skirting board. Alice looked at him for a moment, then swung her legs out.

The freezing winter air swirled around her, nipping at her nose and ears. Although the acrid smell of cordite filled her nose, alongside it was the faintest hint of snow swirling in the atmosphere. Pausing, she looked ahead at the burning docklands for a moment, then as an explosion somewhere to the east of them lit up the navy-blue sky, she said a small prayer, pressed her lips into a determined line, grasped the sheet with both hands and slipped off the ledge.

After what seemed like an eternity of dangling in the air, her feet touched the cobbles below.

Brogan's head appeared above her. 'Are you all right, Alice?'

'I'm fine,' she called up as, with shaking fingers, she untied the sheet from round her waist.

Flapping in the night air, it disappeared upwards.

There was a pause, then Brogan's head appeared again. 'I'm lowering the baby.'

Holding the sheet firmly, he held a small white cocoon of sheeting away from the window. Then he lowered it slowly down into Alice's waiting arms.

In the red glow of the burning warehouses and with the drone of enemy planes flying overhead, Alice gazed down at the newborn infant. Effie's son, not yet an hour old and born with a war raging around him, lay swaddled in knitted blankets, gazing up at her with calm brown eyes. Alice's heart squeezed, then squeezed again as the empty, childless years of her marriage crushed her anew.

'Stand ready,' Brogan shouted.

Pushing her heartache aside, Alice placed Master Fitzgerald securely on a beer crate and then looked up again.

'Copy,' she shouted, spreading her feet to balance herself ready to help her friend.

Above her head Effie's feet appeared over the edge of the window and then, with the sheets tied round her, and Brogan gripping tight to the other end, Effie slowly descended to the yard.

With her arms outstretched, Alice caught her friend. She helped her across the stone-floored yard and sat her down on one of the empty barrels, then collected the baby from where she'd left him and handed him to his mother. When she was satisfied that both mother and baby were unharmed, she turned back, and saw that Brogan had already climbed halfway down the wall. However, as his boots scraped the top of a ground-floor window one of the sheets holding him ripped. Alice watched in horror as in what seemed like slow motion he crashed to the ground.

Alice dashed across to him and threw herself on the cold stones of the yard, where he lay on the ground with his eyes closed.

'Brogan!' she shouted, and put her arms round his neck. 'Brogan!'

His eyes opened and relief flooded through her.

His dark brown eyes held her grey ones for a long moment, then, as she struggled against the urge to press her lips onto his to protect her heart, the baby's cry cut between them and she looked away.

Brogan sighed, then eased himself up onto his feet a little stiffly and strode over to Effie. He lifted her in his arms again and headed for the yard door, which Alice opened for him. The wail of the all-clear started as they walked briskly away from the pub. They turned the corner onto the Highway and continued on until they reached the ARP barrier a hundred yards away.

As they approached, a couple of the wardens, who had been leaning against a warehouse wall smoking, stood up and came towards them.

'I've got a mum and newborn here,' said Brogan as they reached the rope cordon. 'Any chance of you guys fetching an ambulance?'

'Are you warm enough, Effie?' said Alice, her breath little puffs of steam. She was walking beside the stretcher on which two first aiders carried Effie towards the Red Cross ambulance.

Effie nodded as she tucked the blanket a little tighter round her baby's head.

It was now just before nine o'clock and, although the fires still raged around them, the German planes were now on their way back to their bases in northern France, having emptied their loading bays of bombs. Around them the fire brigade, heavy rescue and first aid teams were already whizzing up and down the road dousing flames, shoring up buildings, rescuing those trapped and treating the injured.

As they reached the ambulance, which was in fact a converted horsebox, Alice paused and stood back to let them load Effie on the vehicle, but Effie caught her arm.

'You're coming with me, aren't you, Alice?' she said.

Alice looked across at one of the young women in ambulance uniform, who gave a little nod.

'Of course I am,' she replied, patting her friend's hand. 'I'll jump on board once they've got you both settled.'

Effie released her hand.

Alice stepped back and, as she turned to Brogan, who was standing behind her, a couple of snowflakes fluttered down and landed on her cheek.

Placing a hand on his forearm, she looked up at him. 'Just saying thank you doesn't seem enough.'

With the reflection of the burning city flickering in his eyes, Brogan gazed down at her. 'Seeing you safe is all the thanks I need, Alice, because I love you.' That smile of his lifted the corners of his lips. 'After all, only a man crazy in love would have walked across the top of the twenty-foot-high nine-inch-wide wall at the side of the Maid of Norway. I only wish you could let yourself believe me and allow us to have a happy life together.'

An urgent whistle cut between them. Alice looked round and saw one of the nurses beckoning her.

'I know,' he said. 'You have to go.'

With conflicting emotions swirling in her chest, Alice gazed up at Brogan for a moment, then, bobbing up onto the balls of her feet, she placed her hands on his chest and pressed her lips onto his stubbly cheek. Then she turned and, with tears pressing at the back of her eyes, dashed towards the waiting ambulance.

CHAPTER 25

'I trust you had an enjoyable time at your aunt's Christmas party, Lieutenant, or perhaps I should say, *Captain* Rafferty,' said Harris, as Brogan walked into the Jules Hotel lobby. 'And although it is perhaps a little premature, may I wish you a happy Christmas.'

Brushing the light dusting of snow from his shoulders, Brogan forced a smile. 'And to you too, Harris.'

'Looks like we're going to have a white Christmas,' said the hotel's elderly steward.

'So it does,' Brogan replied.

It was now just after ten in the evening and, after ensuring his aunt and everyone else sheltering beneath the relief centre were safe, Brogan had headed back to his billet. As the jeep he'd come in was parked alongside the Maid of Norway and its unwanted guest, he had walked the five and half miles back from Shadwell. By the time he reached St Paul's Cathedral half an hour later it was falling in earnest, and as he entered Leicester Square it was settling on walls, postboxes and the boarded-up statue of Eros in Piccadilly Circus.

'And chef would like to know if you will be requiring Christmas dinner tomorrow?' added the hotel's elderly retainer.

'Thank you but, no,' Brogan replied. 'I'll be eating out.'

Harris nodded. 'At your aunt's public house?'

'At Rainbow Corner,' Brogan replied, shrugging off his overcoat and hanging it on the hall stand.

To be honest, the last thing he was up for at the moment was socialising, so the anonymity of tucking himself into Rainbow Corner's library all Christmas Day would suit him just fine.

'All of us at the Jules are sorry to see you depart, Captain,' said Harris.

'Thank you,' Brogan replied. 'You've all been very kind, and the stay here's been swell.'

The lobby manager gave him a polite smile. 'Will you require assistance to pack?'

Brogan shook his head. 'Thank you, no. Is Sam in the kitchen?'

'He is,' Harris replied. 'Keeping an eye on the proceedings.'

Brogan went through to the kitchen at the rear of the building.

After receiving his usual unrestrained greeting from the dog and letting him have a quick sniff around in the hotel's backyard, Brogan, with Sam trotting at his heels, made his way to the bar.

He wasn't the only GI who was shipping out after the holidays; he recognised a couple of lieutenants from the transport and logistical corps gathered at the bar. Judging by their unsteady gait and raucous conversation, they had clearly started their farewell drinks and festive celebration a great deal earlier in the day.

Telling Sam to wait beside the door, Brogan made his way over to the far end of the bar.

'Bourbon,' he said. 'And make it a double.'

His drink arrived and, after thanking the barman, Brogan called Sam to him, then made his way over to an empty table in the corner. Knowing the score, Sam settled down under a chair while Brogan slouched in another. Brogan swallowed a mouthful of his drink, ran the glass back and forth between his fingers and stared broodily into the dark-amber liquid.

Seeing as the temperature outside was hovering just below freezing, most people wouldn't have relished the prospect of an hour-long trek. However, after watching the ambulance drive away, taking Alice and his happiness with him, Brogan was pleased to walk through London's wintery streets in an attempt to cool his burning heart. It hadn't worked. If anything, his solitary contemplation while he passed through the bomb-damaged thousand-year-old city had made his pain worse. He'd tried to convince himself that his feelings for Alice were nothing more than one of hundreds of wartime romances, passions ignited by the danger and drama and doomed to fizzle out when peace eventually came. But his heart wouldn't buy it, because his love for Alice would last into eternity.

As he threw back another mouthful of drink, Brogan's attention drifted over to the collection of GIs at the bar.

'A toast,' shouted a captain with fair hair, raising his glass high. 'To all the lovely ladies who have made us very welcome in Old London Town.'

'And in their beds,' slurred one of his friends, sloshing his drink over the edge of his glass as he held it up.

Those around him sniggered as the dozen or so officers raised their drinks high then took a large swallow.

'And,' continued the captain, holding his drink aloft again, 'may the wee lassies of bonny Scotland be just as friendly.'

Ashamed that only few short months ago he would have said the same thing, Brogan knocked back his drink.

'Come, Sam,' he said, rising to his feet. 'Let's get some air.'

'He's such a handsome young man, don't you think?' asked Effie softly without taking her eyes from the sleeping infant in her arms.

Alice, who was sitting on the visitor's chair by her friend's bed, nodded. How could she disagree? Her friend's newborn son was nothing short of perfect. A perfect Christmas baby.

'He certainly is,' said Maeve, who was standing on the other side of the bed.

'He looks like his father,' said Nell, who was standing next to her, her arm slung around George's shoulders.

She was right. Effie's husband Nathan was from Barbados and one of the hundreds of men from the British colonies who had left their homes to help defend Britain from the enemy, and his son had his light brown skin and dark curly hair.

The girls of Woman's Auxiliary Air Force Balloon Command no. 3 crew attached to number 312 site were standing round Effie's bed admiring their friend and one-time corporal's newly arrived offspring, and had been for the past ten minutes.

Effie's bed was halfway down the row, almost opposite the nurses' station, where a couple of nurses sat, with crêpe paper Christmas hats over their frilly one. There was also a foot-high, cardboard Christmas tree with silver foil decoration in the corner of the desk. There was only a dim light beside the two nurses and the blackout curtains were pulled tight, so, other than the odd little cry and the whispers of mothers soothing their children, the ward was quiet.

'What are you going to call him?' asked Maeve.

'Patrick,' said Effie.

Maeve looked puzzled. 'Patrick?'

'Yes, I thought you and Nathan had decided on Charles, after his father,' said Nell.

'We had,' agreed Effie. 'But I remember Florrie mentioning that Brogan's middle name was Patrick, and after all he did to get us out... I don't think Nathan will mind.'

The image of Brogan looking through the window at her flooded back into Alice's mind. The memory of his smile joined it, then the feel of his reassuring arms round her.

'I'm sorry, ladies,' whispered a soft voice, cutting across Alice's dreams.

She turned to see one of the night nurses in her lilac striped uniform, standing at the end of Effie's bed.

'Matron will be doing her rounds in a while,' the nurse continued. 'And there'll be hell to pay if she finds four of you here. One of you can stay for a little bit longer, but I'm afraid...'

'No bother,' said Nell. 'We're on duty at six so we ought to get some shut-eye.'

'You can't go back to the Maid of Norway,' said Effie.

'No, we're having to squeeze in with Millie's number 9 crew in the boys' orphanage until Florrie gets the dear old Maid repaired,' said George. 'Now we ought to go.'

Alice started to rise but Effie stretched out and placed one hand over hers.

'I just want to have a quick word,' she said.

'See you back at the billet,' whispered Nell.

Waving their farewells, the three friends crept out of the silent ward as Alice resumed her seat.

'I just wanted to thank you, again,' said Effie softly, looking at her and squeezing her hand. 'Thank you for coming back and delivering Patrick. I couldn't have done it without you.'

'Well, I think you did most of it yourself, Effie,' said Alice.

'Even so,' said Effie. 'I wanted to thank you – and Brogan. I never had a chance to thank him properly for what he did because the ambulance whisked me away.'

Alice's heart ached at the sound of his name.

'And about Brogan, Alice.' Effie squeezed her hand. 'You love him, don't you?'

Emotion filling her heart, Alice nodded.

'Well then,' continued her friend.

Alice's gaze shifted to the newborn baby in her friend's arms. 'But what if—'

'You can't have children?' asked Effie.

Again, Alice nodded.

'Do you really think Brogan will love you any less?' asked Effie. 'Because I certainly don't. Forget the past, Alice, and grasp your second chance for love and happiness.'

Patrick gave a little cry and Effie's focus immediately shifted to the infant in her arms as he started rooting around.

Shifting her position, Effie unfastened her nightdress and offered him her breast, which he latched onto immediately.

With thoughts tumbling around in her mind, Alice watched her friend nurse her infant son.

The ward door creaked open and Alice looked round, expecting to see the matron in a navy uniform. Instead, a tall RAF officer with light brown skin and wayward black curls strode onto the ward.

As she looked up from her son, Effie's eyes lit up.

'Nathan!' she cried, her voice breaking.

'Effie!' Nathan hurried across, threw his cap on the bed and scooped Effie and his newborn son into his arms.

Rising from her seat, Alice stepped back, and watched as husband and wife, lovers for life, lost themselves in each other. As never before, calm and certainty settled on her.

A smile spread slowly across Alice's face.

After a moment Nathan released Effie from his embrace and turned to Alice.

'I went to the Maid of Norway and Florrie told me what happened this evening,' he said. 'How can I ever thank you and Lieutenant Rafferty, Alice?'

'You don't have to,' Alice replied. 'It's thanks enough to see you safely home, Nathan, so you and Effie can have your first Christmas as a family.'

She went round to the other side of the bed and smiled down at baby Patrick, who had nodded off into a milk-drowsy sleep, then leant forward and gave her friend a peck on the cheek.

'I've got to go,' she said.

'Where?' asked Nathan.

Alice and Effie exchanged a fond smile.

'Where she was always meant to be,' Effie replied.

Wrapped in his greatcoat with the collar turned up and the peak of his cap pulled down, Brogan sat hugging himself as Sam frolicked around catching snowflakes in his mouth. Brogan had taken him on their usual walk into Green Park and then across Piccadilly into Shepherd Market before arriving back in Grosvenor Square. Having brushed off the snow, he was now sitting on one of the benches in front of the American Embassy. He and Sam had been there for some time, but he had no inclination to move. Why would he, when all he had in front of him was a life without Alice?

As if to torture him further, in the dark of the winter night blackout, dotted around the square were couples on benches, locked in each other's embrace, visible only by the dim outline from their muted torches.

Given her obvious love of children, clearly the years of constant disappointment had taken their toll on Alice's emotions. And as much as he'd always wanted a house full of children, he wanted – no, *needed* Alice even more. Perhaps he could have convinced her that he loved her and that she was enough for him and begged her again to marry him if he had

had more time. But time was the one thing he didn't have right now. Nothing short of a Christmas miracle would mend his bruised and battered heart, and they were always in short supply.

A cynical curl lifted one corner of his mouth and, turning his collar up a little further round his ears, Brogan continued his contemplation of the tips of his boots as the snow fell noiselessly around him.

A woman's tinkling laughter drifted over. Brogan raised his head and, straining his eyes, peered into the darkness and looked across the snow-covered bushes towards the gate on the south side. Through the gently falling snow he saw the outline of a woman, wrapped up against the cold, entering the square. Then, stopping, she looked around. Sam, who had been dancing around a bush, suddenly stopped and, with his tail wagging furiously, he dashed towards her. Bending down, the newcomer made a fuss of Sam, then looked over his head to where Brogan was slumped.

With his heart thumping painfully in his chest, Brogan rose to his feet. He started forward and she did the same; then they both broke into a run, but stopped a few feet apart. Hardly believing his eyes, he stared at her as a dusting of snow settled on the shoulders of her WAAF greatcoat and she gazed up at him with her lovely grey eyes.

'Alice? What are you doing here?' He frowned. 'There's nothing wrong with Effie and the baby, is there?'

Laughing, she shook her head. 'No, no. They're both fine. In fact, better than fine. Nathan arrived at the hospital. They've named the baby Patrick, after you, Brogan.'

'Did they?' he said, feeling more than a little touched by the news.

'I'm here looking for you,' she continued. 'The young lad on the desk in your hotel told me you might be here. I would have been here sooner, but it took me ages to flag down a taxi on Mile End Road.'

'Well, it is Christmas Eve,' Brogan replied.

'I know,' she said. 'But I just had to find you.'

'Did you?'

'Yes, I did.' She took a deep breath. 'I had to find you, Brogan, because I love you.'

Alice crossed the space between them and, sending his cap tumbling to the floor as she did, threw her arms round his neck and pressed her lips onto his. It took a second for his mind to catch up with his body, but then his arms closed round her and he kissed her back.

As his arms encircled Alice, all the pain and crushing disappointment she had endured in the past evaporated instantly, leaving only a future filled with love and the man she would love to the end of her time on earth.

Losing herself in his embrace, Alice clung onto him, enjoying the feel of his hard body against her and the magic of his lips on hers. Reluctantly, she drew back and looked up at him through the snowflakes glistening on her eyelashes.

With her arms still wrapped round his neck, she smiled up at him.

'I love you, Brogan,' she repeated. 'And I'm sorry it took me so long to tell you.'

Looking down at her with love shining from his dark brown eyes, Brogan's arms tightened round her.

'You have now and that's all that matters,' he said, in a low, vibrant voice that set her pulse galloping off.

Releasing her, Brogan took off his glove and pulled the signet ring off his little finger. Then he went down on one knee on the snow and took her left hand.

'So, I ask you again, Alice,' he said, looking earnestly up at her. 'Will you marry me?'

Feeling as if her heart would burst with happiness, Alice nodded. 'Yes.'

He slipped his ring onto her third finger. 'I know it's a bit big, but it will have to do until I can buy you a proper one.'

'Don't worry, I'll put it on a chain,' she said.

Brogan kissed her hand, then stood up and took her in his arms again and pressed his lips on hers for another heart-stopping kiss.

Then he raised his head and frowned. 'I have to get permission, which can take an age as the top brass aren't keen on serving soldiers marrying – plus, as I said, I'm shipping out the day after tomorrow, so I can't say when we will be able to tie the knot, but I will come back—'

'I know,' said Alice. 'And I'll wait for you. Why don't you leave Sam with me to keep me company?'

'Are you sure? I was worrying about having him so near to the battlefield if I took him to Africa.'

'Of course,' said Alice. 'The balloon site could do with a guard dog.'

Looking down with love brimming in his eyes, Brogan lowered his lips to hers for a tender kiss but then, as he raised his head, frowned. 'God, I wish I didn't have to go so soon.'

'So do I, my love, but...' Stretching up, Alice ran her fingers through his springy curls and then, grasping them firmly, pulled his head down. She pressed her lips on his again but this time opened her mouth under his for a long moment before she tore her lips free. 'We now have forty-eight hours,' she said, glancing up at him from beneath her eyelashes. 'And I'm not on duty until Tuesday.'

Grinning, Brogan gathered her to him again and kissed her. That kiss that promised everything for the future.

The clock of a nearby church started chiming out midnight.

Brogan took his fiancée's hand. 'Happy Christmas, Alice,' he said, pressing it to his lips.

'Happy Christmas, Brogan,' she replied.

With his free hand he picked up his fallen cap and set it on his head at its usual jaunty angle. Hand in hand and with Sam leaving muddy footprints in the white snow as he trotted beside them, they set off across the square.

Holding his hand as she walked beside Brogan, Alice wondered why it had taken her so long to accept his love, but now she had all the pieces her life made perfect sense.

He would be gone soon, too soon, but Alice knew that, when he returned, she would have the happy marriage and, please God, the children she had always dreamed of, and that was certainly worth waiting for.

A LETTER FROM JEAN

Dear reader,

I want to say a huge thank you for choosing to read the second in my East End Girls series, *Winter Wishes for the East End Girls*. If you did enjoy it, and want to keep up to date with all my latest releases, just sign up at the following link. Your email address will never be shared and you can unsubscribe at any time.

www.bookouture.com/jean-fullerton

I hope you loved Alice's story in *Winter Wishes for the East End Girls* and, if you did, I would be very grateful if you could write a review. I'd love to hear what you think, and it makes such a difference helping new readers to discover one of my books for the first time.

I love hearing from my readers – you can get in touch through social media or my website.

Thanks,

Jean Fullerton

KEEP IN TOUCH WITH JEAN

www.jeanfullerton.com

facebook.com/AuthorJeanFullerton

instagram.com/jean_fullerton

ACKNOWLEDGEMENTS

As always, I would like to mention a few books, authors and people to whom I am particularly indebted.

In order to set my characters' thoughts and worldview authentically to the harsh reality of life on the Home Front during the Second World War I returned to *Wartime Britain 1939–1945* and *The Blitz* (both by Juliet Gardiner) and *The East End at War* (Rosemary Taylor and Christopher Lloyd). However, to reflect the true nature of Alice and her friends' lives as a WAAF barrage balloon crew in wartime East London, I was greatly helped by returning to the autobiographies I'd used previously, including *Our Wartime Days* (Beryl Escott), *Living Dangerously* (Betty Farley), *Spit, Polish and Tears* (Norman Small) and *We All Wore Blue* (Muriel Pushman), along with *World War II British Women's Uniforms* (Martin Brayley and Richard Ingram) and *Balloons at War* (John Christopher). I'm also grateful to the website *A History of RAF Cardington 1936–2000* (www.rafcardington.org.uk).

For Brogan's experiences in the US Army's Office of War Information (OWI) and Public Relations, based in the heart of Mayfair, I am indebted to *Overpaid, Oversexed and Over Here: The American GI in World War II Britain* (Juliet Gardiner), *WWII Letters from England: An American Soldier Writes Home, Book 1* (Susan Sommers Thurman) and *US Army Handbook, 1939–1945* (George Forty).

Lastly, to ensure I had Brogan's uniform correct I consulted *An Illustrated Encyclopedia of Uniforms of World War II*

(Jonathan North and Jeremy Black). Anyone interested in learning more about how GIs were introduced to the British way of life can watch the US Army's *How to Behave in Britain* www.youtube.com/watch?v=SyYSBBE1DFw&t=22s (contains language of the period).

Lastly, I would also like to thank a few more people. Firstly, my very own Hero-at-Home, Kelvin, for his unwavering support, and my three daughters, Janet, Fiona and Amy, who listen patiently as I explain the endless twists and turns of the plot. Kate Burke from Blake Friedmann Literary Agents for her steadfast support and encouragement. A big thanks goes to Lizzie Brien for her detailed and insightful edits, and the rest of the wonderful Bookouture team for all their support.

RAISING READERS
Books Build Bright Futures

Dear Reader,

We'd love your attention for one more page to tell you about the crisis in children's reading, and what we can all do.

Studies have shown that reading for fun is the **single biggest predictor of a child's future life chances** – more than family circumstance, parents' educational background or income. It improves academic results, mental health, wealth, communication skills, ambition and happiness.

The number of children reading for fun is in rapid decline. Young people have a lot of competition for their time, and a worryingly high number do not have a single book at home.

Hachette works extensively with schools, libraries and literacy charities, but here are some ways we can all raise more readers:

- Reading to children for just 10 minutes a day makes a difference
- Don't give up if children aren't regular readers – there will be books for them!

- Visit bookshops and libraries to get recommendations
- Encourage them to listen to audiobooks
- Support school libraries
- Give books as gifts

There's a lot more information about how to encourage children to read on our websites: **www.RaisingReaders.co.uk** and **www.JoinRaisingReaders.com**.

Thank you for reading.

www.ingramcontent.com/pod-product-compliance
Lightning Source LLC
Chambersburg PA
CBHW061520210726
48287CB00006B/1763